CASTLE OF HORROR
ANTHOLOGY

VOLUME 10

CASTLE BRIDGE MEDIA
DENVER, COLORADO, USA

CASTLE BRIDGE MEDIA
Denver, Colorado
Edited by Jason Henderson and In Churl Yo
Designed by In Churl Yo
Cover Photos by Daniel Diemer/Unsplash & Cristian Grecu/Unsplash
Illustration by Andrea Crisante/Shutterstock

This book is a work of fiction. Names, characters, business, events, and incidents are the products of the authors' imaginations. Any resemblance to actual persons, living or dead (or undead), or actual events is purely coincidental.

TABLE OF CONTENTS

INTRODUCTION

THE WORDS '*SATURDAY MORNING*' CONJURE up different feelings for different generations, depending not only on their prospective ages but the strata of entertainment media that was available to them and how that media was being delivered.

The nostalgia driven among us will offer the strongest response back, of a long-ago simpler time where choices of what to watch, while fewer and of debatably lesser quality, were nonetheless better. Where animation wasn't judged by the number of frames per second projected, the complexity of character development portrayed, or even the credibility of the plot presented.

Once upon a time (actually, between the 1960s and 1990s), Saturday mornings were *magical*, where the world seemed to slow down and the only thing that mattered was grabbing a bowl of cereal and plopping down in front of the television to watch a solid block of animated, kid-centric programming.

This was the golden era of Saturday morning cartoons, and for those fortunate enough to experience it, they were more than just a source of entertainment. Those cartoons were a rite of passage, a weekly ritual that brought joy, laughter, and a sense of adventure. From the moment the opening theme song began, we were transported to worlds beyond our wildest dreams. Whether we were following the antics of the *Looney Tunes*, joining the heroic escapades of *Super Friends*, or solving mysteries with *Scooby-Doo*, Saturday mornings were a gateway to a universe of endless possibilities.

These shows became cultural touchstones, creating shared experiences and bonding moments for children and families alike. Saturday mornings often meant gathering around the television with siblings or friends, engaging in discussions about the latest plot twists or imitating the catchphrases of beloved characters. These cartoons became a significant part of many people's childhood memories.

Still, as time and technology both advanced, the landscape of Saturday mornings began to change. The arrival of cable television, streaming services, and on-demand content altered the way we consume our favorite animated programs. The era of waking up early on Saturdays and rushing to catch the latest adventures have slowly faded into memory.

But we here in the Castle of Horror have dared to bring Saturday mornings back by re-animating our favorite shows from the dead with our mad yet talented crew of authors who have used their dark powers to create twisted, thinly veiled versions for your reading pleasure. Could there be a better motif than the beloved tales of our youth in which to play? We have stricken the record of which shows were used for inspiration. Perhaps you can identify the bodies of work from what remains…

The deep, dark blueberry-filled true nature of ███████████ comes to bloody, gory, misogynistic life in **P. J. Hoover's** *What Happens in Blue Dairy*.

A mayor launches a life-or-death mission to save his town from reanimated superwomen in **Jeremiah Dylan Cook's** dark take on ████ ███████████, *The Three Terrors*.

A musician's path to stardom is paved with blood oaths, death, and zombie dancers, in **Dennis K. Crosby's** ███████████ take, *Souled*.

A band of mercenary orc hunters plays a fairy tale RPG for a change of pace in **Alethea Kontis'** violently whimsical *Chaos Crushers' Day Off*.

The ████████████████████████ get a truly bizarre retelling in **Joy Preble's** *Shell Game*.

A very ████████████-like family investigate unnatural deaths and battle an alien ghost in **Steven Philip Jones'** *QED: The Cosmic Spectre*.

████████████████████████ weaves a path of death, destruction, and diabolical terror through the small town of Grubbs, Arkansas in **Heath W. Shelby's** *Act of God*.

A ██████████████-style square-jawed hero battles implacable alien forces bent on conquering the Earth in **Tony Jones's** *The Amazing Adventures of Boom Jackson*.

Close Your Eyes and Make Believe from **Bryan Young** tells a story of how children must retreat to their imagination to cope with the most horrific of everyday occurrences.

████████████ gets a dark update when Lovecraftian horrors rise from the depths in **Scott Pearson's** *The Shadows Under Mariana Base*.

Will McDermott explores the implications of ████████████████████ ████████████████████ in *The Luck of Big Red*.

And in a ghoulish finale, ████████████ and ████████████ come together to terrorize a young mother from the screen of the family's TV in **Katya de Becerra's** *Break Your Mommy's Bones*.

Jason and I are beyond proud and excited to offer such amazing stories to you, showcasing an assemblage of unique voices from the genre's top writers. While we can't have the Saturday mornings of our youth back, this may just be the next best thing. Thank you for supporting independent publishing, and please consider seeking out other volumes from the *Castle of Horror Anthology* series to enjoy even more outstanding tales of the madcap and the macabre.

That's all, folks! ♜

—In Churl Yo, publisher, Castle Bridge Media

WHAT HAPPENS IN BLUE DAIRY

By PJ Hoover

IT HAPPENS TO BE THE case that there's a village deep in the heart of Texas named Blue Dairy. You won't find it on any maps. It's off the path, tucked away in the hill country, beyond the wineries of Highway 290 and the distilleries of Dripping Springs, beyond the Christmas lights of Johnson City and the Nimitz Museum in Fredericksburg. Visitors never come to the town of Blue Dairy, for around Blue Dairy is a boundary crafted ages ago by Papa, the oldest and wisest of those living in Blue Dairy. It's not magic. Papa doesn't need magic. He uses nature, a powerful force not to be disregarded. Papa believes that nature makes anything possible, including the bountiful fruit the residents of Blue Dairy eat.

"It's time for the monthly harvest," Papa says from the center of the town square. He stands on a stage with a golden podium where once a week he gives a sermon on the moral rights and wrongs. Papa insists if there are too many wrongs, nature will get angry and there will be retribution.

"I love the harvest," Harry says. "It always puts me in a good mood."

"I hate the harvest," Grant says. He crosses his arms and offers no more explanation. Grant hates many things besides the harvest, but were we to list them here, they would take up the remainder of the story.

There's a quiet mummering among the residents of Blue Dairy and all heads begin to turn in one direction. Papa claps his blue hands together to once again get everyone's attention.

Right . . . blue hands. Papa's hands are blue. All of his skin is blue, just like everyone who lives in Blue Dairy. It's not unheard of. It's the same reason why flamingos are pink. They each so much shrimp that it changes the color of their features. Why people who eat too many carrots get an orange glow in their skin. For the residents of Blue Dairy, with a diet primarily consisting of blueberries, their skin has turned blue. Scientists would fight to study this phenomenon, turning the residents of Blue Dairy into nothing more than lab rats. It's the reason Papa has worked so hard to keep the town off the map.

Papa claps once more, and everyone turns back to look at him.

"As we've done in the past, we'll pair up," Papa says. "And as in the past—"

"You sure look good today, Scarlette," Charles says.

Scarlette giggles and laughs and tosses her long blond hair over her shoulder. "Why thank you, Charles."

Papa clears his throat. "As we've done in the past, if you've paired up with Scarlette in the last year, you are not eligible to pair up with her for today's harvest."

Eleven guys, including Charles, let out audible groans. A twelfth raises his hand.

"Yes, Dan?" Papa says.

"I paired up with Scarlette twelve months ago," Dan says. "Does that count as in the last year?"

"Yes, genius," Chet says before Papa can respond. "It's still within the year."

Jaz raises his hand. "Can I be with Scarlette? I've never been with Scarlette."

Papa looks at Jaz, considers this, then nods. "Jaz, you shall be paired up with Scarlette."

Scarlette mumbles, "It would be nice if they asked me," under her breath, and then she giggles.

And with that set, the remainder of the residents of Blue Dairy pair up, and the harvest is on.

Now why is pairing up with Scarlette such a big deal? For those unfamiliar with Blue Dairy, it's a valid question. Blue Dairy is unlike other towns in more ways than just the blue skin. Also, what makes Blue Dairy unusual is the fact that there is only one female in the entire town. That's right—Scarlette. This anomaly is another reason why scientists would want to study the residents of Blue Dairy, and another reason why Papa works so hard to keep the town hidden.

Scarlette and Jaz head off in their assigned direction for the harvest. They each carry baskets.

Jaz yawns loudly and holds his basket out to Scarlette. "Could you carry this for me?"

Scarlette pushes the basket back toward him. "Carry your own basket."

"Oh, come on," Jaz says. "It's good exercise. You could use the exercise."

Scarlette narrows her eyes at him. Then she grabs the basket and stomps off toward the blueberry patch.

Every month the blueberries near Blue Dairy are ripe (another anomaly), but some months are better than others. Scarlette fills her basket in a half hour. She turns, looking for Jaz. He's nowhere to be seen, but a sound like a power saw fills the air. It's coming from a nearby blueberry bush. Jaz's basket sits in front of the bush, and from underneath it peek out Jaz's shoes.

"Asleep," Scarlette says. "Figures." She picks up his basket and begins picking blueberries to fill it. All teams must come back with two baskets filled with blueberries. It's the only way they'll have enough to make it through the month without having to go on another harvest. The last thing Scarlette wants is to go on another harvest.

It takes her another half hour, but she fills Jaz's basket to the brim. Then she sets off, carrying both back to the town. Her muscles ache by the time she gets to the town center.

"Look at you, Scarlette!" Brax calls out to her. "Carrying those baskets. Watch out. You don't want to get too muscular."

Scarlette flashes him a smile and laughs like he's said something funny. Too muscular! As if that's a bad thing.

"I'll never have muscles like you," she says, trying to act coy.

Brax flexes his blue biceps in two different poses. "If you want, sometime I can give you a little personal training." Then he winks at her.

Ugh. Seriously.

"I think I'm busy," Scarlette says, then she looks away, hoping to get a couple minutes of silence as the rest of the town returns.

Two by two, everyone filters back into the town square. Two by two baskets are set down. Once all groups have returned, Papa gets back on the stage and stands at the gold podium.

"A plentiful harvest," Papa says. "Benjamin will be able to make all our favorites this month!" He looks around the town square, scanned the group. "But where is Jaz?" His eyes go immediately to Scarlette.

She crosses her arms. "Asleep under the blueberry bush." As if they even need to ask. Jaz can't stay awake to save his life.

Papa narrows his eyes at her, as if to say, "You didn't wake him." But it is not her job to be Jaz's keeper. Instead, Papa claps his hands together and points to two brothers, Thomas and Charles. "You two, go get Jaz. The rest of you carry your baskets to Pie and More."

Scarlette picks up hers and Jaz's baskets and heads toward Pie and More. It's the only restaurant in town, so it's more just like a big cafeteria where everyone eats. Benjamin, the owner, has a team of twenty that help him make blueberry pies, blueberry muffins, blueberry milkshakes, and blueberry pizza. There's even a brewery down the street that makes blueberry beer. Scarlette could seriously go for a beer about right now. Maybe she'll drop her baskets off and then sneak in the backdoor of the brewery.

One by one, the baskets are placed on a long table in the restaurant. She's just set hers and Jaz's down when the two guys that went to find Jaz come rushing back in.

"It's . . . horrible," Thomas says.

"There was a . . . ," his brother Charles says.

"It must've . . . ," Thomas says. He's breathing so hard, he can hardly get out a word.

Papa steps forward and places a hand on each of the brothers' shoulder. "Slow down. What's wrong?"

"A monster," Charles says. "There was a monster."

"It got Jaz," Thomas says.

Papa narrows his eyes. "Where. Is. Jaz?"

Thomas and Charles look at each other. They glance to Scarlette and then look back to Papa. "I don't think we should say in front of her."

As if Scarlette can't handle whatever they're about to say.

Papa looks in her direction. "Scarlette, could you please go wait outside?"

Scarlette opens her mouth to protest, but then shuts it. What is the use? Papa is the worst of the bunch, treating her like she's some delicate flower that will wilt under the first drop of rain.

"Fine," she says and stomps out, her white high heels clacking on the tiled floor of the restaurant. She's out the door and around the corner. Then she ducks down under an open window and listens.

Papa nods his head. "She's gone. Now tell me where Jaz is."

Thomas swallows then clenches his fists. "He's dead."

"Dead?"

"Uh huh," Charles says. "Murdered."

"By a monster," Thomas adds. "It ripped his guts out."

As one might imagine, this revelation causes quite a stir in the town of Blue Dairy. Papa orders the body of Jaz to be retrieved. He also assigns Jeremy, the closest the town has to a detective, to figure out what happened.

Scarlette slips away, thinking how she was right. Jaz really couldn't stay awake to save his life.

\#   \#   \#

Early the next morning, Scarlette is just finishing up her morning pushups when there's a knock on her door. She opens it to see Jeremy standing on her doorstep.

"Mind if I come in?" Jeremy says, then walks inside, bumping into Scarlette who hasn't said yes.

"I guess not," Scarlette says.

"I need to ask you some questions," Jeremy says. "Can I have some coffee?"

"Is that one of your questions?" Scarlette says. Despite what everyone in town thinks, her house is not a coffee shop, and she is no barista.

"This is no time for humor," Jeremy says. "And I take it black." Then he sits at her kitchen table and laces his fingers together . . . waiting.

Scarlette bites the inside of her mouth to keep from screaming. Then she walks to the espresso maker, trying to find a reason why she shouldn't spit in his coffee. She takes her time making it, then brings it over, carefully setting it in front of him so as not to spill a drop.

Jeremy takes a long sip and smiles. Then he motions with his hand. "Please sit."

"I'm fine   standing," Scarlette says. She doesn't want him to stay any longer than necessary.

Jeremy shrugs. "Are you worried that sitting will make your ass flat? I've heard that can happen. I guess I don't blame you. With an ass like that . . . well . . ."

Scarlette really wants to punch him. But instead, she giggles. "Aww you're sweet." Then she sits. The sooner she answers his questions, the sooner he'll be out of here, leaving her to a day of peace and quiet.

He must've gone to the library and found a book on how to solve mysteries, because the questions he asks sound like they've come from a pre-canned list.

"When did you last see Jaz?"

"What was he doing the last time you saw him?"

"Do you know anyone who would have any reason to hurt Jaz?"

"I thought they said it was a monster," Scarlette says. She shouldn't know that since she wasn't supposed to listen, but Jeremy's probably not smart enough to figure that out.

Jeremy slowly shakes his head. "There is no such thing as monsters. Whoever did this was a human, through and blue."

Scarlette shudders and wraps her arms around herself. "That's awful!"

Jeremy reaches over and places a hand on her forearm. "It's okay. I know this is probably too much for you. How about I let you rest a little. Get some beauty sleep. I'll continue my investigation, and then I'll come back later . . . maybe after dark?" And he winks at her.

Scarlette clenches her teeth together. What is it with every single guy in town thinking she'll jump their bones given the chance?

"I'll probably be tired," she says.

Jeremy stands. "Great. I'll see you later. Maybe have a cold blueberry beer ready for me?" Then he's out the door and on to question the next person on his list.

Scarlette shuts the door and tries to cool herself off. The guys in town have always been pretty open about wanting her to be their girlfriend, but in the last year, it's gotten out of control, like there's some virus spreading around and infecting them.

"Maybe I'll just leave," Scarlette says to herself. This is not the first time Scarlette has thought this, but in the last year, it's been a lot more often. There's a whole world out there, waiting for Scarlette to explore. A whole world of possibilities.

One time she asked Papa about visiting other towns, but he'd told her it could never happen. With their unique blue skin, it would be too dangerous. Also, the barrier he's placed around the town would prevent it. And so, Scarlette has been here her entire life. But still, she spends the next couple hours . . . thinking about it. Considering her options. If she were to do it, what would she need?

Around lunchtime, the delicious scent of blueberry pie comes wafting through town. But it's not the blueberry pie Scarlette wants. She really needs that drink. She changes her dress, brushes her hair, puts on some lipstick, and heads out, locking her door behind her. Nobody else in the town of Blue Dairy locks their doors, but Scarlette, being the only female, does. If she didn't, she'd probably get home to at least six guys waiting for her each day.

A bunch of the guys are already walking toward Pie and More. Scarlette tries to trail behind them, but they immediately latch onto her and engage her in conversation.

"Your hair sure looks nice today," one says. "Did you do something different?"

"Have you lost weight?" another says. "Without those extra couple pounds, you really look good."

"You look so pretty when you smile," still another says.

Scarlette says thank you and tosses her hair and smiles—exactly what they expect her to do. And all the while, she keeps thinking about leaving.

The group turns the corner and stops. In the middle of the alley between two buildings, there is blood everywhere. It's splattered against the walls and windows of the surrounding structures. It covers the sidewalk, so much of it that it forms puddles. And in the middle of it all lay a body.

One of the guys in the group rushes up and squats down next to the body. "It's Jeremy!" he says. "He's dead."

No shit, Scarlette thinks. With that much blood, he couldn't be alive. When she hears who it is, all she can think it that she no longer has to worry about him coming back over tonight. And she knows that's an awful thought, but she also can't help it. He was such a douche bag and now he's dead.

But like Scarlette always does, she plays the role she's supposed to play. Her nose and lips quiver a couple times, and she begins to cry.

"Who would do this?" she says between sobs.

And then Papa is there, on scene, and pulling her away from the dead body in the middle of the alleyway. She cries to entire time as he consoles her.

"I'm so sorry you had to see that," he says, rubbing her neck.

She kind of shrugs off his hand, but he's not taking the hint. He begins to massage his fingers into her muscles.

Scarlette stands, brushing off her dress and wiping at her eyes. "I need to go home."

Papa glances back at the alleyway where Jeremy's dead body has gathered a crowd, then back to Scarlette. "Will you be able to get home by yourself? They need me here."

Scarlette pretends to look a little scared but also a little confident. She's practiced these looks to perfection in her mirror. "You have to stay here, Papa. I'll be fine."

Papa doesn't look convinced. "I could get someone to walk you home . . ."

She shakes her head. "No, no. It's okay." And then she doubles the confidence. "I will be A-okay." And before he can change his mind, she walks away. Except she doesn't walk home. She goes in the direction of home, but once she's out of sight, she changes course, taking the backway to the brewery. It's only when she's through the door and inhaling the fresh scent of brewed hops that she finally relaxes.

"Hey, Scarlette," Drew says. "You want the usual?"

Drew runs the brewery and the distillery. He makes blueberry beer, blueberry wine, and Scarlette's favorite: blueberry vodka.

"God yes," she says. Nobody else is around—they're either looking at the dead body or at Pie and More eating blueberry scones—so Scarlette can drop the act . . . a bit.

"You got it," Drew says, and he puts a double shot of blueberry vodka in front of her.

Scarlette grabs it, tilts her head back, and downs it in one swallow.

Here's the thing Scarlette loves about Drew. In this situation, other guys in town would absolutely make some comment about how great Scarlette can swallow. Not Drew. He simply grabs the bottle, fills her glass up again, and pushes it back across the bar to her.

It's been a day, so Scarlette doesn't hesitate. She downs that one too. Drew pours one more and also passes over a bowl of blueberry pretzels.

"Rough day?" he says.

Scarlette nods and grabs a handful of pretzels. "Jeremy got murdered."

Drew is wiping the beer taps, but stops mid-wipe. "Are you kidding? Yesterday Jaz and now today Jeremy? What the hell is going on?"

Scarlette shrugs, not really caring. The vodka is working its way through her system nicely, and everything already feels better with the world. She crunches through the pretzels.

"No idea," she says. "I don't care."

"Do they think it's a monster?" Drew asks.

Scarlette downs her third double shot of vodka then slams the shot glass on the bar. "Jeremy didn't think so. But there was a lot of blood." And she does her best to describe the crime scene.

"Nothing like this has ever happened here," Drew says.

Exactly, is what Scarlette thinks. And because of that, this could be the perfect opportunity. If not now, there may never be another good chance.

"I'm leaving tonight," Scarlette says. Screw what Papa says. There's not some nature-powered boundary around the town. She can leave and go to the real world and she'll just handle the blue skin thing when she gets there.

Maybe if she stops eating so many blueberries, her skin will change back to . . . well, whatever color people's skin normally is.

"Leaving where?" Drew asks. He motions as if to ask if she wants another drink.

She gives a small shake of her head. Six shots has her head in the perfect space. As the plan is coming together in her mind, it's sounding better and better.

"Leaving here," Scarlette says. "The town of Blue Dairy."

Drew's eyes go wide. "Is that even possible? What about the shield? Papa always says—"

"I know what Papa says," Scarlette says. "But Papa could be lying. Nobody else has ever tried to leave. How do we know there's really anything stopping us?"

Drew seems to consider this. As he does, he grabs a shot glass from the bar and pours himself a double. He pounds it and then slams his shot glass down on the bar, hard enough that it shatters.

"I'm going with you," he says.

A flash of anger moves through Scarlette. Not Drew, too.

"I don't need your protection," she says.

Drew grins. "Never said you did, Scarlette."

"Then why do you want to go?"

He looks out, as if seeing beyond the walls. "I want to see what else is out there. See what's beyond Blue Dairy. I've always dreamed of leaving. Never had the balls to. But you . . ."

Scarlette stands. "I have the balls to." And with that her mind is made up. Tonight she is leaving Blue Dairy.

#   #   #

They agree to meet later that day. Papa has called a meeting for the entire town, so there shouldn't be anyone to see them sneaking away. Harry comes by to see Scarlette, "just to make sure she's feeling happy with everything going on." She assures him that she's okay, and hurries him out the door.

Grant comes by next, pretty much to vent. He's upset about the weather, he thought the blueberry scones were burnt at lunch, and he says he has a rash on his butt cheeks. Then he asks her if she'll sit with him at lunch tomorrow. Tomorrow Scarlette will not be here, so what the hell. She agrees and is almost certain a small smile pops through on his eternally grouchy face.

After she gets rid of him, Chet comes by, offering to teach her to add and subtract numbers. Scarlette hates how she has to pretend to be bad at math in this town. It's like because she's a girl, she's not allowed to be smart. That gets so old real fast. But since she's leaving, once again it doesn't matter. Chet gives her some practice problems, and she gets every single one right.

"Nice job, Scarlette," Chet says. "My tutoring is really paying off."

Of course, he credits himself.

Scarlette giggles. "I guess so."

Chet leans in. "Say, later, after the meeting and dinner, do you want me to come by and tutor you some more?" And he winks.

For fuck sake, really?

Scarlette pretends to consider this, putting her finger to her lips in deep thought. "Oooh, I'm so sorry, but I have plans tonight."

Chet's face hardens. "What plans?"

Well, she's sure as hell not going to tell him her real plans, but she's got to come up with something.

"Tonight is the night I'll be cleaning my entire house," she says. There's no way he'll want to join her for that.

"What do you wear when you're cleaning?" Chet asks.

He's probably got mental images of her in some sexy maid costume, bending over, dusting baseboards.

"Sweatpants," she says. "And now we better get ready for the meeting." She stands up and hurries to the door, pulling it open.

Chet leaves, saying he'll see her at the meeting and that maybe they can sit next to each other at dinner. That's a big solid nope. Scarlette will be at neither.

She locks the door behind him and pulls the shades. If anyone else knocks—

Another knock on the door. Scarlette doesn't move. Doesn't dare breathe.

Whoever it is knocks again . . . and again . . . and then finally gives up and leaves.

Scarlette hurries into her bedroom, grabbing a blue tote bag from the far corner of the closet. She stuffs essentials into it: a water bottle, some blueberry snack bars, a flashlight. What else does one need when escaping the town where they've lived their entire life? Scarlette can't think of anything. Hopefully Drew will pack some vodka. She changes into black leggings and a long-sleeved black T-shirt and then throws a white dress on overtop it along with her standard white heels. No need to raise suspicion while moving through town. With the way the guys in town are always gawking at her, someone is bound to be watching. Just to make it look good, she sticks a loaf of blueberry bread into the bag. She can say she's bringing it as a gift to Jaz's roommate. Or maybe to Jeremy's roommate. Maybe both. She sticks another loaf in the bag.

Everyone should be heading to the meeting at the center of town. Scarlette slips out the back door. She's meeting Drew at the park on the edge of town. She's hardly two houses away when someone calls her name. It's Brax.

"Hey, Scarlette, are we going to work out together later?" he calls. "We can work on your flexibility." Then he bends over and touches his toes.

Don't raise suspicion. That's all Scarlette can think. She tries to smile. Gives a half wave. Then continues on her way.

Drew is waiting at the park. He's sitting on a bench on the far edge, in the shadows, dressed in black so he blends into the background. With it nearly being dinner time, it's starting to get dark. He stands when he sees her approaching.

"Ready?" he asks.

Scarlette slips into the shadows and pulls the white dress off from over her other clothes. She stuffs the dress into her bag in case she'll need it for anything later. "Ready," she says.

And the two set off into the woods, away from the town of Blue Dairy.

They walk in silence for the first half hour, stepping through the trees and brush. Each moment it gets darker as the sun sets and the night comes. And only once the final rays of the sun have dipped below the tree line do they dare to talk.

"I can't believe we're really doing this," Drew says.

"Doing what exactly?" someone says, and Chet steps out in front of them, crossing his arms over his scrawny chest. "Is this what your plans were? Why you didn't want any more tutoring?"

Scarlette and Drew stop. She didn't want tutoring because she didn't need tutoring, and even if she did, she didn't want it from Chet.

"It's not what it looks like," Scarlette says.

"What does it look like?" Chet asks, and he takes a step forward. "Because it looks to me like you're trying to find a reason to not wear the sexy maid costume for me." But before he can make another move, something comes toward him in the dark—an axe. It flies end over end until with a loud thunk, it embeds itself solidly in his puny chest.

Chet looks down as blood spurts out of his chest. He looks to Scarlette and Drew in disbelief. Then back at his chest. "I thought . . . I thought . . ." And he collapses.

Blood pools around him, and the world goes silent. Scarlette doesn't dare move. She hadn't thrown the axe and neither had Drew. Which means that someone is out there, right now, very close by, watching them. Whoever it is, this is not their first murder. They've killed Jaz and Jeremy and now Chet.

Drew steps a little closet to Scarlette, and barely, under his breath, he says, "What the fuck is going on?"

"I don't know," she whispers. "But I think we should run."

They take off, trying to stay side by side as they dash through the thick trees. Scarlette jumps over tree roots, cursing the stupid heels she wears. These are not the shoes one wants when running away from home, but it was this or her flip flops.

From behind them, in the dark, a laugh sounds out. It echoes impossibly through the forest. "There is no escape," a hollow voice says, robotic and sinister.

There must be an escape. Scarlette refuses to believe Papa's stories of the barrier around their town are true.

"Keep running," she calls to Drew. He's still next to her, keeping pace step for step.

She pushes ahead, not slowing down. Branches scrape at her face. She stumbles on rocks. She does not stop. Then, there's a thud next to her and Drew is down. She stops only long enough to see a spear protruding from his back. He lays flat on his stomach, head turned to the side with lifeless eyes showing. Scarlette screams once, then begins running again.

The haunting laughs sounds through the forest again. "Keep flying, butterfly," the voice says. "Soon I'll clip your wings."

The air is thin. Scarlette is breathing harder than she ever has in her life. She's got to get out of here. Got to get away from whoever is doing this. Whatever psycho is behind this. That's four dead now.

Drew. If he hadn't been with her, he wouldn't be dead. But there is no time to think about that now.

Scarlette runs, flying through the forest. But then she slams into something invisible. It knocks her backward, smashing her face, making her land on her butt. All the air is knocked out of her. She's stunned, and it takes her a few moments to reorient herself. Shit shit shit. She has to get up.

She gets to her hands and knees and then slowly stands. Her head is spinning, but she gives it a moment to settle. Then she walks forward, feeling for whatever it was that stopped her.

There, woven among the branches and trees and vines is a chain link fence. It's got to be ten feet high, and it's green to blend in with the forest. Not magic. Not nature. Just a fence.

Scarlette begins to climb. She kicks off her heels after the first one gets caught in one of the links. But before she's more than two feet off the ground, hands grab her from behind. She's pulled downward and tossed onto the ground.

"Where are we going?" a voice says.

Scarlette turns to see Papa looking down at her.

Papa. The leader of the town. The wisest member of their community. The murderer.

"You killed them?" Scarlette says.

Papa smiles and leans forward, brushing a lock of her golden hair out of her face. "Of course, I did. They didn't treat you right. None of them treat you right. Not the way I would treat you. How could I ever tolerate the thought of you having to spend time with any of them when you should be spending all your time with me?"

"But you killed them," Scarlette says. She may not have liked—okay she hated—the way the guys in town talked to her, but that didn't mean she wanted them dead. "Even Drew. He never treated me bad." Drew was going to escape with her.

"He was the worst of the bunch," Papa says. "I know what would have eventually happened between the two of you if I hadn't intervened. I saw the way you looked at him."

Papa is wrong. Papa is insane. And as Scarlette realizes this, she knows she must proceed very carefully.

"What are you going to do with me?" she asks. Her voice is shaking because she's scared as shit, but she also tries to batt her eyelashes the way all the guys in town—including Papa apparently—like.

A smile creeps onto Papa's face. "I have it all worked out. You are going to be all mine. I won't have to share you with anyone." Then he leans down and kisses her, long and hard. His lips feel like dried blueberry crumble cake. His breath smells like fetid fruit.

Scarlette pushes him away and scrambles backward. Her back is up against the fence.

"Don't be scared," Papa says. "It will be you and me forever, here in Blue Dairy."

"I'm leaving," Scarlette says.

Papa tsks her and slowly shakes his head. "You can never leave. I will make certain of that."

And Scarlette realizes the only way she'll ever get out of here—ever get free—is to kill Papa.

He leans forward once more. She thinks he's going to kiss her again. But instead, he pulls a cloth out from his pocket and presses it toward her face. It smells like a mix between blueberries and chemicals, and then the world goes black.

# # #

Scarlette wakes with a start. She's lying on a bed—not her bed. Not her house. She makes it a general rule to never go into anyone else's house, but one time Papa had insisted. That's the only reason she knows where she is. She's in his house now, lying on his bed.

She sits up. Papa's house is right near the center of town. Out the window, she sees him there, on the stage, talking at the podium. But she can't hear a word. The windows are too thick. But the crowd stands there, fixed on his every word. Whatever he's saying must be pretty heavy. Some of the guys have tears running down their cheeks.

Maybe he's talking about Drew and Chet, now also dead. Or maybe . . . The guys in town have to have noticed that she's not out there. Being the only girl in town, her presence would definitely be missed. Maybe he's talking about her. But where would he tell them she is?

She hurries to the door and turns the knob. It doesn't budge. She shoves all her weight against it. Nothing. It's locked and as far as she can tell, there is no deadbolt for her to turn. There is only a numerical keypad with a red light illuminated.

Scarlette runs back to the window. Pounds on the glass. Surely she can get someone's attention. They'll look over and see her and she can motion for them to come let her out. Except when she pounds, the thick glass doesn't hardly make a sound. And beyond it, Scarlette sees three layers of the thick glass. There is no way anyone will hear the pounding. But there's still a chance someone could look over and . . .

Oh wait. Papa's house is central to town. And as such, he used privacy glass for his windows. When looking at them from the outside, they look like shiny mirrors. Nobody can see in.

She sinks to the ground and lets her situation filter through her system. The door is locked. The windows are thick and triple-paned. Nobody can see in. And Papa's plan becomes abundantly clear to her. He plans to keep her here, as his prisoner, forever. And as for what he told the others? Maybe he said she was dead. Maybe he said she was sick. They believe everything Papa says. They have no reason to doubt him. And they certainly don't know that he's the murderer. In short, she'd kind of screwed.

The next two hours Scarlette scours the place. What she discovers is that this is no house. This is a prison. There is nothing sharp. No unlocked doors or windows. No way out. But Scarlette is not going to give up.

She hears five beeps as if a keypad is being pressed. The front door! This is her chance. While it's open, she'll scream out at whoever is there to listen. She rushes to the door just as it swings open. Scarlette begins to scream and yell as Papa walks through the door.

He laughs. "It won't do you any good." And he holds the door open so she can see. Beyond this door is another door, that one closed, preventing the sound of her screams from escaping.

Her voice dies in her throat. He's thought of everything. Of course, he has. This is Papa. She steps back, trying to not lose it. But she has got to find a way out of here.

Papa steps forward and places a hand on her shoulder, rubbing his fingers into her blue skin. Wait, she's not wearing the black leggings and T-shirt she'd had on before. She's in a white dress—way sexier than her normal dresses, with a low neckline that almost shows her nipples and a hem that barely covers her ass cheeks—and white high heels—at least three inches higher than normal. Had he changed her clothes?

She shrugs his hand off. "Someone is going to find out what you're doing."

Papa smiles at her like she's a child. "No one will ever find out. They all think you're dead. And yes, they are very sad; they will be for a while. But they'll get over it. And as for what we have going on here . . . well, that will be our little secret forever."

Forever is sounding like a very long time.

"Oh, and if you ever think to try to hurt me and escape, you'll never be able to get the door—"

Before Papa can utter another word, Scarlette grabs a high heel off her foot and swings it at Papa. It smacks into his head, making a sickening sucking sound as the stiletto digs into his skull. He drops to the floor, and then he doesn't move again. She only spares a moment to look at his lifeless body. Then the door begins to slowly close. Scarlette wedges her other white high heel into the door and the frame, stopping it from closing. She pulls it open and steps through. But before she's all the way out, a hand reaches out and grabs her ankle, pulling her back in.

Scarlette drops to the ground, landing hard on her chest, smacking her nose. She kicks at the hand holding her.

"Never . . . let . . . you . . . go . . . ," Papa utters and he tries to hold on.

"Oh yes you will." Scarlette kicks again, smashing a spikey heel into his fingers. He releases his grip, and she pulls the door closed. Then she crawls to the outer door, stands up, and turns the knob. Like a small gift from the universe, it opens. Fresh air rushes in. Scarlette kicks off her other high heel, and then she's running. Guys from town call her name, try to chase after her, but she doesn't slow. She rushes to the park, then onward into the forest. In the daylight, it's easier to see. And when she finally reaches the chain link fence, she climbs. ♜

THE THREE TERRORS

By Jeremiah Dylan Cook

1

"THE TOWN OF CITYSVILLE BELONGS "The town of Citysville belongs to us now." The leader lands on my front stoop while the other two remain dark silhouettes in the evening sky.

In the porch light, I make out the woman's unnatural red irises through her mess of long, auburn hair. Her head is disproportionately large compared to her slim body, with a line of neck stitches illustrating where her incongruous anatomy was joined. She wears a white dress, presumably the one her body was buried in, stained with large splotches of blood.

My pulse races as I briefly consider suicide by argument. I take a deep breath and stroke my curled, white mustache. Summoning every bit of decorum I've learned in my thirty years as a politician, I respond. "Of course, I will resign as mayor immediately."

"A pointless gesture. We have no desire for titles. Citysville will remain as is. You'll be our dollies, our little town of toys, and we want the town to have a mayor. You'll inform the others. Let them know that if anyone tries to leave, we'll break them." She smiles as she floats back into the air.

In the blink of an eye, the other two are within inches of me. I stumble backward only to be stopped by my closed door. They resemble the first with their disproportioned heads and neck stitches but are otherwise unique. The one to my right wears an emerald dress, has her black hair in a flapper's bob, and chews on a mostly skinless human finger.

The one to my left reaches forward and rubs my head. "Oh, he looks just like an egg. Can I crack him?" She wears her blonde hair in pigtails and sports a blue skirt and black blouse.

"Only if I get to lick up what comes out." Replies the girl to my right.

The leader returns. "You've eaten enough, Belladonna. The mayor lives for now."

Belladonna smirks with the finger still jutting from her mouth. "I'm not the one who wanted to kill him. That was Baubles."

Baubles cackles as she twirls her pigtails. "Don't be mad, Bloom. I just ain't never seen a head that looks like an egg afore."

"Let's go." Bloom, the leader, returns to the sky.

Baubles and Belladonna roll their eyes and follow. Alone, I turn, re-enter my home, and shut the door. Now that they can't see me, I collapse and try to catch my breath. Sweat and shivers break out across my body. This is all my fault.

I pull out my phone and call my secretary. "Grab Craig and meet me at Town Hall."

2

There's an enormous plop from outside my office as another broken piece of concrete from the destroyed Cavadini Bridge falls into water. The Daily Bridge, on the other side of town, is in the same situation. Citysville, existing on an island between the bifurcated Strong River, was now disconnected from the rest of the country by road. The few boats on the island had been destroyed along with the bridges. Some people might be willing to brave the currents, but the swim is long and unbearably frigid this time of year. I turn away from the window and await my conspirators.

The office is modest. Pictures from various events I've assisted with cover the walls. I'd dedicated my life to Citysville, helping fund the Citysville Redevelopment Committee, CRC for short, in the early 90s. We managed to change the area from a failed Steel fiefdom to a thriving accumulation of kitschy shops and bed and breakfasts. Day trippers and couples came from miles around to visit. My desk is small with two chairs opposite my own. A collection of political biographies sits on a bookshelf to my right, to my left is a mini fridge.

Ms. Hale, my longtime secretary, enters with Craig following. Both look ready for clandestine activities in practical, black outfits. Hale has a good six inches on Craig's height. I'd heard many people remark on her model's physique over my time in City Hall. She has her long, red hair hidden in a beanie. Craig puts his hood down revealing his curly hair, bloodshot eyes, and beard.

"Thanks for coming on such short notice." I start.

"The military didn't stop them, did it?" Ms. Hale asks.

"No. I watched them demolish a squadron of planes before the sun set. They stopped by my house after to tell me we were their playthings."

Craig runs a hand through his hair. "No good news on my front either. I found Professor Plutonium's corpse today in the trash behind his lab. His heart had been ripped out."

Ms. Hale walks to my window and draws the shade. "Did you make it inside?"

Craig paces from wall to wall. "My access to the back door still works, but I didn't want to risk going further. These girls aren't exactly sugar, spice, and everything nice!"

"You were supposed to verify that the subject was still alive." Ms. Hale lets out a sigh.

Before morale gets any lower, I interject. "It doesn't matter now. Craig can get us in the building. We'll have to hope they haven't killed him."

Craig stops. "I don't know if I can do this."

"We need you to navigate us through the facility. Neither of us have been there before." I respond.

"If you'd just listened to me when I first told you about what Professor

Plutonium was up to, we wouldn't be here right now!" Craig punches the wall.

I stand. "You're right, and I'm sorry, but we need to try this. We can't let their occupation of our town continue. It's only a matter of time before the military decides to try nuking them along with everyone trapped here."

Craig shrugs. "I can draw you a map and give you my access badge."

"It'll have to do. What about you, Ms. Hale? Last chance to back out."

"With you to the end."

3

Ms. Hale and I stare up at the huge smokestacks and the long building, reminiscent of a giant loaf of bread, which used to be the Tartakovsky Steel Mill. A chain-link fence surrounds the property with signs dissuading trespassing and advertising Plutonium Inc. We make our way around the property to the side next to the river. A small gatehouse stands out from the old Steel Mill with its sleek, modern design. I pull out Craig's badge and swipe it. There is a flash of green light above the door, and I grasp the handle.

Inside, there is a metal detector and an abandoned security desk. We proceed through and enter the desolate yard between the building and the fence. The dumpster with Professor Plutonium is next to the back entrance. A bloody hole pierces his white lab coat, dress shirt, and tie. His normally stoic face displays a rictus of pain in death.

I can't help remembering the life changing interaction I had with him three years ago. Victor Kane, who the press had dubbed Professor Plutonium after a breakthrough that enhanced the military's nuclear arsenal, entered my office offering to provide Citysville with free electricity in exchange for the Tartakovsky Steel Mill. His timing was impeccable as I needed something big to sway voters in my favor to fend off a tough mayoral challenger. Plutonium made good on his promise, the residents responded with record turnout in my favor, and I signed the mill away. My debt to him kept me working to hush all the rumors about what he was doing here until it was too late.

I avoid taking in any more of the grisly details and continue to the back door. Ms. Hale searches the skies above us for any sign of the girls our residents have aptly dubbed the Three Terrors. I scan Craig's badge again, and the door, which is a handle-less metal slab like something off a science fiction spaceship, slides up. We enter.

Automatic running lights spring to life on the floor and ceiling of the immaculate, white hallway. A small screen to our right displays a "Welcome Back Craig" message. I reach into my pocket and pull out the map we'd been given.

"It's not far." I whisper. "He should be just ahead."

"What are the odds they're somewhere in this facility?" Ms. Hale asks.

"Who knows? They were born here, and we've observed them returning since their emergence, but they could be miles away at this moment. Plutonium added dozens of labs inside this building, so there should be somewhere we can hide in a pinch."

We walk down the hallway, cognizant of keeping our steps quiet. Locked doors appear on our right and left with name plates. There's a room labeled "Her" and one labeled "Gangrene." I avoid mental speculation on what other horrible things Plutonium was up to without my knowledge. Looking down at the map, I see our destination is around the corner a few steps away.

A grinding, metallic clang rings through the hallway. Ms. Hale and I stop abruptly and look for the source. Nothing appears behind us meaning it must be from just around the bend. Voices echo off the walls to our location.

"The government has agreed to our terms." Bloom says.

"They're giving us Citysville?" Belladonna asks.

"How nice of them." Baubles cackles.

"Nice has nothing to do with it." Bloom says. "They're not going to waste the resources to save a couple thousand people. Easier to just say the town is irradiated, cut off communication, and keep people away."

There's another ear-splitting crash as metal is twisted and destroyed. Ms. Hale and I remain where we are as silence resumes its rule. I hold a hand up to indicate Ms. Hale should remain as I proceed. Taking a deep breath, I lean my head past the corner.

The passage ahead is clear of deranged super women, but it's littered with debris. Girders bend inward from a hole in the roof, and a pile of concrete sits where Plutonium's creations must've landed. A metal door has also been shredded into several pieces. I glance down at Craig's map. Our destination is at the end of this hallway and takes us right past the openings. If the Terrors are lingering, they'll spot us as we pass. I beckon for Ms. Hale to follow and make my way to the edge of the holes. While I've never been particularly religious, I find myself making the sign of the cross as I peek, first into the hole in the roof, which is clear, and then into the space that used to be a door.

The hallway over the threshold is the same as the one we're in, with running lights and white coloring. Another door, thirty feet away, is also gone. Inside the revealed room, I make out a couch, a kitchen, and something else. My heart leaps as I realize it's Belladonna.

Her back is to us, and she flies out of view. This might be our only chance. I chart my path across the debris on the floor and go. Ms. Hale follows. We don't wait to find out if we've been spotted. If we have, we'll be dead soon anyway. I raise Craig's badge to the door we've sought out, and it slides open. We step inside, and the door shuts. Relieved to have something between us and them, even if it won't hold, we both sigh.

"Good of you to come, Mr. Mayor."

The voice startles us both. I spot a glass cylinder sprouting from a computer console. Inside sits a chimpanzee with black fur and greenish skin. He regards us with intelligence far beyond any usual simian. His skull is elongated and covered by a metal contraption connected to various wires and tubes that lead up to a dome-shaped machine in the ceiling. This is who we've come to see.

The chimp smiles. "Don't worry, they can't hear us with the door closed. The professor ensured all his rooms were soundproof to keep workers from hearing the agony he put his subjects through."

"Craig told you we were coming?" I ask.

"No. Craig and I rarely spoke as the professor was often present."

"Then how did you know I'd be here?" I step forward toward the computer console.

"A simple computation of variables. Craig, knowing of my intelligence, was destined to tell an authority figure about me after the professor lost control of his girls."

Ms. Hale approaches. "Then your reputation proceeds you. Do you have a name? I assume you don't want to be referred to by your subject name of Mental Oscillating Judicious Organism."

"Certainly not. A title designed to remove my rights as a living creature. You can call me Jo, short for Johann Wolfgang von Goethe, a favorite historical thinker. We can keep up the small talk if you'd both like to die, but I recommend we move to the endgame."

"Alright, Jo. What do you have in mind?" I ask.

"The professor has dart guns filled with a fluid he designed to negate the reanimation liquid he bought from All Purchaser Commodities." Jo scratches where the metal contraption covers his elongated head.

"APC sells reanimation liquid?" Ms. Hale looks puzzled.

Jo rolls his eyes. "It's a company secret. But that story is for another time. I know where the dart gun is, but you'll need to let me out of here."

"Of course." I search the control panel for some way to release the chimp.

Ms. Hale stands next to me. "No offense, Jo, but how do we know we aren't letting something worse than those girls out of confinement?"

Jo bares his teeth for a moment before closing his eyes. "I am worse than those girls. But what I will do with my freedom is conquer the system, leaving the average person alone. Places like Citysville have nothing to fear from me. I'm not some mad cannibal or would-be despot. I am a chimp who's had his brain enhanced and connected to the internet. Sentience was thrust upon me, and I was forced to endure pain and torture. I was made to watch as the professor created superhuman dolls for his own sick fetishes. I reject his ways and means, but I am also the most fit creature to oversee this planet. Given my freedom, I will work toward my goals. Make your choice. Either you leave me here for the girls to discover and kill or you let me out with no strings attached."

"We don't have a choice." I say. "Tell me how to free you."

Ms. Hale's features are conflicted as I follow Jo's directions to work the console. After several button selections, and the switch of a lever, the cylinder around Jo slides down. The various tubes and wires quickly detach from the mechanical device covering the chimp's brain.

Jo slides off his chair and his head wobbles. "I must ask one of you to carry me. My body cannot support the weight of this brain."

I step forward and offer my arms. Jo climbs in, and I cradle him like a large baby. He's heavy but most of the weight comes from his head covering, which he rests against my chest. My chin contacts the metal, and I find it cold.

Ms. Hale takes the map from my pocket and holds it up. "Where to?"

Jo taps it. "Directly opposite my room is where the professor created the girls. That's where you'll find the guns."

I and Ms. Hale move to either side of the door to be out of view when it opens.

"We're going to have to be incredibly careful and quiet. We just heard the Three Terrors nearby on our way here." I swipe Craig's badge.

The hallway outside remains empty, and we move quickly to the destroyed section. Ms. Hale risks her life this time by peeking to see if the girls are in view. Thankfully, she survives and beckons for me to follow with Jo. We make it to the door we need. A plate above reads "Daughters." I scan Craig's badge, but nothing happens.

Jo reaches out for the scanner and works quickly at removing the face plate and accessing the wiring underneath.

The sound of scraping metal echoes from nearby.

"Stop that." Screams Bloom.

"I'm boredddd." Baubles responds.

A television smashes behind us, thrown from the hallway with the broken door. Ms. Hale squeezes my arm tightly. Baubles floats into view behind us. She's focused on the shattered television and doesn't see us. The door slides open with a barely perceptible woosh, but the airflow causes Baubles pigtails to rock in the breeze. She starts to look in our direction as we hurry into the room. The door shuts automatically.

Inside is a horror show. Three blood-stained medical gurneys occupy the center of the room. Beside each table sits a see-through plastic bag filled with discarded female anatomy. It's obvious that Plutonium created the Three Terrors through a process of mixing and matching. On a workbench, behind the gurneys, are robotic contraptions. They look like metallic hearts. I'm no scientist, but I assume these are what give the Terrors their superhuman powers. The final bit of ugliness is a white board filled with Plutonium's notes saying things like, "flexible," "moisture," and "erotic."

"There." Jo points.

I follow his hand to a locker in the corner. It's open, and several dart guns sit inside with dozens of rounds of darts filled with a glowing blue liquid. There's a knock at the door behind us.

Ms. Hale is already running for the guns when I follow. She collects two, which are pre-loaded and turns to aim at the door. Jo and I do the same just as Baubles rips through the metal hiding us.

"Little pigs, little pigs, come out or I'll blow your house in." Baubles cackles.

Ms. Hale fires both shots of her dual wielded dart guns. One clanks off a remaining bit of door while the other connects with Baubles forehead. Her invulnerability has made her unconcerned with projectiles. She finishes off the remains of the door blocking her way and steps toward us. Baubles is smiling, but green ichor begins leaking from her nose, followed by her mouth and ears. She takes another step and falls to the ground. Her stitched neck begins leaking the same fluid streaming from her face. She continues trying to approach as she crawls through the growing puddle of green liquid. Finally, halfway to us, she ceases movement.

Bloom flies around the corner and stops at the doorway. "What the hell?" She steps over the threshold. Her large eyes inspect the scene as I raise my weapon. "Is that a monkey?"

Bloom dashes toward Ms. Hale as my gun sends the dart in her direction. It ricochets off the wall as she grabs Ms. Hale by the neck. Bloom lifts my secretary up but drops her suddenly. I see a dart sticking out of Bloom's arm, and I look down to see Jo's weapon has been discharged.

Ms. Hale chokes from the force of the initial grab and lashes out, sending Bloom tumbling backward. The ghoulish creature slips and stumbles in her sister's remains. Her body rapidly deteriorates in the same fashion as Baubles.

"One left." Jo announces.

"The worst one." I reply.

We re-load and proceed out of the disgusting room back to the destroyed door. We round the corner to look down the hall together. Belladonna stands at the opposite end, waiting for us.

"Looks like dessert just wandered in." Belladonna flies at us.

I fire and hear at least one other dart discharged, but then I feel the wind knocked out of me. Jo tumbles to the floor, his metal container clanking off the ground. Ms. Hale is down, and her eyes are closed. We came so close only to fail. Belladonna reaches down, grabs my hand, and lifts it to her mouth. She bites into my flesh. Despite the surging adrenaline, I feel the horrible pain. She chews on the piece of bone, muscle, and skin that once resided between my thumb and index finger. Blood spurts out. She releases her grip on my arm but puts a foot on my chest so I can't wiggle away. I clutch my bleeding hand.

Even though I want to give up, I frantically search for any signs of hope. Jo is up but struggling to crawl away from us and flee. Ms. Hale's eyes are fluttering. She's not dead. Her gun is still in her hand, and it's loaded. I just need to give her time.

"Your sisters are dead!" I shout.

Belladonna isn't phased by the declaration. She continues to relish the piece of me she's eating. The front of her emerald dress is dribbled with blood.

"Did you hear me you psycho? We managed to kill two of you, and you're next!"

Ms. Hale's eyes are open now. She's coming around. The gun is rising, but it's wobbly. She fires, but the shot bounces off the wall and lands next to my head.

Belladonna laughs as she turns to regard Ms. Hale. "Don't worry. I'll be eating you next."

I let go of my bleeding hand, grab the dart, and jam it into Belladonna's leg.

Faster than the others, she collapses as green liquid flows from her orifices.

"It's over." Ms. Hale makes it back to her feet.

I re-cover my wound and look for Jo. To my surprise, Craig appears and picks him up.

"Right on time." Jo says as he gets comfortable in his new carrier's arms.

As the chimp and the young man vanish around the corner, heading for the exit, I can't help wondering about what I've just loosed into the world. Will Jo be worse than the Three Terrors? ♜

SOULED

By Dennis K. Crosby

"ALL RIGHT, JUNIOR. JUST ONE more document to sign and we'll be all set."

"Cool."

Junior Coleman pushed the dreadlocks from his face and skimmed over the words of the contract, once again pretending the legalese made perfect sense to him. This had been the way of things for the past couple of years. Pretending. He was talented, sure. Not necessarily a prodigy when it came to guitar, but most certainly talented. He'd learned quickly. His mother said it was in his blood. Told him he was destined for great things on the stage and that his music would change the world. She'd said those things so often he started to believe it. He got better over the years. He was recognized, but in the end, he always felt like he was pretending—still waiting for the moment when he would truly be a star.

Today was the day.

Today he'd be able to stop pretending.

Junior signed the contract, handed it to his manager, Grady Sanford, then sat back in his chair. He looked around the greenroom and closed his eyes for a moment to allow the enormity of what was about to happen fill his soul. He pushed away the echoes of the word "pretender" bouncing around in his head. He let his music replace it. He allowed what had come to be called the "Junior Coleman Sound" to fill his mind. The music began to fill every part of his body. First his foot tapped, then his index finger, followed by a shoulder bounce.

He smiled.

He opened his eyes.

He was present.

"You ready for this?" asked Grady.

"Hell yeah," said Junior.

"You ready for this?!" shouted Grady.

"Hell to the yeah!" shouted Junior.

"You ready for THIS?" repeated Grady, holding his arms out.

"HELL YEAH!" yelled Junior.

"My man," said Grady, holding his hand out.

Junior grabbed it, pulled himself up and embraced his longtime manager. This was a part of their performance ritual. Ever since he was booked at the Apollo in Harlem, when word about the incomparable Junior Coleman was making its way around music circuits, Grady would ask if he was ready. Always three times, always increasing the intensity. This performance wasn't just any performance. This was a featured spot on the hottest morning music program in the country. A program that shined a spotlight on black performers. Junior Coleman was making waves on the R&B charts with his first album. When the call came from Don Cornell, both Junior and Grady knew everything was about to change. He was offered two songs on Music Moves the Soul, on the main stage, and he jumped at the chance. This was about to be the best deal since…that night.

That night at the crossroads.

#   #   #

On his knees, in the center of the crossroads, Junior held the dagger tightly. His fingers wrapped around the ornate crimson and black handle. It was shaped like two serpents coiled around each other, with their mouth opened on either side of the blade as if that's where the sharp metal sprang.

38

He grabbed the blade with his right hand, then pulled the weapon toward him with his left, to cut his palm for the bloodletting.

"Gah! Dammit!" he screamed.

He dropped the dagger to the ground, retrieved the white porcelain bowl at his side and positioned it underneath his right fist, allowing the blood to stain and fill it. After a thirty count, Junior removed the scarf from around his neck and wrapped his hand with it. He realized the folly of his actions as he made a fist around the cloth and winced.

"Damn! How the hell am I supposed to play now? Dammit! I should have…"

Junior let the words trail off. He'd gone too far for regret. He looked around and wondered if anyone was lurking, serving as witness to an idiotic plan thought up by a desperate musician. But there was no one. There was nothing for miles. No homes, no cars, no…nothing. In the distance, the sun was setting. A beautiful reddish orange blaze of fire and light ready for its evening slumber. Junior stared at it, mesmerized, as it dipped below the horizon.

He still wasn't sure if this would work. According to the legend, the crossroads, the location where Robert Johnson had allegedly made his deal with the devil, was in Clarksdale, Mississippi, at the intersection of highway sixty-one and highway forty-nine. But according to the book he'd found in his father's trunk, the crossroads could be anywhere. It wasn't about the location—it was about the ritual. Junior chose a remote location in central Illinois, between the towns of Bloomington-Normal and Champaign-Urbana. The roads seemed to have little traffic, and when they did, hours passed before another soul showed up. It was the perfect place to test out what he'd learned.

"All right. I guess I'm doing this."

Reaching into the backpack at his side, Junior grabbed a vial of ashes. The ashes were but a sampling of a larger harvest from the burned corpse of a young man, a saxophonist in Junior's last band. A saxophonist who'd runoff with Junior's girlfriend. He remembered the moment he'd discovered them together and his fist tightened. He winced again, the sharp pain a reminder of what he'd just done. The pain caused him to get angrier and more determined to make this deal. When he'd discovered Nicole and Marcus together, he'd said nothing. He got drunk, he broke things, and during the lashing out, he'd discovered his father's trunk and the treasure inside—two treasures really. The first, his father's leatherbound black journal that chronicled his life and his experience with the true treasure—the brown leather journal of Aleister Crowley. Since reading that book, terrible things had been done to get this point, to get to the crossroads. Terrible things that had been justified at every turn.

There was no turning back.

Junior sprinkled the dead saxophonist's ashes over the blood in the porcelain bowl. Reaching into his bag again, he retrieved a lighter, the type with the elongated neck so people could protect themselves from sparks and pain when lighting fires and grills. The final piece for his ritual was a business card. It was the card of a manager named Grady Sanford. Junior heard he was the best, and he desperately wanted to work with him. On the back of the card, an ancient prayer handwritten in Aramaic. Junior had barely passed English back in high school, so this was going to be interesting.

"Okay. Okay. Here we go. Read the words. Light the card. Drop it in the bowl. And wait. No problem. I got this."

Junior repeated the last three words at least a dozen times before finally taking a deep breath and actually executing the plan. He recited the prayer, surprisingly well, lit the card and dropped it in the bowl. The card went up in flames like it was doused in gasoline. It was a wonder he'd not burned his fingers. He watched as it rested atop his ashen mixed blood, then gasped as it dipped below like a drowned man giving up his fight for life.

And there was nothing.

No light. No sound. No…nothing.

Junior remained there for several minutes, waiting, wishing, cursing, before finally rising from his knees. Twenty minutes passed. Defeated, Junior packed the dagger and vial in his backpack, slung it over his shoulder and turned to walk away.

Then the rumbling began.

The porcelain bowl shook as if caught in an earthquake.

Junior turned at the sound of an inhuman wail and watched an eruption of fire and magma escape the bowl.

Reddish orange liquid oozed out, forming a deadly pool of heat and fire. Dumbfounded, Junior walked just to the edge and despite the small pockets of fire and steam rising from the mini lava flow, he felt nothing but cold air. The center of the lava pool, where the bowl once was, began to bubble. From it, more lava and fire rose. It reached a height of six feet or more before it began to take form. First legs, then a torso, then finally arms, and a head. Red eyes formed in the center of the figure's head. The fiery figure stepped forward, and the burning man spoke despite having no mouth.

"Welcome to the crossroads, Junior Coleman. How can I be of service?" it asked.

#   #   #

"Here we are, my friends, with another episode of Music Moves the Soul. A show that'll get you outta yo seat, so you can jam and move ya feet. I am your host, Don Cornell, here, as always, to shine the light on the next up and coming artist…and to have a little fun along the way. Junior Coleman will join us live in a little bit, but for now, let's dig on the musical stylings of the royal genius known…as Prince."

Junior heard the smooth-talking Don Cornell on the speakers as he walked through the hallway of Johnson Studios where the hit music show was filmed. As the funk-filled sounds of Prince swam through the hallway his heartbeat quickened as he was closer and closer to achieving his dream.

When he was a boy, his mother would turn on the black and white television in the kitchen every Saturday morning as she cleaned. She would crank it as loud as it would go so she could hear the music over the clanking of dishes and running water. Junior would join her after he'd finished cleaning his room and together, they would dance and sing along to every tune they heard, stopping only to watch whatever artist or group was featured live that day. They'd even challenge each other to see who could solve the jumble board the fastest.

"Mama, I'm gonna be on Music Moves the Soul one day. Watch and see."

He'd say that. Word for word. Every Saturday morning. Now, twenty years later, that dream was about to come true. The culmination of years of hard work, practice, and faith.

Murder and that deal at the crossroads didn't hurt either.

"Right this way, Mr. Coleman," said the producer leading the way.

Junior was led to another room, just off stage, where he'd be able to watch the show and await his time on stage. The room was a bit psychedelic. The multi-colored walls were covered in shapes and far out images that defied imagination. They seemed to move. Not so much with the beat of the music, they just moved, swirled, and spun in all directions. Furnished with a red couch, a black loveseat, and a green recliner, the room was an assault on the visual senses. A flat monitor was attached to the wall to watch the taping, and the music from the show came in through large speakers mounted in the upper corners.

"I know, it's a trip, right?" asked the producer.

"This is definitely something else," said Junior.

"Just hang out here, and I'll be back to get you in about twenty minutes. We'll head on up to Section Wild Wonder."

"Wild Wonder?"

"Yeah, that's where you'll go to play for the local affiliate."

"Local…wait…I thought I was gonna be featured on the main stage? I'm supposed to be on Lower Reality." said Junior.

"Oh, you are on the main stage. But the main stage for the local broadcast," said the producer.

"But that's not what I was promised, man."

"Look, I don't handle that side of things, so I can't speak to what you were promised, only what I was directed to do," said the producer. "Look man, local or national, this is still the chance of a lifetime. Don't let your ego blow it. I done seen too many cats come up in here thinkin' they all that, just to get kicked to the curb. Don't be that dude."

Junior sat with that for a moment and allowed his anger to subside. It was a slow process, but after he relaxed his shoulders and took a deep breath, he nodded his head then walked to the green recliner to take a seat and wait.

"My man," said the producer, pointing at Junior to acknowledge his happiness with the decision he'd made.

When the door closed, Junior slammed his fist on the arm of the chair in frustration.

"Well that's not very professional."

Junior shot up from the chair, searching for the man behind the voice. The room was too small to have missed anyone. There was no place to hide. No closets or hidden rooms. With the exception of the recliner, the couch and loveseat were back up against the wall making it impossible for someone to hide behind them.

"Easy Junior, I'm right here."

Junior stood frozen as a shadow stepped from the corner and took the form of a man. The black shape was tall and faceless yet kept moving forward. Junior took a step back, then another, and another, before falling back into the recliner from which he'd sprang.

"Whoa. You okay there, Junior?" asked the shadow.

"Wh-wh-what the hell are you?" asked Junior.

"Oh come now," began the shadow, "you know me. Stop acting like we don't go back a few years."

Junior tried to push himself further into the recliner in a childlike attempt to retreat, his mind absent of all rational thought.

"Maybe it's my appearance," said the shadow. "Here, let me fix that."

The shadow snapped its fingers and instantly burst into flame. The red eyes in the center of its head were trained on Junior. The musician felt his heart skip several beats as awareness dropped over him.

"Y-y-y-you," stammered Junior.

"Mm-hm. Me," said the shadow. "Now, I believe we have some business to tend to."

#   #   #

"So what happens now?" asked Junior.

"Well, you've just called me to the crossroads, young man. What happens now is, you tell me why."

"Are…are…are you the devil?"

Junior's question was met with low laughter that sent vibrations through the ground, up his leg, and straight to his heart. Pressure around his heart increased. The beating slowed. Junior dropped to his knees and clutched at his chest. Unable to speak, he screamed…in his mind. He screamed for help, for an end to the pain. But of course his pleas went unheard.

Or did they.

The laughter stopped and with it, the vice-like grip Junior felt within his chest. He inhaled deeply as if it were his first breath on Earth. On all fours now, Junior coughed and spit as his eyes watered.

"Does it still matter who I am?" asked the flaming, red-eyed figure.

With effort, Junior lifted his head, and slowly shook it from side to side.

"Good. Now then, collect yourself, and tell me why I'm here."

Junior coughed for another minute before pulling himself together and sitting back on his haunches to face the being before him. The flames were bright. The thing was a walking inferno, yet there was no heat. What really sent chills through Junior were the eyes. Blood red irises encased in a jet-black frame. It was impossible. Everything about the moment should have been impossible. But it was happening.

Just like the book said it would.

"I…um…brought you here to ask for your help," said Junior.

"Let's assume I know that already. Get to it."

"I'm a musician…a singer," began Junior, "and I want to be famous."

"So practice," said the flaming figure.

"I do. I always do. It's what I've always done. But…but…it's just not—"

"Happening fast enough?"

Junior lowered his head and let words sink in before he nodded. It was the truth. It wasn't happening fast enough for him. He wanted to be famous. He wanted the accolades. He wanted love. His mother stood by his side from childhood till her death. She encouraged him, supported him, believed in him, at every stage of his development. She'd sunk every dollar and cent she had into his lessons. From rent to his cellular phone she'd paid his bills so he could focus on the music. When she died, he'd all but given up.

Until he found the book.

And now, here he was, kneeling before a fiery supernatural being, about to sell his soul for fame.

"I'm good. I'm *really* good," said Junior. "I just…need a break. I want to be great. I want to make my mother proud."

"Your mother is dead," said the fiery figure sending up a burst of flame into the air.

Junior held up an arm to shield his eyes. Once again, there was no heat. Just light. Impossible light.

"I…I know. But, after all she sacrificed for me…I can't just live a life that amounts to nothing. I want to be famous, and I want my music to live on for generations."

The figure chuckled. Junior felt the ground vibrate again. He absently grabbed his chest and lowered his head, but nothing happened. Daring to look up, Junior stared into the red eyes before him. The being gestured for Junior to stand…and he obliged.

"Do you know what it means to ask something of me?"

Junior nodded.

"And you're prepared to make that sacrifice?" asked the being, stepping closer to Junior.

After a short hesitation, Junior nodded.

"You're certain," said the being, now face to face with Junior, who, to his credit, did not flinch. "I need to hear you say the words."

"I know what I'm asking, and what I'm sacrificing. I'm prepared," said Junior.

Within the flame, Junior thought he saw the face of a man, smiling.

"Very well," said the being.

The fiery figure pressed its hand against Junior's chest, right over the heart. The flames increased and the light hurt Junior's eyes so much that even closed, it felt as if he were staring into the sun on a summer's afternoon. There was no heat…still. Only the cold. Junior heard the crackling of flame speed up. The light was brighter, brighter, and brighter still.

Then nothing.

The light beyond his eyelids was gone and Junior slowly opened them. He was shocked to find nothing in front of him. The fiery figure was gone.

Junior looked all around and saw only darkness, save for the cluster of lights coming from the small town in the distance.

"What the…?"

Junior reached down for his backpack, uncertain if what just happened *actually* happened. As he bent over, he felt a pain in his chest. He immediately moved to rub the area and felt something strange beneath his shirt. Junior retrieved a flashlight from his bag, lifted his shirt and shined the light on himself. There, over his heart, was a handprint burned into his skin.

Just like the book said.

#   #   #

"Looks like you made it," said the shadow.

Junior said nothing. Not out of fear, but out of surprise. This wasn't how things were supposed to go for him. He'd made a deal. He'd done terrible things to get to this moment. He'd promised his very soul.

And he wasn't getting the top stage?

"This isn't what you promised me," said Junior, finding his voice.

"I beg your pardon?"

"You promised me fame. You promised me people would be talking about me in two years' time. Well, it's been two years!"

"And look where you are," said the shadow.

"I'm on the damn Wild Wonder stage. Wild. Wonder. You don't get famous there. They don't spread that feed to the world. That's only for the locals. The locals already know me, man!"

It took Junior a few moments to recognize that he was standing. Not only was he standing, but he was also face to face with the shadow. His heart was racing, but again, not in fear. The surprise he once felt morphed into anger. It filled him.

"After everything I've done. All the sacrifices I made. *This* is what I get?" spat Junior.

Junior heard a rumble. The floor buzzed and he felt a tingle in his feet. The shadow's red eyes narrowed and in that moment, Junior realized where the rumble was coming from. The shadow became blurry, vibrating at an unnatural speed. The tingle in Junior's feet traveled to his legs, his thighs, and his torso, before stopping in his chest.

"Oh no. No. No, no, no, no, nooooo!"

Junior dropped to his knees and clutched at his chest. It was worse than before. More intense, more malicious. The first time this happened, years ago, he didn't know what to expect. This time, he was willing to bet everything he was about to die.

His chest tightened. His breath was rapid and shallow. The end was coming.

"Understand this, boy," began the shadow, "you are not in control here. And you NEVER question my integrity. We made a deal, it's true, and I am bound by our covenant to honor that. But make no mistake, if you disrespect me one more time, I will break that deal…and I will break you."

Junior heard a snap, and pain shot through his abdomen. Then a second and third snap followed by increased pressure around his lungs. The sound of breaking bones did not stop. His fingers became displaced, he fell to the side from the pain of broken femurs. More ribs cracked, further constricting his breathing. Pressure in his skull made him scream at the top of his lungs.

"Mr. Coleman are you okay?" asked the producer after bursting into the room.

Confused, Junior looked around, searching for the shadow. He saw nothing but the psychedelic walls, furniture, and dancers on the monitor enjoying the sounds of Luther Vandross. He patted himself and found that he was whole. No broken bones. The only thing out of the ordinary was the fact that he was on the ground uncoiling from a fetal position.

"Mr. Coleman?"

Junior said nothing.

"Mr. Coleman?"

Finally, awareness washed over him.

"Uh…uh…yeah. I'm uh…good. I was, um, meditating. I must have dozed off."

He'd done it before, so it wasn't out of the ordinary. It wasn't the truth at this moment, but the producer didn't need to know that. Besides, who would believe the truth anyway?

"Yeah, I dozed off and fell out of the chair. Had a dream just that quick that I was falling. Crazy, man."

"For sure," said the producer. "Here, let me help you up."

Junior grabbed the producer's extended hand and rose. He made minimal eye contact. The absurdity of what had happened filled him with embarrassment. He wanted to move on from the moment.

"Is it time?" asked Junior.

"Yes sir," said the producer. "If you'll follow me, I'll get you to the stage."

The producer exited the room and Junior followed. He took one last look, searching for the shadow, but there was nothing. The only thing he felt was heat from the mark on his chest. The intensity was low but rising.

"I'm sorry," he whispered into the room.

The heat on his chest cooled.

#   #   #

Junior walked the long hallway behind the producer. Everything seemed…off. The hallway seemed to be never ending, and eerily quiet. Junior couldn't even hear the telecast anymore. There was no music, no shuffling feet dancing to the soulful sounds of…anybody. The lighting was dim. Bulbs flickered or were completely out.

"Are we almost there?" he asked the producer.

Silence.

He saw the producer just ahead of him one minute, and in the next moment, he'd vanished.

"Hey. Hey, man. Where'd you go? Where are we at, man?"

Junior stopped. He spun around, trying to get his bearings. Behind him there was darkness. Ahead of him, the same. To his right, though, there was a door. He could see purple light pulsating through the cracks. On his left, another door. Golden light escaped its cracks. There were no sounds coming from either, but they were the only source of anything in the otherwise pitch-black hallway.

Junior stepped to the right and grabbed the doorknob. It would not turn.

He tried again and again but it simply would not budge. He knocked. He called to whomever was inside, only to be met with silence. He tried the same on the door to his left and found it to be the same. Defeated, he rested his head against the door, and repeated the same word over and over.

"Why?"

"Because you have not committed to a decision. This is where the true path to stardom begins, Junior."

Junior jumped.

"Who's there?" he asked, his voice barely audible over his heartbeat. "Show yourself!"

The hallway lights flickered. At the end of the corridor Junior saw a dark figure with long wavy arms. The only thing he could truly make out were the red eyes in the center of its head. It was him. The figure began to walk closer as the lights flickered before finally going out completely. Junior heard nothing. Not even his own breathing which was out of control. Suddenly the lights came on and the figure was directly in front of him.

"Hello there," said the man.

Not a shadow this time. Not a fiery entity of living flame. A…man. With bright red eyes, dark weathered skin, and a sinister, bloody grin. Junior fell back, landed on his ass, and tried to scoot backward, only to bump into to something…no…someone. He looked back, then up, and found the same man looking down at him.

"That's not very polite, Junior."

The man bent down, grabbed Junior and hoisted him up. Junior dangled for several beats before he was finally lowered to the floor. The dark man released him, and Junior stepped back.

"Wh-wh-what the hell is this?" asked Junior.

"If you'd just calm down, I'll tell you."

The lights overhead came on, then dimmed. Ahead of him and behind the man, Junior saw people moving about. He could hear the music from the show overhead and the shuffling of feet. Junior turned and looked behind him. He saw people wearing headsets, holding clipboards, and talking into microphones. They all walked about as if nothing strange had occurred. He turned back to face the man before him and what he saw sent electricity through his body.

"You…you're…you're…"

"Don Cornell. At your service. For quite some time actually."

"You mean…all this time…it was you? The fire? The shadow? The—"

"Everything, young man."

The man now before Junior was about his height, maybe slightly taller. He wore his hair in a short afro, groomed well, with short sideburns. He was clean shaven and wore wire rimmed glasses which framed regular brown eyes. His suit was impeccable. A tailor-made three-piece ensemble in black, with a white shirt, red tie, and matching pocket square. The man carried himself in such a way that no one doubted he was the alpha.

"How? Why?"

"The 'how' is complicated. But the 'why'? Oh, my brother, that's very simple. Because you asked. You summoned me years ago. You made a request. We made a deal. And now we're here to see the culmination of all your efforts over the years. This show is the way to get you there."

"The deal isn't over yet though. You promised me stardom. You said—"

"Look, we're not going through this again, Junior. I did promise you stardom, but even I can't do anything until you've made the right choice."

Junior wasn't sure what that meant. Hadn't he been making the right choices the last couple of years? He did everything he was supposed to do, everything the book told him to do. He'd lied, he'd cheated, he'd stolen, and he'd killed. He did everything. What more could there possibly be?

"You've got two doors here, Junior. The door with the purple light will lead you to the Wild Wonder stage and you'll play the local broadcast. It will lead to more gigs, a radio show, a few parts on television, and in about five years, you'll get picked up by a major record label and your career will flourish. You'll have a long stable career that you can be proud of."

Junior let that sink in for a moment. Five years? He'd been paying his dues for years already. He was ready for more. He deserved more. He'd *earned* more. As the thoughts played out in his mind, his gaze drifted toward the other door.

"Ahhhh," began Don, "you get it now."

"What's behind this one?" asked Junior.

"Everything. The door with the golden glow will lead you toward the main stage, the national stage. The Lower Reality Section is what they call it. It fits in with the psychedelic atmosphere around here, you dig? It's the path to instant stardom, and everything you've earned. Money, fame, women, travel…everything."

Junior looked at the door, the saw the sign on the wall just to its right. It hadn't been there before. But now it was visible, right in his face. It read SEC. LOWER REALITY. It was the stage to be on. The one rumored to be the end-all-be-all for stage performers. The greats had played there, and their music endured for years and years.

"Well?" asked Don.

"Man, this ain't even a question that needs to be asked," said Junior, turning toward the door with the golden glow. "I've made my choice. Will it open this time?"

"It'll open," said Don. "If you're sure that's what you want."

"It's all I've wanted. That's why I called you in the first place. It's taken too long to get here as far as I'm concerned. The clock is ticking and I'm ready to move on."

A beat passed before Junior heard that familiar chuckle. Don Cornell, the host of Music Moves the Soul, and whatever else he was, was laughing at him.

"What's so funny?" asked Junior.

"You, my brotha. You…and this notion of time. Thinking that there's not enough, or that you're running out."

"I don't know what you are man. Maybe time is different for you. But there's not enough of it for me. I done put too much into this life to wait around another second to get what I earned. I've got work to do, and I want it to last for as long as possible."

"Time doesn't mean what you think it does, young man," said Don, shaking his head.

"No! It doesn't mean what *you* think it does. The clock is ticking, and I've got to make my move."

Don Cornell shook his head at Junior.

"Time means nothing," said Don. "I lose patience with people who work on a clock."

"Whatever, man. Look, I'm ready to do this," said Junior, grabbing the doorknob.

"So be it," said Don.

Junior turned the knob. The golden glow illuminated the entire door and he walked into the light. Once through, he found himself backstage of Sec. Lower Reality. Junior smiled wide as he looked on.

"This is where I'm meant to be," he said. "It's my time."

"Indeed it is," said Don, his brown eyes now bright red. "Indeed. It. Is."

#   #   #

"Ladies and gentlemen, we are about to bear witness to a new sound. But before we do, let's unscramble some letters," said Don, standing next to a couple.

Junior looked on, anxious for them to get through this. The couple had been chosen to work on the jumble board and spell something out with the letters while people danced to the music. He'd done this with his mother a hundred times or more. After that, he'd come on stage. He wanted his moment, in front of them, in front of the cameras, in front of the whole country. After today, everyone would know the name Junior Coleman.

"And what's your name, ma'am?" asked Don.

"Evelyn. Evelyn Coleman."

Junior heard the name and his jaw dropped.

"And you sir?" asked Don, turning his microphone to the man next to Evelyn.

"Thomas Coleman, Sr."

Junior's eyes welled with tears.

"All right then, Thomas and Evelyn. While we groove to the sound of The Whispers, you've got sixty seconds to work the jumble board. Right now it spells out Sec Lower Reality, the name of the place we're currently groovin' in right now," said Don, his words met with cheers and whistles from the crowd. "Move these letters around though, to spell out the name of someone you, and everyone in this room, should know."

The music played, the couple worked the letters, and Junior stood off stage in shock. He caught a quick glimpse of Don Cornell off to the side, smiling, eyes glowing brightly, before returning his gaze to the couple. But they weren't just any couple. They were his parents.

His very dead parents.

"What the hell is this?" he asked himself in a whisper.

"This is Music Moves the Soul, brotha," said Don Cornell.

Junior shuddered at the sudden arrival. He looked at Don, then, with a shaky hand, pointed to his parents.

"How is this happening? How are they here?"

"What? You don't want your parents to see you shine?"

"But…but…they're—"

"Dead?" finished Don. "I told you, time doesn't mean anything to me. I've got a job to do, too."

"And…what is that job?" asked Junior, fearful of the answer.

"To move souls, brotha."

Don vanished in a burst of flame and reappeared on the other side of the stage. Returning his gaze to his parents, Junior found them dancing, but staring back at him with dead eyes and mouths open, black ooze dripping down their chins. They continued to dance, but separated slightly, revealing the jumble board behind them. The once scrambled letters now spelled out a name. Junior knew the name. He knew the name because it was written in the book that began the nightmare he was now in.

"Aleister Crowley," whispered Junior.

"All right folks, it's time to jam. The young man about to step onto this stage is going to dazzle you. He's got his own sounds and he's making local waves with his voice. Let's give it up…for Junior…Coleman."

Junior found himself on stage but had no idea how he'd arrived there. He heard the applause from the audience and the first notes from the band. Looking toward the jumble board, he found that his parents were gone. All he saw was a sea of young men and women beginning to sway to the music.

"Get it together!" he said to himself.

And then he sang…somehow.

The words came out, one after the other, just as he'd written them.

He was on autopilot. Uncertain at first, Junior allowed the music and the words to energize him, and suddenly, all the madness he'd been through drifted away.

Minutes later, Junior was bowing to a roaring crowd. The applause was deafening. And he loved every second of it. He smiled. He waved to the dancers and blew kisses to the ladies. This is what he'd dreamed of. His time had finally come.

"Yes. Yes. Yes," said Don, walking up to Junior for his post-performance interview. "Junior Coleman. Amazing. Welcome to the program."

"Thank you. It's a dream come true."

"Tell us about this Junior Coleman sound," said Don.

"Well, it's really a combination of things. It's my feelings, it's my experiences, it's my hopes and dreams. You know, my dad always said…"

Junior's father had returned, dead eyed, slack jawed, oozing black liquid from his mouth. His mother stood next to him, ashen colored, with mangled hair. They stood in the center of the crowd and as a hush ran through the room Junior saw that it was filled with the dead. The woman next to his mother held her head under her arm. Men and women swayed side to side in rotted clothes with bits of hair and skin falling to the floor. There was a low hum, a rumble. It was the sound of the dead moaning, their dead eyes fixed on Junior.

"Wh-wh-what is this?" asked Junior.

"This is you, getting everything you've earned," said Don.

"Wait…what? I don't understand."

"You wanted fame. You wanted success. You wanted your music to live on. There are not bigger stars, my brotha, then young phenoms who die young."

The crowd parted, forming a row of dead on each side, and they continued to sway from side to side. Junior looked from them to Don. The host's red eyes brightened, and he burst into flame. He raised his fiery arm and pointed down the path.

"It's your time," said Don.

'It's…it's…it's not supposed to be like this," pleaded Junior.

"Everything you asked for is right there at the end of that dance line," said Don.

At the end of the dance line was an open door. Beyond that door, Junior saw a subway train. The doors to the subway car opened, and inside were the wandering corpses of well-known musicians. Musicians Junior grew up loving, idolizing.

Musicians who'd died soon after their meteoric rise to fame.

Two of the dead dancers came onto the stage and grabbed Junior. He struggled against them, but their strength was overwhelming. They took him to the edge of the stage and pushed him off. He landed hard, the taste of copper filled his mouth. He felt cold dead hands grab at him again to help him up. It was his mother and father. He looked from one to the other as they both pointed toward a door at the end of the double row of dead dancers. He looked back toward Don, but he was gone. In his place, a cloaked figure holding a scythe. Music played as the dead swayed, and Junior Coleman moved down the dance line toward his fate. At the end of the line, he went through the door, then boarded the train.

He looked back once last time before the doors closed and the train left.

#   #   #

"Well that's gonna do it for us this week, my friends. Special thanks to Junior Coleman for his magnificent performance. We're no doubt gonna watch his star rise in the next few months. Thank you to all the dancers here today. Join us again next week when we'll have another very special guest. And you can betcha last money it's all gonna be a stone gas, honey! I'm Don Cornell and as always in parting we wish you love, peace, and sooooul! ♜

THE CHAOS CRUSHERS' DAY OFF

By Alethea Kontis

"WHERE IS THAT BLIGHT-BRAINED halfling?" Hands on hips, Persimmon Petalwhisper stomped a foot in exasperation. A burst of glitterspark and forget-me-nots sprang up beneath her heel and fell blessedly short of her rose-colored dress. Persi enjoyed wearing pastels whenever the guild wasn't adventuring hither and yon. But she couldn't afford to singe another hem with her temper.

When the Chaos Crushers were saving the godsforsaken world from orcs, Persi's uniform consisted of a dull but useful conglomeration of rags that concealed a variety of supplies for mischief-making, and no shoes whatsoever. But as a result of the sleeping sickness that still held their leader and mastermind, High Wizard Vasim, in its thrall, all their daily wear was receiving a much-needed cleaning. The Chaos Crushers had suddenly found themselves with some time off.

Which meant that today was game day. A nice, relaxing, orc-free game day. The guild gathered around the table in their usual abandoned barrow. Most of them, anyway.

"Yenry's always late." Kian tied his shining locks of black hair back into a queue, revealing the dusky pointed elf ears he normally kept hidden.

"Mithrax knows why we put up with him."

"Because, even late, he always shows up." Azorius slid his black shield beneath the stone bench. "And he's usually very amusing."

"Unlike Bob." Nex crossed her very long legs. The curl of her blood red lip revealed a pointed dragon's tooth.

"You know Bob is a very private person," said Azorius.

"Bob's probably a double agent," said the dark elf.

"Bob's not a double agent," said the dragonborn. "Bob's a *jerk*."

"It's tough being a gelatinous sphere," said the ever-optimistic Azorius.

"Try being a dragon stuck in a human-sized body needing to depend on that gelatinous sphere for backup. Why is he part of this guild again?"

"He can kill *anything*," said the dark elf.

"Bob prefers 'they,' not 'he,'" said the paladin. "Be sensitive."

Nex's nostrils flared and smoked. In a gracefully sinuous move, she tossed the violet waves of her hair over one turquoise shoulder. "Our guild is the Chaos CRUSHERS, not the Chaos SLIMERS."

"We can play without Bob," said Persi. "But if that lunkheaded halfling doesn't bring us the game soon, I'm going to kick him so hard he'll poop flowers for a fortnight."

Nex raised an eyebrow. "Your date didn't go well then?"

"Our date didn't happen at all! The numbskull 'lost track of time while acquiring a shining treasure.' Shocker, right?" Persi crossed her arms. "I knew it was a bad idea. I never should have said yes to him in the first place."

"But we've been dancing around this for *years*," said Azorius. "You two are perfect for each other. Give him a chance."

"Nah." Nex snorted. "Cut his heart out and eat it instead."

"What she said," Kian chimed in. "I've got a blade or twelve you're welcome to borrow."

Persi smiled. Not one for the front lines of battle, she was more suited to the role of spy, thief, healer, or good luck charm. But that never stopped her dark-hearted guild mates from suggesting that there might be a bloodthirsty soul deep down inside her. It made Persi feel powerful. And that was why she loved them.

Well…all except Yenry.

As if summoned by thought, the halfling tumbled through the opening of the barrow in a cloud of dust. He jumped quickly to his feet, spread his arms and cried, "TA-DA!"

"Are you being chased?" asked Azorius.

Yenry tousled his wild hair and brushed off his shirt and trousers. "Not anymore."

"Did you get the game, half-bite?" Nex asked with a toothy yawn.

The rucksack of holding hung flat against Yenry's back, but that didn't mean anything. He could hide a horse in there without causing so much as a bulge. And had, on occasion.

Yenry unbuckled the leather straps and extracted a box from the sack. He got down on one knee and presented it to Persi as if she were Queen of All. The title inscribed on the lid read *The Princess Trial: A Fairy Tale Adventure*.

Any other day, Persi might have squealed in delight. This was exactly *her* sort of game, not something the others would have chosen. Ever. Not even Bob. Instead, she looked down her nose at Yenry and in a very Nex-like tone sneered, "You're late."

"I lost track of time while acquiring this shining treasure."

"Ooh," Azorius whispered. "He *does* say that, doesn't he?"

"You only just noticed?" Nex asked the paladin.

"If Persi doesn't hurt him, I might," Kian muttered.

Persi scowled at Yenry. "You are such a…hobgoblin."

Yenry rose back to his full height, only half a head taller than she. "Watch your mouth, little lady."

"*Little?*" Persi couldn't stop herself. "Bite me, shortbread."

His green eyes flashed. "Sure thing, wingless."

Sparks flew from Persi's fingers. She didn't punch him in the face, but her fistful of glitter did. The small barrow instantly filled with the scent of jasmine. Azorius sneezed.

Yenry bent and put a hand over one cheek. He coughed and scraped what he could from his lashes. When he looked back at her with one bloodshot, shimmering eye, he didn't yell. He just grinned.

Enraged, Persi's arm pulled back for another volley.

"As amusing as this is," said Nex, "can we just play the game already?"

"Pity," muttered Kian. "I was about to put money on the pixie."

"I don't believe anyone would have taken that bet," said Azorius.

Persi smiled broadly and sat next to the elf. Yenry took the only bench left, on the opposite side. He slid the box onto the table with a glittery finger.

Nex read the title. "*The Princess Trial.*" She stared at Yenry with fire in her eyes. "Seriously?"

"Looks can be deceiving," said the halfling. The dust still graying his boar-brown hair made him seem a decade older, lending a certain gravity to his words. Granted, the glitter caking the left side of his face took much of that away. "Surely any game from Vasim's shelves is a game worth playing."

They all drew in breath at this pronouncement. None of them—not even Nex—would have dared pilfer an item from the personal store of the High Wizard himself. Especially for something as trivial as game day.

But this was exactly the kind of thing that set Yenry apart. The halfling seemed to have been born with skills that other Master Thieves might never acquire…and the arrogance to go with them. Persi was a decent enough burglar—quiet, light of foot, and great at squeezing into tight places—but Yenry put the artist in con artist. He could stumble naked into a kingdom overrun by orcs and leave fed and clean and fully dressed, with a handful of freed prisoners, the most dangerous monster in the dungeon, and the queen's best horse.

The Chaos Crushers formed that day, though they hadn't made it official until the High Wizard had taken the motley crew in hand for their first quest.

"Then by all means, let us play," Nex said in a reverent tone. "I shall take the role of the princess."

Persi bit the inside of her lip until she tasted blood. If she so much as snickered at the mental image of Nex as a princess, she could kiss this dress— plus her hair, her eyebrows, and probably three layers of skin—goodbye.

"No, no, that's not how this works." Yenry opened the box and lifted up a faceted stone the color of Nex's skin. "We roll. The die chooses which part we play."

Nex snatched the die out of Yenry's hand and examined it. "How many sides does this thing have?"

"Twenty."

"And what number are we trying to get?"

Yenry lifted a parchment from inside the box. "It says here that whosoever rolls the lowest number shall be the Game Master. The other parts are assigned in ascending order—there's a list here."

But the dragonborn had already rolled. "Five," she said proudly. "Beat that."

Kian did almost immediately. "Two."

Yenry shook a finger at Persi. "Your turn. Go on. There's still a chance for you to get the princess part. We all know it should be you."

Persi grimaced. She really didn't see the point. She was fine with Kian being the Game Master and Nex playing the Princess, but Yenry was right. Persi really did want to be the princess herself. Dutifully, she lifted the die. It was cool to the touch. She casually tossed it back onto the tabletop. It clattered to a stop in front of Azorius.

The paladin bent over the die. "One!" he bellowed.

"What?" Persi could hardly contain her shock. That meant she was…

Kian patted her on the back. "Well done, Game Master."

Azorius got an eight. Yenry got a seven.

"So the roles are as follows," Yenry announced. "Lokian, Prince of Seven Enemies, will be the Princess Brittany."

Kian tilted his head gracefully. Well, he certainly had the hair for it.

"Nex, you will play Prince Tyler."

Nex's smile would have frightened an orc. "I'll take it."

"I shall take on the role of the princess's most trusted companion. A"—Yenry's finger slid along the parchment—"skunk frog."

Laughter echoed off the barrow walls. "What will I call you, O trusted companion?" Kian asked him.

"Booty," Yenry said without pause. "After my two favorite things."

"And who shall I be?" Azorius asked.

"You will be…the princess's horse."

"An honorable steed," Azorius said with great confidence.

"Sure," said Yenry. "Here are the character cards for each of us—they list how many damage points we have left until we die, and what sort of items and weapons we have on our persons. Now, hand this booklet to our Game Master and let's start setting up the field of play."

Persi accepted the Game Master's guide from Azorius. It wasn't terribly thick—perhaps this would be a nice short game. The yellowing pages seemed soft, but sturdy. Persi opened the cover. The words scrawled across the first page made her eyes widen.

I BELIEVE IN YOU.

Thank you, book, thought Persi. I believe in you, too.

Persi turned to the next page. It was blank. And then it wasn't. Words wrote themselves onto the parchment right before her eyes.

Your job as Game Master is to control how the story unfolds. Read each section as it reveals itself, and communicate the situation to the players. Remember, above all else, that you have ultimate control over this game. YOU.

The words faded as she read them, all but that last, emphatic **YOU.**

All right then, book, thought Persi. Mission accepted. Let's do this thing.

"Let's do this thing."

Persi's head flew up from the booklet at the words Nex had spoken. There was obviously some serious magic afoot. It didn't seem that any of the others had picked up on it yet, but they probably would as the story unfolded.

On the table, the guild had arranged nine plain grid squares into one larger square. Randomly scattered across the squares were silver figurines of their characters, rendered in perfect miniature.

Yenry picked up Princess Brittany for closer examination. "You know, Kian, she looks a little bit like you."

"Yours looks like you too," the dark elf responded, referring to Yenry's skunk frog.

"Once upon a time," Persi began.

"Yes," Azorius said of his figurine. "A very honorable steed."

"SHUT UP, MEAT STICKS. PERSI IS TRYING TO START THE GAME."

The barrow fell silent.

"Thank you, Nex," said Persi, and she began to read from the booklet again. "Once upon a time, a beautiful young princess lived in a shining castle."

Kian rested his chin in his hands and batted his eyelashes at the company.

"Princess Brittany was kind and generous, but her mother was far more"—the word took a moment to appear—"complicated."

The company grunted as one at that assessment. Even Persi sympathized. If any of them had had perfect families, most likely none of them would be here now.

"On the eve of Princess Brittany's thirteenth birthday, the mad queen sent her best huntsman into the woods with the princess."

At this, the squares on the table sprang to life. A miniature forest grew before their eyes and soon towered over the figures of the princess, the horse, and the skunk frog. The prince figurine disappeared from the board and reappeared in front of Nex.

"I take it I'm not in this scene," said Nex. "Pity." She sounded more bored than sad.

When the magical wood had settled, Persi went on. "The huntsman's orders were to kill the princess and return to the queen with her heart and liver as proof that the deed was done."

"Wow," said Azorius.

"Yummy," said Nex.

"I kill the huntsman instead," said Kian.

"Can he do that?" Azorius asked Persi.

"I don't know. Can he do that?" Persi asked the booklet.

All players must state their desired actions, said the book. Persi conveyed this answer to the table.

"Attack the huntsman with my..." Kian consulted the princess's character card. Unimpressed with whatever he found there, he tossed the card back onto the table. "A really sharp rock."

Azorius checked his own card. "Attack the huntsman with my iron-clad hooves."

Yenry did not look at his card. He looked at Persi. "Search for treasure," he said. The twinkle in his eye was not from the glitter on his face. Persi scowled back at him. When the rest of his party glared too, Yenry pointed to his figurine on the leaf-strewn path in the miniature wood. "*Skunk frog*, remember? What sort of damage could I possibly do to a highly skilled huntsman?"

Roll for damage, said the book.

"Really?" Persi said. "You guys are just going to attack? You're not going to try to talk to the man? Find out why he's doing this? Try to convince him to be on your side?"

Her guild members had no response.

ROLL FOR DAMAGE, said the book.

Persi shrugged. "Roll for damage, then."

Each player rolled the twenty-sided die, and then Persi rolled on behalf of the huntsman. The fight took several rounds—in small part because the princess and her horse could only inflict so much damage on the huntsman; in large part because Persi's rolls for the huntsman all turned out impressively low numbers. They finally did manage to defeat the huntsman, but not without great cost to their damage points.

"Let's move on," said Kian.

"Wait," said Azorius. "I only have one damage point left."

"I have three gold coins and a griddlecake," Yenry said proudly. Even Persi had been shocked that the huntsman had so much in his pockets.

"That's not helpful unless you're going to pay for a healer," said Azorius. "Do we know a healer?"

"Nope," Persi said proudly. Perhaps they'd respect her potions a little more after the Chaos Crushers' next skirmish.

"Perhaps I have a healing potion in my saddlebags." Azorius studied his card. "Nothing. You?"

Yenry held his card close to his chest, so that Azorius could not see its contents. "Nope."

Kian did the same. "Not a thing. What do we do now?"

Choose a direction and roll to walk, said the book.

"I walk east," Kian said as he rolled.

"I walk east." Azorius rolled and passed the die to Yenry.

"I kick the horse," Yenry said. Nex laughed. Yenry rolled before the rest of his companions could respond.

The princess's noble steed perishes in the dark wood, Persi read from the book.

"Hey, it worked!" Yenry cheered.

"Why would you do that?" Azorius bristled. "I only had one damage point left!"

"Because if you die, you'll have to choose a new character card now," Yenry explained. "I'd rather go into the next fight with someone at the top of their game instead of a horse that's going to bite it in the first round and leave the rest of us hanging."

Nex nodded. "It's the smart move."

"Aw…" Azorius hung his head. "I didn't even have a chance to name him."

The horse figurine toppled to one side. The other figurines gathered around him, as if mourning. Then the horse shimmered and disappeared.

"My card went blank," said Azorius.

Persi read the details of what had transpired. "Ha!"

"It's bad enough that I can't play yet," said Nex. "No fair skipping ahead."

Persi looked up from the booklet. Instead of continuing to parrot everything word for word, she decided to paraphrase. "The sun is beginning to set. The trees cast long shadows over the path. There is a slight chill in the air."

The game board animated Persi's story as it unfolded. Shadows twisted this way and that around the figurines left on the board. Even the barrow felt dimmer. The sound of frogs and crickets emanated from the darkness.

Persi smiled. She decided to exercise her ultimate control as Game Master.

"The wind whistles through the trees," said Persi, her voice low and ominous. A slight breeze kicked up in the barrow, and the smell of dried leaves and loam rose up from the game board. "The howl of it sounds like a mournful cry." A keening tone echoed from somewhere; instinct caused everyone in the guild to glance around for the source.

Everyone except Persi.

"There is a rustle in the bushes—" A rustle came from behind Kian's chair. The dark elf snapped his head around, hidden blade already to hand.

When he realized what he'd done, he shook his head. "You're getting good at this, Petalwhisper."

Persi took the compliment and continued. "The noise scared Princess Brittany, but there was no need to worry. From the brush emerged a very nice-looking donkey."

"That's me!" Azorius said brightly. He showed off his card, refilled with information on this new character. The figurine of a donkey now stood on the board with the others.

"From whence have you come, good Sir Ass?" asked Yenry.

"From whence have I come?" Azorius whispered to Persi.

"The donkey came from the north," Persi read. "Where he was employed by a brotherhood of dwarfs."

Nex chuckled. The rest of them groaned.

"I guess we go see these dwarfs then," Kian said reluctantly.

The trio continued to roll and walk their way through the woods. Since Booty the skunk frog rode in the Princess's pocket, Yenry used every one of his turns to search for treasure. By the time they arrived at the dwarfs' well, he had acquired a penknife, a vial labeled "Powder of Life," a handful of berries, seven mushrooms, three acorns, a canary feather, and a withering look from Nex.

"You are trying my patience, halfling."

"You never know when any of this stuff will come in handy," said Yenry. "Now hush and play the game."

"I'm not even in the stupid game yet!"

At the well, the princess and her friends meet Prince Tyler, said the book.

"It's about time!" said Nex. "Now let's kill these rock-sniffing dwarfs!"

The rest of the party cried their agreement and scrambled for the die.

Persi opened her mouth and closed it again. Seriously? Had they read any books at all? Listened to any stories? Didn't they know that these dwarfs were the sort to harbor and care for princesses, not the grumpy, smelly, foul-mouthed weapons dealers they encountered in the orc-ridden wastelands?

Persi might have had ultimate control over the game, but she had no control over how ridiculous her guild mates could be. Fine. If they wanted to ruin the storyline for themselves, she'd help them along…as painfully as possible.

Princess Brittany and her headstrong party had a sword, a dagger, a penknife, and a donkey. Persi's seven dwarfs were armed to the teeth, and then some.

Persi assumed the dwarfs had pickaxes, because she knew pickaxes were essential to mining, so she started the attacks with those. When the book hinted at the existence of a brass lamp, she had the brilliant idea to douse someone in the oil and set them on fire.

That someone ended up being Azorius's donkey. He hadn't made it.

From then on, the book followed Persi's lead. She would suggest a weapon and, if it was appropriate, the book would put it into play. The game board—now the dwarfs' house—was covered in blood and broken bodies. Every plate and piece of furniture was smashed, and almost every window was broken.

Nex's prince fought valiantly. He disarmed all of the dwarfs at least twice, but Persi kept finding new objects for them. A rock hammer. A chair. The broken handle of a broom. But Prince Tyler, so far the strongest character in the group, killed them all. He chased the last dwarf out to the barn and cornered him between two bales of hay.

"I have you now," Nex said through her teeth.

"The dwarf reaches into one of the hay bales and pulls out…a stick of dynamite!" *Can I do that?* Persi thought.

Roll to light the dynamite, said the book.

Grinning, Persi rolled. The dynamite fuse ignited. The figurines scattered. The barn burst into a giant ball of light and heat. Even Nex looked mildly impressed, and that was saying something.

"What's your move now?" Persi asked calmly, as if the game board hadn't just violently exploded between them.

"Drink one of my healing potions," said Kian.

"Ditto," said Yenry.

Azorius pointed at them. "You said you didn't have healing potions!"

"What did it matter?" Kian said. "You were essentially dead at the time."

"And you're dead now," added Yenry.

"Let's take shelter in the house if it's still intact," said Nex. "Perhaps we can shore up here for a few rounds and nurse our wounds while we decide what to do."

The rest of the party agreed. No surprise. They usually did everything Nex suggested in the real world, too. But Persi thought she recognized this fairy tale. If she was right, she knew what was in store for them. And she wasn't about to spoil the fun.

After the first round of resting and healing, Azorius asked, "Can I come back as another character?"

Persi started at the book, but the page remained empty. She looked at the game board, still littered with bodies. "I'm not sure how. You all killed everyone that lived here."

"Wait!" Yenry ran his finger down his character card. "There. I carve a face in that broken handle of a broom with my penknife and sprinkle it with Powder of Life."

"That's not going to work," said Nex.

"It worked!" said Persi.

The large man whooped as his character card refilled again with script. His bushy brows furrowed as he read. "But my only attack seems to be…a saving throw from Booty the skunk frog." Slowly, Azorius's pursed lips spread into a wide smile. "I'm alive! I'll take it! Thanks, Yenry!"

"Don't mention it, Stick."

On the next round, there was a knock at the door of the dwarfs' cottage.

"I'll get that," Kian said in a ridiculous falsetto. "Who is it?"

Persi bent her head over the booklet so the others could not see her smile as she read the scene she knew she'd find there. **At the door is an old woman. She has a basket of beautiful, fresh apples. And you are all very hungry**.

"I take an apple," said Kian.

The apples cost one gold coin each, read Persi.

"That's ridiculous!" said Nex. "Who in their right mind would charge that much for an apple?"

"I don't have any gold," Kian said, checking his character card.

"Booty the skunk frog does," Azorius volunteered.

"Rat," Yenry said to Azorius.

"Stick," corrected Azorius.

"Give her the gold, Yenry," ordered Nex.

"The name is *Booty*," said Yenry. "And no."

"Come on," said Kian. "There are three of us and you have three gold coins."

"No way," said Yenry. "Find your own apples."

Nex snarled. "I pick up the skunk frog and shake him until the coins fall out."

Persi raised an eyebrow. "That's your move?"

"Yes," said Nex.

Prince Tyler gains three gold coins, said the book.

"Bully." Yenry crossed his arms. "I hope you choke."

Persi coughed to cover what was almost a laugh at Yenry's comment. Her throat was very dry from all that reading. She wished one of them had thought to bring snacks.

"I buy the apple from the old woman and eat it," said Kian. "Or does that count as two moves?"

Apparently, it did not.

Princess Brittany dies from eating the poisoned apple, said the book.

"What?" Kian yelled.

"You cannot speak," said Persi. "You're dead. Sorry."

"That woman is a witch!" cried Azorius.

"Wait a minute." Kian's head perked up. "That old woman is—"

"Shhh!" Persi hissed at the dark elf.

"But all I need is—"

"YOU ARE DEAD, BRITTANY." Persi raised her voice enough to drown out the rest of Kian's sentence. The dark elf gave up and slumped back in his chair to watch the carnage unfold.

"Attack her!" Azorius bellowed.

"But should we?" Nex hedged. "I mean, witches can be useful under the right circumstances…"

"Attack the witch!" Yenry cried, rolling the die.

"And throw Stick!" Azorius added.

"Fine. Attack I guess," said Nex.

Booty the skunk frog scored a nasty bite on the witch's ankle. Stick gave her a splinter. Once again, Prince Tyler was left with the dragon's share of the fighting. Which gave Persi a fabulous idea.

"Roll to turn the witch into a dragon," Persi said on the next round.

The old woman turns into a dragon, said the book. Lightning flashed over the game board. Somewhere far away, thunder rolled. From magically conjured clouds, a shadowy dragon rose to loom over the figurines. There was a hint of sulfur in the air.

"Oh, huh-uh." Yenry held up a hand. "Stick and I are running away from that nonsense. Good luck, Prince Tyler!"

Nex leaned in closer. "Attack the dragon. Aim for the soft area at her throat." And then she rolled the die.

Five.

The sword glances off the dragon's scales, leaving barely a scrape, said the book. The shadow dragon roared and belched flame.

Persi took the die in hand. She leaned in, too. "Bite off the prince's sword arm."

Yenry hooted and slapped the table with both hands. Azorius gasped. Kian chuckled.

"That's a harder move than you think," said Nex, who would know.

Persi took a deep breath and rolled.

Twenty.

Persi blinked in astonishment. The shadow dragon on the board bent and tore into the prince figurine. There was a flash of red. Persi half expected to see blood splattered on Nex's face. There might as well have been. Both of the dragonborn's eyebrows were raised. An astonished Nex was such a rare sight that her very countenance looked strange. The whole situation felt strange.

And Persi gaining the upper hand? Unheard of. Part of her almost wanted to apologize. The other part knew that if she did, she'd lose the smattering of Nex's respect that she had earned in this moment.

The dragon lost a few more damage points. The damage points on Prince Tyler's card, however, fell precipitously. They continued to slowly diminish as the prince's figure continued to bleed.

"We have lost," Nex said quietly.

Yenry stood up. "Not yet, we haven't! Stick, let's come out of hiding and take one last shot at this dragon. What do you say?"

Azorius stood as well. "I am with you, brother!"

Yenry rolled the die. Twelve.

The skunk frog bites the dragon on the ankle. The dragon loses three drops of blood. The skunk frog loses a tooth.

"Your valiant effort is appreciated," Nex said without energy, as if she were the one bleeding out on the table.

Azorius snapped up the die. "Saving throw!" he cried as he tossed it in the air. Yenry bellowed and clapped as well, cheering him on. The die clattered to a stop in the middle of the bloody battle.

This time, they all leaned in to see what the die read.

Twenty.

Azorius and Yenry let out deafening whoops of triumph. Persi sat back and read from the booklet.

In his saving throw, Booty tosses Stick into the air…and straight down the gullet of the dragon.

Azorius's character card went blank once more. The shadow dragon on the table writhed, choked and finally fell on the table, dead.

You have defeated the dragon, said the booklet.

Yenry and Azorius exchanged high-fives, but Nex remained despondent. "We beat the dragon, yes, but we did not truly win the game. Look at this." She waved a turquoise hand over the mess they had made. "None of us survived."

"Speak for yourself," said Yenry. He raised his chin and puffed out his chest like a peacock. "I may be toothless, but I'm not dead. And if I'm not dead, then that means the game's not finished."

"What else could there possibly be left to do?" asked Kian.

Yenry pointed at the figurine of the prince. "I take a cup of the dragon's saliva and pour it over Tyler's arm to staunch the wound." He pointed to the dragon. "Then, I take the prince's sword and cut through the soft part of the dragon's neck to retrieve Stick. Finally, I kiss the princess and wake her up."

Azorius's character card refilled once more. Prince Tyler's dangerously low damage count stopped shrinking. But Princess Brittany's figurine stayed dead. Kian's card remained blank.

"It didn't work," said Kian.

Nex shook her head slowly. "It's me," she said to the table. "I should have been the one to kiss the princess." Her opaline eyes met Persi's. "You knew that all along, didn't you?"

Persi merely smiled a little and shrugged. Nex knew she'd been defeated. There was no need to rub her nose in it. Any of the others might have, but that wasn't Persi's style.

"Prince Tyler kisses Princess Brittany," said Nex.

There was no need to roll for this action. The one-armed figurine of the prince rose from the table and limped over to the prone form of the princess. Gently, he bent over her and gave her a kiss.

Nothing happened.

"Make sure the poison apple's not still in her mouth," Yenry offered.

At that, the figure of the princess turned to the side and coughed up the piece of poison apple.

Kian's character card filled once more. "I'm back!"

The figurines on the table gathered together in a group hug. Above them, the guild members clapped each other on the backs.

Nex extended a turquoise hand across the table to Persi. "Well played, Game Master." The pixie clasped it warmly as they shook. "I look forward to our next adventure."

The scene on the table vanished. It was replaced by a large castle. On a high balcony stood the princess, her one-armed prince, and their companions.

Persi looked down at the booklet once more.

And they lived happily ever after, she read to the table.

As she spoke the words, bright balls of color exploded in the sky above the castle in celebration. The guild members watched in awe and wonder. And then the castle vanished.

It was replaced by the image of the High Wizard Vasim.

"Congratulations, Chaos Crushers," said the wizard. "I hope this adventure has been illuminating. Just as I hope this game is soon returned to the very spot from whence it came." Vasim's image looked directly at Yenry. "You and I will be having a talk, thief," it said before vanishing.

Azorius whistled. "Somebody's in trouble."

The comment caused another round of laughter…which ceased when another object appeared on the game board: a sparkling tiara, worthy of a princess.

"To the victor goes the spoils," Yenry said as he reached for the tiara.

Nex slapped his hand away. "This is not for you, halfwit." The dragonborn snapped up the tiara in her turquoise hands…and presented it to Persi. "I believe this goes to the true winner of this game."

Speechless, Persi accepted the tiara and placed it on her brow. "Thank you," she said, as the High Wizard had taught her to say when she could think of nothing else.

"Now I think we should leave the pilferer to clean up," said Nex. "Add to his punishment."

"Agreed," said Kian. "I don't know about all of you, but I need to stretch my legs."

"Let's walk down to the inn," said Nex.

Azorius picked up his shield. "First round's on me!"

"Thanks, Stick. You coming, Persi?" Nex called over her shoulder.

"In a second," the pixie said to her guild mates. "I'll be right there." She turned back to where Yenry was putting each square of the game board carefully back in the box. "So how did you do it?"

Yenry put on his most innocent face. "Do what?"

"How did you rig the game?"

Yenry's eyes sparkled almost as brightly as her tiara. "Give me another chance at our date, and I'll tell you."

Persi put her hands on her hips. "Tell me, and I'll think about it."

He gave her a crooked grin.

"Tell me *the truth*."

Yenry's grin fell. "You're no fun. The truth is…I had nothing to do with winning, losing, the tiara, any of it. As soon as I saw this game on Vasim's shelf, I just knew you needed it."

"But why?" she whispered.

Yenry shrugged. "Why not? You're always going on and on about the fairy tales your family used to tell. I thought we needed to play a game you would be really good at. And you were. *Incredibly* good. Maybe too good."

He placed the figurines inside the box and secured the lid. "Taking Nex down a peg was just a bonus."

Persi couldn't believe her ears. "So you stood me up because…?"

"Because it took me too long to find the right game."

She narrowed her eyes at him, but he didn't flinch. Could he actually be telling her the truth? "You really did this all for me?"

"Yes," he said. "Did it work?"

"Maybe," she said, but Persi let her smile answer for her. The tiara seemed to give her a courage she never had before. She lifted a hand and brushed some of the glitter off Yenry's cheek with her fingertips. "Sorry about earlier."

"Don't apologize," he said, taking her hand in his. "You making me shine is not a bad thing."

Game Master Persi, still flush with power, was suddenly seized by a wicked desire to see just how much more of Yenry she could make sparkle. But there was a noise in the doorway, and the two of them leapt apart.

Inch by slow inch, a thick green ooze slid into the barrow.

"Hey there, guild mates!" Bob lifted up a large bag. "I brought snacks!" ♜

SHELL GAME

By Joy Preble

IT WAS, AT FIRST, A very tight fit. Even tighter as she realized there was no going back, no way to reverse what had happened. But tight fits were her specialty. At least they had been.

You don't become a successful thief if you're not willing to get yourself jammed up now and then. Not willing to risk it all.

Caterina Von Eckstein was at the top of her game. She had risked everything and then some. You calculated the odds, and then you leaped. Sometimes literally.

Like that museum job back in December. It had been going so well until the silent alarm went off. The one her contact swore had been disabled. The one that required her to rappel off the roof in a raging thunderstorm and slam the last ten feet into a fortunately placed set of topiaries when her soggy hands slipped off the soggy rope and sent her tumbling.

She'd plucked tiny, well-manicured branches out of her ass for days.

Still. It wouldn't have been like her not to take the job when it was offered. The payoff was too big, too tantalizing to give up.

"It's dangerous," the gruff voice on the message had said. "You should know that." He cleared his throat. His voice stayed husky. "Are you in?"

It was the raspy voice that did it. Cat was a sucker for voices, especially ones that sounded like their owner had just rolled out of bed, rumpled, slightly hung-over, smelling of whiskey and sex—a fair amount of both. Preferably with her.

Cat was a woman of specific tastes and fantasies. She went after them like she did everything else in her life—with a dogged intensity until she got what she'd come for.

So yeah. She wanted the job. Bad. She should have known better. But the more he talked, the more she wanted it. That damn sexy voice.

He gave her the rundown.

A crumbling Gilded Age mansion on the far north side, couple blocks from the lake. New owners were doing a gut-rehab. Cat's phone caller had a contact who did real estate and gave him a heads-up anytime a house might have a history.

This one did.

Back in the 20's the original owner had done business with some gangster types. A few not-quite-honest politicians, too. Did side work for Al Capone and others, fencing artwork and the like. Laundering ill-gotten cash. The usual, but there were rumors, persistently, about hidden treasure. A fortune of money and bonds never recovered from unsolved bank robberies. Maybe even a few gold bars. The stories varied but the rumors persisted.

They intensified when the owner was gunned down on his front lawn one crisp October afternoon in 1928. The house went to a nephew. Rented out over the decades but staying in the family. As far as anyone could tell, no fortune had ever been found.

"It's there, though," said Cat's caller. "They just don't know how to find it."

"And you do?"

"Absolutely," he said, with enough confidence that Cat let him continue.

The new owners' contractor, he explained, had found a hidden door in a wall panel. The discovery was causing a delay—was there really something there?—but it had all amounted to nothing. A passageway that led to an empty room. No secret fortune. Except the thousands that would come out of the owners' pockets to wall the whole thing up permanently.

"But we," Cat's caller said, "are going to get there first. It's there.

Another hidden room. I'm sure of it."

"Are you?" Cat was always skeptical of total assurance. Except when it was her own.

"If I wasn't, we wouldn't be talking."

The plan—the how and when of it— was what they'd discuss when they met. Tomorrow, he said. Give Cat time to do her own research. She gave him props for knowing she was already quietly tapping her laptop as they spoke.

"If I do this," Cat said because sexy voice aside, business was business. "What's my cut? Being as you're so sure there's some huge payoff waiting for us. Exactly how much do you think we're going to get?"

She bit back a gasp when he answered. Then countered with ten thousand more.

He sighed and told her yes. The ease with which she won the bargain should have warned her.

So did his suggested meeting place.

But people were quirky. They had their kinks and habits and weird shit. Or maybe he just liked crappy pizza joints. She was willing to overlook it. Pineapple on a pizza? A travesty, for sure, but no worse than the jewel thief she partnered with two years ago—the one who liked blueberry bagels, which was an afront to humanity. But no one—other than Caterina herself— was a better safe cracker, and if you're going to break into ten safes in 20 minutes, then you have to divide and conquer, even if it means splitting the take with someone who was also fond of chocolate hummus, a product that made absolutely no sense at all.

She'd listen to his spiel, Cat told herself. This guy from the phone. Then she'd tune in her inner-voice—the one she'd foolishly ignored with the museum heist. A sort of premonition was how she saw it, this sixth sense she'd experienced since childhood—as close as Cat ever came to believing in things that went bump in the night. All she knew was that when she trusted herself, she was better off.

So she'd hear the guy out. Then she'd make up her mind.

But imagining him in her bed surrounded by heaps of cash, she knew she already had.

"Meet me at Sammy Mozz," phone guy said, and at first, Cat thought she'd misheard. Her would-be heist partner wanted to talk business at a pizza chain known for its cheap all you can eat buffet and lurid topping options? What was he? Twelve years old?

"8:45," he added. "Out front. Look for the giant mouse."

She waited for him to laugh. He didn't. Just snapped out directions like maybe she didn't have GPS. A tickle of annoyance knocked a chip off her fascination with that husky voice. So maybe less sexy and more demeaning, misogynistic bastard? Usually, Cat was a highly accurate judge of character. But something—she wasn't sure what—was making it harder to read the signs.

She arrived at 8:35. By 8:40, she was tapping her foot. The place closed at nine on Thursdays. So what had been the point of the whole side conversation about whether or not she appreciated the finer points of fruit on her pizza?

Also, there was no giant mouse—unless you counted the peeling-paint one on the window. The neighborhood around the joint wasn't much better—Sammy Mozz sat half-under the El tracks in a dark spot just west of Broadway.

By 8:47 (Cat was a stickler for starting things on time), she figured he had ghosted her. Already her brain was ticking off contingency plans for the evening, erasing her mental plans for all that money she probably wasn't going to have.

She was, despite the fake-cheese and mildly rancid grease smells off-gassing from the Sammy Mozz kitchen, absolutely ravenous. She'd hit up that little sandwich place on Montrose, get a large Italian sub with extra mortadella and extra hot peppers and wash it down with a bottle of Stella. Curl up with a movie and remind herself that these things happen.

At 8:51, she called it.

Just as a giant mouse rose from the street like a specter, half-tripping over his red clown-shoes as he lumbered heavily toward her.

The mouse waved. An El train roared by overhead.

Cat frowned.

The costume was shabby—some kind of grey, vaguely fuzzy material and a comical head with a pointy, red-ball-tipped nose, one of the ears drooping like something had bitten it half off. Its gloves were drooping, too, as though whoever was inside had hands too small to fill them.

It lumbered closer. The whole outfit was pulled way too tight against the chest and arms, and as it plodded along, she saw why. The back was bulging hugely, like there was a giant backpack underneath or something else dome shaped. Like a tiny mountain. Had to be some kind of gear, but what?

The mouse waved again. "Sorry for the delay," he hollered.

Well for fuck's sake. This was the guy? Dressed as a mouse? A pizza-place mouse in a shabby-ass costume. And he smelled. Not terribly bad, but even from here she could sniff out a damp, mildew odor, as though he had been swimming in a stagnant pond or…

Oh. She saw now why it had looked like he'd risen from underground.

Because he had. Yup, this damn waving giant mouse had just climbed up from the sewer. The round disc top was still wobbling askew, half on the asphalt.

The fucking sewer. In a fucking mouse costume.

Jesus.

That Italian sub and beer was sounding better and better. Hell, grilled cheese and a juice box would be fine. It's not like her research into his mansion story had turned up anything but rumors.

"I don't do late," Cat snapped, and turned on her heel.

The blow came fast from her left, a shove and a punch and something painfully sharp that drew blood when she blocked with her hand. Mouse Guy? He was too far way still. No it was—

Another strike from her right, a fist plowing into her belly, leaving her bent and gasping, and another hit before she could straighten—a kick to the ankles, tripping her up and sending her sprawling, knees hitting, then hands and arms. She skid on the cement, her strength from years of climbing ropes and hoisting herself up walls so she could drop through skylights, the only thing that kept her head from slamming.

It did not keep her from being kicked again, a brutal jab to the ribs.

Pain shot through her. Whatever breath still in her lungs expelled itself with a harsh whoosh. *Get up,* she told herself dimly. She willed herself to breathe. Her vision was going spotty.

Then something grabbed the collar of her hoodie, yanked her up and away and somehow a small trickle of air found its way to her lungs. She yelped hoarsely, flailing, trying to get her brain to explain what was happening, who was doing this, where they had come from. Anything. Something.

"I got you," rasped a familiar voice in her ear. "Hang on."

Pineapple-pizza mouse?

Was he saving her? Or was he in on the attack? Everything was happening too fast to process. And the searing pain pretty much everywhere, wasn't making things easier.

Shit. Shit. Shit.

From her new vantage point as Pizza Mouse lifted her, she could finally make out her attackers. She now counted three, black-hooded and massed in a scrum, and from the looks of things, they were getting ready to come at her again.

Pizza-Mouse plodded off—quickly and strangely gracefully—with her cradled in his arms. He was a strong mother-fucker, she had to give that to him. His biceps felt like steel and the top of his chest… was he wearing armor? Maybe that explained the fit of the costume.

He set her down gently by the dumpster. "Stay put," he said. "I'll be back."

Stay? Was he kidding? She needed to get up. She needed to run. Her heart was exploding in her chest. Blood trickled from somewhere on her forehead, so while her head hadn't hit the ground, it had definitely scraped over something.

She swiped at her eyes. Pain radiated everywhere each time she sucked a ragged breath.

Get up, she told herself. Get the hell up. Cat staggered to her feet. Took a step, but the world spun and her feet began to slide from under her. She gripped the dumpster. Bent and puked. More blood dripped in her eyes.

The impulse to slump to the ground filled her every fiber.

She would have, maybe, but then "Dude!" she heard. "That knife better be made of titanium. Otherwise, you've got a problem on your hands."

The voice was that familiar rasp. Mouse guy? Getting quippy while Cat was trying not die here by a smelly dumpster?

The scrum of her attackers chuckled. Cat tried to walk, but her equilibrium was shot to hell. Her ribs screamed in agony.

All she could do was cling weakly to the dumpster with one hand and swipe blood out of her eyes with the other.

"I warned you, dudes," Mouse guy drawled. "We could all be eating pizza but you wanted to do it the hard way." He snorted a laugh. "Although with me, there really is only the hard way these days."

Again with the quips?

They really were both going to die here, weren't they? Weird Mouse-pineapple pizza-loving guy and Caterina Von Eckstein, whose real name was Catie Joan Rubin, although she hadn't gone by that in a very long time. Catie Rubin who had grown up with crummy parents in a series of crummy apartments—the kind where you can hear the El train going by all night—and promised herself there had to be something better—which she quickly realized she had to acquire for herself because clearly these things did not fall from the sky no matter how much you wished for them. Not even if your senior English teacher Ms. Simmons told you more than once that you were destined for greatness.

Probably teacher bullshit, but Cat had smarts and perseverance, that much was true.

The world underestimated her at its peril.

She had a brother, too, Silas—five years older that Cat— but he'd left when she was just twelve. He'd turn up now and then, occasionally with a girlfriend, more often with one slimy buddy or another-- all who looked to be on the take.

'Little Si' one of them had called her; a muscle-bound guy who was always chewing Wrigley's Spearmint and yammering with Si about how soon, they were going to make it big. Doing what, no one ever said.

Cat hadn't seen Si in years, until about a month ago, when there he was, walking down Marine Drive. Their parents were long gone – her dad to a trailer park outside Orlando, making a living with odd jobs, card sharking, and the occasional phone scam gig. Her mom—last anyone heard—had been hopping from one small New Mexico town to another, where she claimed to be working on her artistic calling. In reality, she and her current boyfriend Oscar were selling cheap throw blankets, velvet paintings—Elvis, The Last Supper, dogs playing poker— and Confederate flags at temporary truck stop stands along I-40.

Silas knew what Cat did for a living, at least generally speaking. As for Silas, last time Cat checked, he was running ghost tours in Milwaukee, which seemed an unlikely place for paranormal shenanigans yet seemed to have a lot of them.

"Si? Silas!" Cat called her brother's name. He started to turn, then hooked a right on Hutchinson, and by the time she jogged to the corner, he was gone. Probably it wasn't even him. Too busy scamming tourists with Midwest spook stories. Cat was not one to mourn her losses. She had reinvented herself. Had nice things and a decent life, and a tidy apartment with a lake view and smooth wood floors.

Would any of her family even know she was dead? She supposed it didn't matter.

It was not like Cat to go down without a fight. But here she was.

No. Damn it. No.

"Stay put," Mouse guy shouted, but Cat realized she was stumbling toward him.

In her dizzy head, she told him off. Said she didn't take orders from fake rodents. Or real ones.

In reality her voice was barely a croak. Surely, she really was dying because that was the only explanation for what she was now seeing. Mouse guy no longer Mouse guy.

As in: the mouse suit was gone. But what the hell? A second costume? Was he now dressed like… a giant turtle?

The world was spinning again. No… Pizza Mouse/Turtle Guy was doing the spinning. He had weapons, from somewhere Cat couldn't fathom. Nun-chucks and a curved sword, no, two swords!—all spinning and moving, and Cat vomited again just watching.

Smack. Kick. Spin. Twirl. Grunt. Wallop! The air rang with the sound of metal hitting heads and knees and arms and bellies. One guy screamed—a furious bellow turned higher pitch shriek, and then he was sprawling and bleeding and not moving. Another wallop and another assailant down, hitting hard, gasping and then going quiet as he smacked the ground.

Pizza Mouse/Turtle was slowing, sizing up the situation.

But the third of the attack pack kept coming, closing the distance fast between him and Pizza Mouse/Turtle. He slapped away the nun-chuck that flew at him, like swatting a fly.

Cat was seeing double now, but something made her keep moving—even later she couldn't say what, except that Caterina von Eckstein, nee' Catie Joan Rubin, always paid her debts. Loyal to the core, or perhaps more accurately, unwilling to let an ugly death claim someone who had helped her. Admittedly, the guy had invited her to this place under what she was certain now were vastly overestimated assumptions, but no matter! He'd carried her to dumpster safety. Some dim, still-functioning piece of her said she owed him.

Especially since he was at least temporarily disabling the bad guys.

Cat put her head down. Didn't stop to remind herself what a seriously bad idea this was. Just screamed like a banshee or one of those ancient blue warriors or Berserkers or… shit.

Bad guy 3 reached into his pocket and pulled out a gun.

Somehow—some primordial reflex kicking in— Cat launched herself into the air, tackling Bad Guy with a side attack, sending them both flailing to the ground.

The gun flew from his hand on impact, skidding into the street. He smelled rank. But underneath there was a scent of something herbal and faintly familiar, but there was no time to identify it. She was punching him then— in the face and the neck and realizing that this time her head had smacked the ground. Hard.

Cat's vision went spotty. Then black.

"Dude," said the husky voice. "I warned you about doing things the hard way. You need to make better choices. Didn't your mother teach you not to point a loaded gun?"

There was noise then—loud popping sounds—and vaguely she saw a hand retrieve the gun. Cat knew she should do something, but nothing in her body was working right.

And then Cat felt herself being gently rolled and Bad Guy—she was still sprawled on top of him—was not there anymore. Her cheek pressed against the dirty cement. She wanted to get up, but she didn't even know how. Her pulse was fluttering.

Someone lifted her, also gently, pressed her against what felt like body armor. She was being carried, and the husky voice was saying "It'll be fine. You'll be fine. We can do pizza later if you want. Pizza always makes things better."

They were moving down, then, sinking into the earth. She heard a metal clanking.

"Caterina," the husky voice said. "You're really something. I knew I called the right person."

Then the whole world went black, and it was a long while before Cat surfaced.

#   #   #

When she finally pried her eyes open, gritty and blinking, Caterina found herself tucked under a soft olive green blanket on a not uncomfortable couch, a musty-smelling pillow cradling her head and the scent of cheese and spices and—was that tomato sauce?—filling air.

Her mouth was dry, her throat aching as she swallowed. Her head hurt, but not as much as she thought it should, given what had happened.

What *had* happened?

Was it all some kind of hallucination?

She touched her hand to her forehead. The bandage there told her she was not imagining.

So where the hell was she?

Cat eased herself up.

"Hello?" she said. No answer. Just quiet and that food smell, which should have turned her stomach but was actually making it gurgle in hunger. What time was it? What day? How long had she been out?

Vaguely she remembered being carried. Mouse guy? Turtle costume?

Were the bad guys dead? She remembered the gun.

Her heart beat faster now, and she swiveled and put her feet on the floor, and when nothing was spinning from that action, she hoisted herself to stand.

Assessed the situation.

She was in one piece. Her clothes were on and did not seem to have been disturbed. Her face – she could tell as she rubbed a hand over it—had been washed and as she'd already noted, bandaged.

Someone had also bandaged her ribs. Slowly, she sucked in a breath. The pain was there, but muted.

Cat narrowed her eyes. Had she been given pain killers of some sort? All details pointed to yes. She didn't feel drugged, but that didn't necessarily mean she hadn't been.

Nothing felt broken—the ribs were questionable but she'd manage— just deeply bruised. A lot of bruises. Her jaw ached. Her forehead was tender, shoulders and wrists, too.

She looked around. The room was cozy, but no windows. Low lit lamps everywhere. A small kitchen. A desk in a corner, a laptop and more low lighting. A long table –wood, polished. A couple doors—bedroom? Bathroom? She'd need to look.

Her shoes were on her feet. Her tote and phone neatly resting a small table near the couch. No missed calls. The time read 2 am. She'd been unconscious for almost five hours.

She rifled through her bag and wallet. Everything seemed in place.

"Hello?" she called again. Her voice echoed. The smell of something cheesy and yeasty still lingered in the air.

Her stomach growled again—audibly enough that she followed her nose to the tiny kitchen. Opened the small oven.

Pizza. And was that pineapple?

"You're awake!" said a familiar voice, and Kat whipped around.

Pineapple pizza was now officially the least of her worries.

"Maybe you should sit down," he said, and nudged her toward a chair by the long table.

"I…" said Cat. "You…" She sat. Heavily. Looked him up and down.

Her brain tried to catch up. It was going to take a minute. A lot of minutes.

Towel in hand (were those actually hands?), he opened the oven and extracted the pineapple pizza. Cut her a slice, which he placed neatly on a paper plate and set in front of her.

"Maybe you should eat?"

"Maybe I should." Cat sniffed cautiously, then hoisted the slice and took a bite. If she ate, then this new hallucination would go away, right? She was just faint with hunger and all these bruises and in shock. Definitely in shock. Only explanation.

She nibbled another bite. Then gobbled a third.

Damn if pineapple on pizza wasn't delicious. A little sweet, but there were jalapeno slices, too. Thinly sliced, spicy, and crispy from the oven, which somehow was exactly right.

"Told you," he said.

The mouse costume was—she saw now—folded tidily underneath the small table that held her tote and phone.

As for the turtle costume, well. Except...

It wasn't a costume, was it?

She burped aggressively. Mouse/Turtle guy who was no longer a mouse and absolutely not in a costume, gave a soft chuckle.

"Um," Cat said slowly. "You're a..."

"Turtle," he said placidly.

No. No way. But he was. An actual turtle. A giant turtle, to be exact. Upright like a human, and talking like one, but definitely turtle-y. And how the hell was that possible?

A giant, nimble turtle-guy who liked pineapple jalapeno pizza and had a sizeable stash of dangerous-looking weapons (she noticed the armoire now, and everything in it), that she'd observed with her own eyes he knew how to use. Lethally.

He had mad fighting skills. Quick on his feet (Two feet. On the ground like a person). Super quick. Stealthy even.

He was wearing a green ninja bandana around his forehead.

The fight that he'd rescued her from flashed through her memory. He'd been wearing a mask then, too, forehead to nose, with openings for his eyes.

He'd grabbed her attacker's gun. She was sure of that now. Was it in the armoire? Another quick glance but she'd didn't see it.

Turtle-guy reached for his own slice of pizza, devouring it in two swift chomps.

So maybe his table manners left something to be desired.

A million question filled her brain. She asked an easy one first.

"You saved my life," she said, assessing. Then, "Are they dead?"

He shrugged. "Nah. Just not doing very well. Tied 'em up and left 'em for the cops. This time, anyway."

He held out his hand. Paw? Her brain spun some more, trying to dredge up turtle facts. Seems she had none. At least not for this particular scenario. "I'm Leo," he said.

She hesitated for a few awkward seconds, then cautiously pressed her hand against his. His palm (she didn't have another word for it) was warm and dry to the touch. He squeezed her hand briefly, then let go.

She remembered the metal clanking and the sense that the earth was swallowing them.

"Are we in the—"

"Sewer," he finished for her even though she'd already figured that one out for herself.

"But how?" Cat managed. "Why?" She gaped at him some more. "Who the hell were those guys?"

And more importantly, had they been after her or the turtle?

"Not sure," Leo said, rubbing his chin with a sizeable thumb. So had he been—was he —human? Because turtles didn't have opposable thumbs, did they?

"They came at me first," Cat said, leaving the thumb issue aside for now.

Leo snagged another pizza slice. "True. They still may have been coming for me. But you have to admit you looked like easy pickings."

Cat straightened. Dropped the remains of her slice on the table. She stalked toward him, supremely pissed now. Enough that she could (mostly) ignore the fresh pain that intensified in her ribs with each step.

"You know they blind-side me, right? Because I was too busy watching you rise up from the stupid sewer. So if anyone is to blame here, it's you, *dude.* But if that's what you think then—"

Cat didn't bother to finish. Just grabbed him by that meaty arm, twisted, and using her body as leverage, slammed him to the floor.

He hit with a thud, eyes wide with a look that was part shock, part admiration, part amusement.

Maybe that last part owing to the fact that she was now wincing in pain as something in her bandaged ribs popped and crackled, sending sharp jolt of pain from the top of her scalp to the soles of her feet.

But she'd taken him down. That's all that mattered. Enough of this shit. She'd sort out the bad guy attack later. Leave turtle man down in his sewer turtle hole and sort that out later, too. Someone had to know about him, right? Cat had many discreet sources.

As for the heist, no fucking way. She didn't need her possibly on-the-fritz Spidey sense to tell her that.

"I'm outta here," she snapped. She should have been gone as soon as she was conscious. Not hanging around some weird underground hide out eating fruit pizza. She'd swing by one of those free-standing ERs and get checked for a concussion.

Cat grabbed her bag. Grabbed her phone. No bars no and no service now even though it had been working a few minutes ago. Whatever. As soon she was streetside, she'd—

"Not that one," Leo said calmly as she yanked open what had to be the front door. It was a bedroom.

Other door. Bathroom. She had to pee, badly, but it would wait til she found the door.

Except there *were* no other doors.

The quick uptick of her heart only pissed her off more.

Leo pushed from the floor. A little less graceful now, Cat noted, and that calmed her heart.

He nudged the throw rug by the bathroom with his foot, revealing a trap door. "You gotta go down a short way and then the tunnel takes you to a ladder, and then you're up and out."

Cat peered down as he pulled open the hidden door by its metal handle.

It creaked open slowly.

Dark as midnight down there, but dim light coming from above and yes, a few feet away, rungs leading up a wall. She couldn't see where they ended. Probably the manhole this absurd turtle man had popped out of.

"I'll take you," Leo said, but she was already crouching by the trap door. "Don't you want to know about the heist?"

"Nope," she said and swung her legs into the opening. It didn't look like much of a drop.

"Or how I got this way?" he added, and it was the regretful tone of his voice that stopped her from leaping in. Okay, that and the money he'd promised her if she took the job.

She cursed her neediness. But damn, it was a lot of money.

She waited for her inner-voice to pipe up. It didn't. Possibly it was mildly concussed along with the rest of her.

"Go then," Turtle Guy said brusquely. "Just be careful. I can call you an Uber. If you want."

From the opening into the sewer tunnel, she could hear whooshing sounds like traffic going by overhead and above that, the even fainter sound of the EL train clackety clacking. Up and out and she could make a run for it.

But if she left now…She swiveled her legs and pushed herself standing, wobbled a little, then steadied.

"Why me?" she said. "For this job, I mean. And what the hell are you? I know what you look like, but looks can be deceiving. So yeah, I want to know how you got this way. How you found me to call about this job — if there actually is a job. Cause treasure in an old mansion? It's a classic trope, wouldn't you say? The kind of story you spout out if you want to con someone. Only I'm not someone you can con. It's not like you're connected to anyone I know. It's not like I've heard your name in, well, any of the circles I run in."

Cat's hands slid to her hips. She hoped this made her seem more menacing than she felt at this moment. "And for the record, I think you're lying. I think you absolutely do know why those guys attacked me."

"I don't," Leo said. He sounded sincere. But lots of people in Cat's life had sounded sincere, *sounded* being the key word. And he hadn't denied being a liar, had he?

"Lots of burglars and thieves in this city," she said when Leo offered no further comment. "I'm just one of many."

"You're the right one for this job."

Maybe it was the quick way he spit out his answer that nudged her muzzy brain into offering up one very helpful thought. Maybe having seen Silas the other day wasn't a coincidence. Which meant that this whole… thing—hadn't come out of the blue. Because with Cat's family there was always an angle. And if that angle was connected to Leo and this supposed job, then she needed to know more.

But to get that truth, she'd have to trust a giant talking turtle whose intentions were still unclear. Even if he had possibly saved her life. Even if his voice had previously sounded, um, interesting. But that was *before* she met him.

Was Leo playing her? Very possibly. Was she safe here? Probably not. Did this have something to do with Silas? Who the hell knew? Cat's family was forever a wild card.

Still. Despite everything, she was curious. And okay, greedy for what she could possibly get if she played this right. Even if she had to risk doing business with someone who, let's face it, wasn't exactly human. But Cat was used to risk. She was, after all, a burglar who'd renamed herself Cat. Courting that whole 'nine lives' thing was her brand.

There was only one thing she was absolutely sure of. If there was a treasure in that northside mansion, she wanted it.

So when Leo offered her another slice of that damn pineapple pizza, she didn't refuse.

"Tell me what you are," Cat said. "Let's start there. After that, we'll see if I want to know more."

#   #   #

Leo's Origin Story—recounted over the rest of that ridiculous pizza—went like this:

He'd been an actual turtle. She tried to wrap her brain around that. It wasn't easy. He'd been tossed into the sewer by the little boy who'd been gifted him as a pet. Not every eight-year-old boy wanted a turtle. They certainly didn't know about indigenous Illinois species and how maybe taking said turtle to the Forest Preserve marsh would be a better idea than just abandoning it into the muck. Maybe you flushed those goldfish you won at the school carnival by tossing a ping pong ball into their little bowls. But not a box turtle who helps cycle minerals and seeds and does his bit for the food chain, insect control, and the environment. (So said Leo, who was— perhaps not surprisingly—a font of turtle factoids).

"Box turtles are ancient," Leo told her. Like 260 million years old! Older than snakes and crocs. "If we're doing well, so is the environment."

"But you, um, aren't exactly a box turtle anymore, are you??"

Leo shrugged. "Yes and no."

Turned out the sewer was near a semi-secret lab up tucked in a quiet northwest suburb. A lab that conducted all sorts of dark matter experiments and other research. Someone got sloppy with disposal. Or maybe someone dumped it on purpose—like the boy had dumped the turtle— just to see. Either way, something green and radioactive and definitely experimental leaked into the water. Little turtle Leo swam right through it. A few hours later, he was transforming.

A scientist from that same lab had gone checking the water and found him. Turns out the chemical was part of a highly dangerous experiment designed to create a group of super-powered warrior types. A safety force, if you will: Strong, fast, smart, fearless.

Cat made a face. "Like Marvel super heroes?" Was he kidding? Clearly not. It wasn't quite Marvel territory, but it was damn close. And real.

"He knew," Leo said of the scientist—the man he called Dr. K. "Or suspected. I think he assumed anything that the chemical touched would be dead. But there I was. Not dead. The first thing I remember understanding was him saying, 'Dude! What happened? Look at you.'"

As best as Leo understood, the process had gone like this: First his body grew and changed. Taller, humanoid. But with a turtle exterior, including the shell. He was strong and fast and nimble – a stocky turtle now about 5'5 and muscular as hell. His brain developed next—his new human brain already stocked with knowledge and filling his new, extra-large but still humanoid head. With it came speech. And memory. And all the rest.

"Dr K. took me in. Gave me my name. Kept me hidden in the lab while I adjusted. They'd put a stop on the original experiment by then. But Dr. K, he wanted to know more. Was I turtle? Or human? Could the process be reversed? Altered? How strong was I? What could I do? What could I be taught to do?"

Turned out that range was pretty vast.

Cat listened and listened. She tried—and failed—to imagine what it would be like to be plodding along as a reptile and suddenly find yourself something very different. The thought made her feel like she'd been dropped into an alternate universe.

At some point, Leo tossed another frozen pineapple pizza in the oven and when it was done, they chomped it down, too. "Dr. K—he loved his Hawaiian pizza," Leo said. "Dude knew a good thing when he saw it."

Almost two years, Leo told her, since it had happened.

Three months ago, Dr. K turned up dead. (Here, Cat gasped, but quietly. She should have seen it coming. Blamed her potentially concussed head for having missed it). "Heart attack," Leo said. "Maybe from keeping all those secrets. Maybe it was just his time."

But Leo had been on his own for awhile by then. "Doc said he couldn't keep me under lock and key forever. He set up a bank account. I get by just fine down here."

He grinned at her, showing teeth. Gestured his chin toward the armoire of weapons. Something in the smile and the gesture and the weapons, made Cat shiver. "I'm a crime-fighter when I can be. As I guess you've noted. Helping the helpless and all that. Doc said that's what I'm made for. Well, remade, I guess."

The doctor had checked in with him periodically. Took blood samples. Kept track of Leo's vitals. At least that's how it had been until Dr K's untimely demise.

By the end of the tale, Cat had collected her wits. "So," she said, wiping the last bit of pizza grease from her fingers with a paper napkin that had seen better days. "Exactly when did you decide to be a criminal?"

That was the bottom line, right? Regardless of the turtle super hero makeover, he wanted her to help him steal a bunch of money that wasn't his. So much for the 'help the helpless' sob story.

Leo grinned another creepy toothy grin. Was he blushing? It was hard to tell.

"Yeah," he said. "That account Dr. K set up? It's running out. Economic downturn and bad investments and all that. Plus the lab closed. So yeah. A turtle needs to live. All that mansion cash is just sitting there, waiting. So, I asked myself when I heard about it. Why not use it to fund my good-guy gigs? Pay it forward once I take it." Another grin. "Sound good, right?"

Cat did not grin back. "It sounds illegal. Not that I'm opposed. It sounds like thievery. Again, not that I care. But just so we're clear. Doing something good with something that's not yours does not exactly make you hero of the week."

"This mean you're not interested?"

Cat gave a short, sharp laugh. Her ribs gave a long, sharp jolt of pain in response. "Not at all. I just like to be on the same page. We're not doing some version of *Les Miserables* here. We're not stealing a loaf of bread because we're starving in the French Revolution."

"Was that a movie?"

Cat sighed. "Yes. But I was referring to the book. Whatever. Why do you need *me*?"

Leo aimed his thumbs at his turtle-shelled chest. "Do I look like I blend in? I had to wear a fucking mouse costume to meet you. It's not a subtle look."

"Okay. But let me repeat one last time before I walk out of here for real. Why *me*? Why Caterina von Eckstein?"

He was quiet for more than few beats.

Cat used them to decide that she still wanted the job. She had no interest in his moral compass or if he even had one. Did she trust him? No. But if the payoff was enough, and she was careful, it wouldn't matter.

Leo cleared his throat. "I've heard good things," he said.

He mentioned a few of her most recent jobs. "There was a museum job," he continued. "Went a bit south is that the story is. But you recovered like a champ and got the job done. That's what I need. Someone who doesn't freak out when something goes sideways. Not that I expect it to. But you're solid. You keep going. That's what I want."

"You make me sound like a battery," Cat said, and she was not amused, either at his clichéd banter or at the museum guy who'd clearly talked his head off and put her in this position.

"Daniel Orsoff tell you that?" she asked, and Leo blinked, so she had her answer. "Don't believe everything you hear. Does he know you're giant reptile?"

"Nope. I've got a sophisticated grapevine that doesn't involve public appearance unless I want it to."

Cat narrowed her eyes. She had her own grapevine. And lately, it had been telling her that the stupid museum job had made people touchy about hiring her. Subtlety had been her specialty. Falling hard into a bunch of prickly topiaries and getting away by the skin of her teeth as any number of cop cars barreled into the compound was as far from subtle as she could get.

A little redemption might serve her even more than the money.

"And how do we get access to this mysterious hidden room you seem so sure of?"

Leo's eyes lit up. "Let me tell you," he said. When he was done, she'd agreed to do the job.

Cat wondered if he knew she wasn't telling him everything. After all, she still didn't know why those guys had come after her. It could have been random. The world was a crazy place. Lately, more than ever.

That Leo might also have left out a few crucial details would only occur to her later.

# # #

At home, cleaned up and showered and dressed in fresh sweatpants and old, soft t-shirt, Cat called the number she hoped was still Si's.

Her diminished status in the high-stakes burglary world was true. But had it come from Daniel Orsoff running his mouth? Probably not. Orsoff knew better.

The phone rang and rang.

Cat waited.

"You telling tales?" she said when Silas finally answered.

He snorted a laugh. "And how are you, sis?"

"Annoyed. Interested. Wondering why you've been ghosting me."

"That all?"

She chewed her lip. But only briefly. She had to know. There was no way around it.

"Leo says you've got a big mouth," she said matter-of-factly. "I didn't know you kept up with me that closely."

She heard the soft tell of her brother exhaling a long breath through his nose. Silas had always been an easy read.

"Is that why I saw you the other day? But you didn't want to see me, did you?"

Another long, nasal exhale on Si's end.

"Jesus, Si. He's fucking giant turtle. You didn't think that was worth mentioning to me?"

This time, her brother laughed. So did Cat. It was, after all, too bizarre not to laugh.

"Blood's thicker than water, Silas. Even our dysfunctional family ooze. You gonna side with a chemically enhanced reptile or your own sister?"

"Was waiting for you to call," Silas said. "Didn't figure you for an idiot."

"Flattery, flattery," Cat told him.

That established, they hammered out a plan.

If Leo wanted that money, he'd have to agree.

Of course, that wasn't the full plan. Like Si had said, Cat wasn't an idiot.

#   #   #

Two days later, Cat and Leo headed to the mansion. Si drove. As Cat had observed, it wasn't like Leo could just walk in with her, big as day.

The reno team was expecting an expert on tile and flooring and renewing the mansion's gardens. All of those would be Cat. She'd pulled an all-nighter researching. Had memorized buzz words like bull nose edging and subway tile and whatever else was currently trending. For flooring, she'd recommend wood. Easy peasy. The new owners had no interest in keeping the house's historical style intact. They just wanted new and fresh and pretty.

Cat could do that. Maybe she'd even make the contractors a few extra bucks while she was it.

She'd studied the floor plan Leo had given her. The room with the hidden door didn't contain the hidden treasure, but if they were lucky, it led to it. She and Si had scaled the roof last night in the dark and their infrared scan showed what Leo had promised. There was another passageway hidden in the back wall, and it led to a smaller room where, according to rumor, the money had long ago been hidden.

"It's narrow as hell," Cat whispered to Si as they crouched on the roof, the wind blowing her hair wild and sending chills deep into her bones. It really was. No way could she get through there without excavating or drilling. The owners had put in a new, fancy alarm system. They'd have to short circuit it or all hell would break loose once they started drilling. The tiniest bit of smoke would set it off.

The inner-voice that had been annoyingly silent for so long was hollering up a storm. *Drop this thing. Don't do it. Something is off. You know it.*

But she wanted to prove herself. To the potential clients who had backed off. To Si, who had always made it clear he thought she didn't measure up. (Although to what standard she was unclear. Si was not anyone's version of success). To her parents who had left and never come back. To Leo, who she was positive thought he could con her. To anyone and everyone who had ever doubted that little Catie Rubin would amount to something. (except you, Ms. Simmons. You always believed in me.) That she was worthy of anything, even a mansion the size of this one, not that she wanted it. Cash was fine. Cash gave you options.

Mostly she wanted to prove it to her own self. Because she had set a goal. Cat von Eckstein never ever gave up.

And now it was time. The plan for today was this: She'd go in. She'd wow them with her reno skills and tile and flooring recommendations. She'd help them plot out the garden. And then she'd pretend to leave but instead, she'd tuck herself away until everyone else was gone. After that, Leo could join her. They'd do job. Get in. Get out. Take the money and run. She'd rely on his muscle if she needed to. Her own smarts if she didn't. Si would work the roof with the infrared, then hustle it back to the car for getaway.

Hell, if they did this right, no one would even know something had happened. The place was still ripped apart from the reno. On that, Leo was right. The timing was perfect.

Cat would take her cut and it would be over.

This is what she was thinking as she rang the bell and the heist began.

"I'm Jen," she announced, decorating books stacked in her arms, when the owner opened the door. "Let's start with those bathrooms, why don't we? I've got lots of ideas for you."

#   #   #

It was fully dark when she tiptoed down to the hulking front door and opened it for Leo.

He sauntered in, gaping at the high ceilings and the general enormous scope of things. "This place," he said.

"Let's do this," said Cat. They headed quickly to the hallway with the first hidden door. She was feeling jumpy. The day had dragged –so many tile choices; so much endless discussion about shades of wood flooring. And that feeling hadn't gone away. That something was coming and it wasn't something good.

Si had been jumpy, too. She couldn't put her finger on it, but she felt it nonetheless. Heard it in his tone while they'd been up on the roof last night and again a few minutes ago over the walkie. He sounded on edge. Freaked out even. He tried to hide it, laughing and joking about how easy this whole gig was, but she could feel it nonetheless.

No matter how long Cat and her brother were apart, she could still read him like a freaking book.

But that was silly, right? Everything was going precisely according to plan.

Which was exactly when Leo said, "There's something else I need to tell you."

Cat raised a brow. "You're going to offer a bigger cut?" Her voice was steady, cool even. Inside she was anything but.

"The thing is," Leo said. "That passageway. It's not going get any less narrow. Or any bigger. And it can't be smashed through or blown apart."

"Because of the alarm system," Cat said. "I know. Old news. We'll have to disarm it. You said you knew…"

She stopped mid-sentence. "What exactly are you about tell me?"

"There's another way," he said. "No alarms. No broken walls. No digging. No smashing. No blowing things ups. They won't even know we were here."

"And exactly how are *you,*" (here she looked Leo up on down pointedly) "much less me, going to get in there if we don't widen the damn thing?"

He slipped three medium-sized bottles out of the messenger bag that only now did Cat notice was slung over his giant shoulder.

"Dr K did a lot of experimenting over the past years," he said.

Cat's heart beat its way into her throat. She looked at the bottles. One was labeled with her name. One with Leo's.

"Drink it down," he said. "It will transform you into a turtle. Small enough to get through a narrow passageway. But only temporarily."

"And that one?" she pointed to the one labeled Leo.

"Makes me small, too. Regulation turtle size. But we're still us." He tapped his head. "In here. We can think and talk. Just like now. Trust me. It's the only way."

He opened the messenger bag. "We've got a couple rounds in here. Just in case. Some emergency reversals, too. All labeled. But we should transform back without it in about an hour. Give or take. We get big. We load up the cash. Shove it through the opening, then swallow another potion, get small and crawl our way out and wait to transform. Then we're out of there. No one will be the wiser."

"Um," Cat said. "No. You don't need me to do this. You can shrink down all on your own. No fucking way. I'll wait for you outside, thank you very much. In fact, I won't wait. I'm going."

"It's going to take two of us to haul it all out of there."

"Absolutely not."

"Think of all the jobs we could do together," Leo said. "You and me."

"Leo," said Cat. "There is no you and me."

"Si said you might balk."

Si? Her brother who had convinced her they could take the majority of the haul and leave this turtle in the dust?

"But I saved your life," Leo said.

In that moment, something finally sunk in. She remembered the attacker with the weird herbal scent. Not so weird, actually. Just Wrigley's Spearmint. The gum that Si's old asshole buddy use to always chew.

She had been set up from the beginning. He'd saved her so he could con her.

Son of a sea biscuit.

"We could be partners," Leo was saying. "I knew it the moment I first saw you."

It was at that very exact second that the security system began bleating and blaring.

Even Leo looked surprised.

Sometimes, a girl has no choice but to go along with game. This was one of those times.

It was swallow the potion, get small and do the job, or stay Cat-sized and go to jail. Damn. Damn. Damn.

"Strip down," Leo said. She did as he directed her. He balled up the clothes in a corner. "They'll think it's just junk," he said. Cat hoped he was right.

"And once they're gone, Si will disarm the fire alarms. After that, we can hack our way out. No problem." He stuffed the other potion bottles through the small hole, one after another.

Si. Her stupid, betraying brother.

She opened her bottle. Leo opened his. They swallowed it all down. Bitter. Gross. So gross. The transformation happened slowly, then faster, like a freight train picking up speed. Shrinking. Shell. Legs. Tail. Holy crap.

"It won't be permanent," Leo said. His voice sounded tiny and far away. "I promise you."

The cops were coming through the hidden door as Cat and Leo scurried through the tiniest of openings and disappeared.

\#   \#   \#

The thing about experimental chemicals is that they're just that. Experimental. They don't always work like you expect. It was clear even to Cat's now turtle-sized but human brain that she was more turtle at this moment than human. Leo, too.

Also, the security alarms had stopped blaring. The cops had come and gone. An hour had passed—at least as far as she could tell.

This posed a variety of problems.

One: She was still a turtle.

Two: There was indeed a fortune in here—stacks of cash and bonds and yes, even a gold brick or two. But she needed to be human sized to get it out of here.

Three: Her clothes were still in the other room. She hoped.

Four: Now small-sized Leo seemed to be performing a mating ritual right there in front of her.

Here was the problem with being a turtle, even one that still knew she was a human named Cat. You acted like a turtle. You felt like a turtle. You did what turtles do. This was clearly not a side-effect Leo had mentioned.

He nuzzled her face, then lumbered quickly behind her, shell to shell. She squeaked then moaned, her eyes widening as his claws latched under her shell so he could hang on while they, well, did what turtles did.

His turtle legs entwined with hers.

Eventually, they stopped, and she slept.

In her turtle dream, she was laying eggs. Turtle eggs. Egg after egg slipped from her.

Not a woman-turtle anymore, waiting for the promised re-transformation to the old Caterina von Eckstein, master thief, long-con expert, a woman who took what she wanted when she wanted it and never, ever looked back.

Just a turtle, normal turtle size with turtle eggs falling out of her, waiting to hatch. Trapped in the basement of this crumbling mansion while the treasure of lifetime remained right here, taunting her.

She woke with a gasp.

She was still a turtle.

Leo was still sleeping. Or dormant. Or hibernating. Or whatever the hell it is that turtles did.

Well. This was not how things were going to end. Nope.

He had lied to her about the automatic reversal. Or the stuff didn't work like he thought. Either way, she was going to fight this until she figured it out.

After that she moved pretty damn fast for a fucking turtle.

She scurried over to the other bottles Leo had shoved into this room. Found the one labeled Emergency Reversal and clawed it open.

She managed to suck down the entire bottle just to be sure.

She waited. The full transformation took awhile, longer than she expected, so long in fact, that she was beginning to think he had once again conned her and that she had failed. She'd crawl into traffic if she had to. And hope some good Samaritan didn't stop his car and save her.

But then it began, the stretching and growing into a human-sized turtle, and then back to herself. Regular Cat von Eckstein, with just the tiniest scaly dry patch on the side of her left calf.

Leo was still sleeping but starting to stir. Guess whatever they'd done had worn him out.

Sometimes the full plan doesn't reveal itself until opportunity arises in the form of a burlap sack of cash with the very tight drawstring.

Leo awoke when she picked him up by the shell. But he was still a small turtle. What could he do? She poured the other bottle of shrinking potion down his little throat just in case. Smashed all but one of the other vials to the floor, careful to avoid stepping in the liquid.

A few minutes later, she slammed her fists into the wall. Kicked and punched and when she'd loosened some dry wall, used it to punch and pry some more. She was strong by nature, stronger still from adrenaline. No alarms went off. Probably still disarmed from the cops.

She slipped on her clothes and shoes – thankfully still in the corner of the other room, then hoisted five bags of cash (so much cash) over her shoulders.

Tucked the remaining bottle of potion in gingerly in her pocket. She'd need it later.

Inside his burlap sack, Leo wriggled furiously, scrabbling back and forth but going nowhere. She drew the drawstring tight. Then knotted it to be sure.

"One down," she said, and headed out.

Si was in the car. He looked mildly surprised to see her. But his eyes lit up at the bags of cash. A couple gold bars, too, that she'd added at the last minute.

"Leo's on his own," Cat said, ignoring the wriggling in the lightest burlap bag. "Let's get the fuck out of here. I'll drive."

Si hesitated only a second. But fortunately, her brother was loyal only to himself. It made things a lot easier.

"Si," she said. "I am never doing this again." She laughed like maybe she didn't mean it. She could tell her brother thought she was joking. Why would she turn down another deal like this? Even without Si's cut, she was rolling in dough, right?

"We need to celebrate," Si said when they'd driven away and headed toward Cat's apartment. They were just passing the hole in the wall pizza place on Irving Park. Thin crust. Tavern cut in those little squares. It was in the bottom floor of an old brick apartment building. There was a giant moose head on the wall over the front counter, a cigar jammed in its mouth.

"Pineapple/jalapeno pizza?" she offered. And when, on the drive home, he announced that the pizza had made him thirsty, his tongue tingle with the spicy peppers, she offered him a drink. Fortunately in some ways, Silas Rubin was a dumb bastard. He guzzled the whole bottle.

What happened next was of his doing, she told herself. He had sold her out to the turtle. This part of her plan seemed only fitting.

"Your buddy who always chewed Spearmint tried to kill me the other night," she said conversationally as Si grew smaller and smaller, less and less human, right there in the front seat of her Altima. "Did you think I wouldn't figure it out? Blood is thicker than water my ass, Si."

By then, Si was silent. She picked him up by the edges of his shell and tucked him into the sack, right next to Leo.

A while later, she dropped him them both into the branch of the Chicago River that ran by Horner Park. It was a pretty area. Not too many predators. She wasn't a monster, after all. Just protecting her own self-interests.

As for the money, she'd have to be careful. But Caterina Von Eckstein was a meticulous sort. She abhorred loose ends.

#   #   #

And so it was that Caterina von Eckstein—formerly Catie Rubin— retired from thievery, at least for now and ensconced herself in a bigger apartment on Lake Shore Drive, one with a 24- hour doorman and great security that would make sure that any unwelcome visitors never came her way.

Somewhere near the Chicago River, two box turtles plodded their way out of the marsh.

In her shiny new apartment on the 8th floor, Cat poured herself a glass of champagne.

In the tall grass of the Forest Preserve, two turtles struggled through the grass. One had what looked for all the world like a ninja mask over his tiny face. The other one would have answered to the name Si, if anyone had known to call him.

They might have even gotten somewhere had it not been for Mrs. Garrity, looking for a turtle for her 4th grade science class.

"You'll do fine," she said. If a tiny voice muttered, "Shit!" Mrs. Garrity didn't hear it. She was too busy striding toward the second turtle, who was now wobbling his way forward.

"My lucky day," she said. "A two-fer!" She scooped them up and tucked both reptiles safely into an air-holed studded box and snapped the lid. Her 4th graders were going to be so excited.

In the trees nearby, just out of sight, someone in a dingy lab coat was watching. This was a stunning development. One that could prove very useful.

He'd bide his time and keep watch. They'd watch the girl, too. After all, she'd downed two different potions. You never knew what could happen. Or when.

So they'd keep an eye on all of them.

And wait. Time would tell. He was sure of it. ♜

QED: THE COSMIC SPECTRE

By Steven Philip Jones

(To Doug Wildey)

September 1964. 12:34 CST, several miles north of Wichita, Kans.

Model 853-21 Quiet Bird, a top-secret scout plane, makes its initial test flight over a desolate stretch of the Great Plains. The first reduced radar cross section aircraft to reach this stage of development, her pilot is Captain Ned Lynch, a decorated fighter pilot, graduate of the U.S. Air Force Test Pilot School, and an alternate for the spaceflight program. The sky is Lynch's home and he has experienced almost everything a flyer can encounter in the wild blue yonder.

But a meteor crossing his flightpath is a new one.

Its black tail momentarily blocks out the sun as Quiet Bird flies through the stream, but there are enough flashes of what could be chemiluminescence that Lynch can discern the meteor's peculiar corkscrew motion.

"Ground Control, this is zero-3-7. Just had a near collision with a bogey. Over."

"Roger, zero-3-7, we see it. One-eighth mile west. Turn right to heading 1-5-zero. Over."

Quiet Bird does not reply.

"Zero-3-7, do you read? Come in. Over."

No reply.

Ground Control scrambles four search planes, one to each compass point. At the same time GC contacts local and state law enforcement agencies to inquire if they have received reports of a meteor or unidentified flying object or anything else that might aid their search. GC also scans ham radio frequencies for same.

Within minutes a search pilot spots Quiet Bird's distinctive twin vertical stabilizers crumpled in a ravine five miles north of where the meteor transected the RCS's flightpath. A rescue team is dispatched while the search for Lynch continues in case he ejected before impact.

The rescuers arrive to find the plane's bubble canopy intact and a mangled body inside the cockpit. The team is acclimated to disfigured corpses, yet one team member gasps, "What happened to him?"

Another gulps, "Wasn't Lynch in his thirties?"

Thirty-seven, to be precise, but the carcass in the G-suit appears to have been a man who was one hundred years old if he was a day.

Three minutes later. A bend of the Dismal Tributary, Wild Horse Valley, Nebr.

The stream snakes southeast through sandhills and canyons. Wide but not very deep, its water comes from the Ogallala Aquifer which boils up in places to create pockets of quicksand.

Meanwhile the meteor is in dark flight and plummeting fast.

It impacts into a pool of spring water with a splash and a plume.

Coyotes, deer, and sandhill cranes scatter.

The meteorite is snared by a quicksand hole and sucked underneath as the colloid bubbles, ripples, then flattens.

Sunlight sparkles on the water.

All is still. Not even the Magicicadas sing.

Four hours later a United States Air Force 6x6 shop van follows a Chevy C/K with a pinto rust pattern along the west bank of the Dismal, the vehicles bobbing and swaying like Conestogas through chophills pockmarked by blowouts and warted by soapweeds. Sunlight is starting to wane and the air beginning to cool as the party reaches the base of the Brady-Moorefield Road crossing and parks.

The pickup's driver climbs out. Lloyd Ohman is a farmer in his seventies, leathery, calm, reticent, and every inch a sandhiller from his short-sleeve shirt to his round toe boots. Exiting the passenger side is meteoriticist Captain Jean Joseph. A little shorter than the average Zoomie, she is thirty, fit, and dusky. Joseph holds a Geiger counter in one hand and rubs her backside with the other. "I thought Nebraska was flat."

"It is along Old 30," Ohman replies with the whisper of a smirk.

The van parks behind the pickup and Colonel Dwight Way exits the cab. A trim man with trim thoughts, he is followed by two young airmen, Cpls. Chick Watson and the driver Hobart Fenton, the latter noticing a varicolored war surplus jeep parked beside one of the crossing's pillars. "Is somebody else down here?"

Way asks Ohman, "You recognize that leaping Lena?"

"Oh yeah, that's Wayne Amsler's jeep. He's a senior over in Svea-Dal. Him and two friends scrounged every half-empty paint can in the county to give it a fresh coat."

Fenton checks the fuel gauge. "The tank's half full."

Watson lifts the hood. "The motor and all the works look A-OK and it's basically clean inside. I don't think it was dumped here."

"Maybe Amsler spotted the meteor and came to check it out."

"So where is he now?" Watson cups his hands around his mouth and shouts "Hello?"

No reply.

"That mystery can wait," Way tells his airmen then asks Joseph, "Are we sure the meteorite is around here?"

"As sure as we can be, sir. Calculations based on radar and seismometers tracking of the meteor indicate this should be the endpoint."

"You don't sound very confident."

"I'd feel more confident if we saw an impact crater or I could pick up more iodine-129 than is normal for a mixed-grass prairie." Joseph turns on her Geiger counter, which hardly crackles.

"All right, then let's start searching. Should we unpack the NBC suits?"

"Not for these readings."

"Fine. You and I will wade over and check the east bank."

Ohman says, "It'd be safer if I drive you across."

"Thank you. Corporals, scour this side."

Ohman warns the young men, "Watch where you plant your feet. Those little cacti have needles that go through anything thinner than metal. And try not to step in any quicksand if you stray off the bank."

The corporals split up, Watson going north and Fenton south. As Fenton approaches the spring pool he spots a light like an aurora rippling beneath the water and bends over for a better look, unsure if it is a mirage or maybe an oil slick.

Way notices Fenton from the other side of the Dismal and asks, "You find something?"

"I don't know, sir. There's some sort of illumination in the water. I've never seen anything like it."

Watson walks back towards Fenton. "Could it be a reflection off the meteorite?"

"I don't… wait!" The light darts like a fish in Fenton's direction but vanishes upon reaching the waterline. "It's gone."

Joseph asks, "Did it evaporate?"

"No, ma'am, not really. It… Bodies! Bodies in the water!"

Watson reaches Fenton and points at the pool. "There are! Three of them!"

Three old men's corpses wearing highschooler clothing stare out of the water, faces contorted in agonized fear.

At the same time an *ignis fatuus* begins glowing amongst the airmen's shadows. Neither realizes it is rising around their legs until Joseph hollers, "Something's seeping out of the ground! Get away from there!"

Too late.

The corpse-light geysers like dark steam peppered with twinkling ash over the corporals to sap the airmen's youth. The last thing either one sees is a shadow person floating within the swirls, its inhuman face glaring at them. In unison the dying men scream: "Cassavius!"

Way shouts "Let's get over there!" but Joseph grabs his arm. "It's too late!"

The smoke seeps back into the ground as its victims collapse like abandoned marionettes.

Ohman can barely swallow, more afraid than he has been since the Meuse-Argonne offensive. "Did you see them?"

"Yes." Way shivers as he looks at Joseph. "Just like Lynch."

Joseph, pale, nods.

"That word they shouted? What was it?"

"I've never heard it before, but we have to divert people away from here until we have control of the situation."

"I'll notify the State Patrol to shut down this road."

"And, sir, we're going to need people with a lot more letters after their names than I have to figure this out."

"All right, I'll have Offutt get the government's best brains out here pronto."

20:36 AST. Lost Key, British Overseas Territory of Bermuda.

The most isolated of the Bermuda Archipelago's 182 islands, Lost Key has been occupied only twice, once during the seventeenth century when a coalition of freebooters known as The Wandering Buccaneers used it as a pirate haven and now as the home of explorer-scientist Peregrine White and her family.

The Whites live in Linndorsa, a home of the future constructed of tungsten steel, prestressed concrete, and acrylic windows. Designed by Peregrine and her father, Dr. Duck Hawk Linn, descendants of the Buccaneers' leader, the semicircular edifice is recessed inside the hollow of a coral ridge that divides the island's beachline from its forest, where an egg-shaped seapod observatory connected to the house by a sequoia-thick stanchion peers over the treetops. A walkway leads from Linndorsa to Kepler Cove and a neomodern dock where the *Sappho I* (a 21' Chris Craft Cobra), the *Sappho II* (a 1962 Lake 'n Sea 14' Caribbean), the *Nova III* (the latest in Peregrine's line of prototype submersibles), and the *Charlotte* (a DeHavilland DHC-2T Turbine Boss Beaver seaplane) are moored.

T. Paine White stands on the dock contemplating a waxing gibbous moon and the Northern Cross. This is his favorite time of evening. The kids are busy with homework, his wife and father-in-law are tinkering in their workshops or writing an article for some journal, and he has the world to himself to recharge his soul and regain his bearings. Six feet two, two hundred sinewy pounds, and in his early forties, White isn't handsome but there is something about his weather-worn face, cobalt eyes, and the mischievous smirk he employs instead of a smile that more than compensates. A retired sergeant in the Special Investigation Branch of the Royal Military Police, White's two concessions to civilian life are his shaggy brunet hair and casual dress. Right now he is wearing an ebony polo shirt, khaki shorts, and cowhide sandals. The weather is perfect, as usual, and he is free to savor a Ramón Allones Superiores without upsetting one of Peregrine's smoke-and-fire extinguishing tocsins.

White's downtime is interrupted by a message coming over the two-way communicator in his dive watch, another Peregrine innovation. Pressing the answer button: "Yes, pet?"

"Hoyt is calling. He needs us." Peregrine's Low Country Georgian accent is pronounced, a sure tell she is eager to plunge into a conundrum brought courtesy of Hoyt Curtain, Director of USINT, a covert agency answerable to the Office of the President. Peregrine is the top consultant for the agency's Scientific, Prototypical, and Unique Research (SPUR) Branch, a department dedicated to expanding the limits of technology and science.

"But we've only been home a week." The Whites just spent half the summer at Edwards Air Force Base where Peregrine assisted on the Lunar Landing Research Vehicle.

"It's a code Critical."

"Oh, I see." What White really sees is there is no dissuading his wife when her curiosity is piqued. "When do we leave?"

"ASAP."

"Where to?"

"Nebraska. Hoyt is handling the flight plan. I'll fill everyone in on the way to Kindley."

"I'll call Waldy to get the *Falco* prepped and then I'll get *Charlotte* ready."

"Can you get Dalton and Zoey ready, too?"

"Of course."

"Thanks. I'll notify Dad. Love you, P."

"Love you more, P." As White disconnects he watches a shooting star streak across the sky. He hopes it is a good omen.

12:33 AM CST. Svea-Dal, Nebr., ten miles west of the Dismal bend.

Ralph Wingate has lived alone for twenty years. A World War I vet and employee of forty years with the Union Pacific Railroad before retiring, Wingate bought a house in the one-horse town of Svea-Dal after inheriting and selling his family's nearby farm. His wife Vera died in 1944 and their six children have not seen him since her funeral even though the furthest one only resides in Lincoln. Coarse and unimaginative, Wingate is not prone to daydreams or wishes, only some occasional dark whims, but tonight he wakes from a nightmare panting, sweating, wondering if something has gone wrong with the world. He heads to the kitchen, pours water from the faucet into a tumbler, adds a jigger of vermouth, and downs it. Setting the glass in the sink he walks to the living room, switches on a lamp, sits in his lounge chair, and relives the nightmare.

It felt at first as if he was trapped somewhere dark without air, which was unpleasant since he has vivid memories of nearly drowning during the Third Battle of the Aisne. Then, suddenly, he was free but his brain was assaulted with inhuman compunctions and incomprehensible calculations. These thoughts were all beyond him and left him lost and confused and frightened. Wingate had no will of his own as he moved or drifted forward, sometimes slowly, sometimes rattlesnake quick, each spurt of progress leaving him weaker and more famished. Then he saw the sign for Lindberg Cemetery, hand-painted on two planks nailed to fence posts standing beside the rutted entrance. Wingate has family buried here, grew up around here, yet everything struck him as foreign and strange, as if he didn't recognize or couldn't fathom the surrounding sandhills, canyons, and farmland bisected by dirt roads or the night sounds or the temperature or even the wind. He was a stranger to everything. All was alien to him.

Then Wingate woke up.

And now an impulse consumes him.

It is ridiculous. Senseless. He should return to bed. But he knows he will only stare at the ceiling until succumbing, dressing, and driving east towards the Dismal Tributary.

22:37 AST. Kindley Air Force Base, St. David's Island.

White brings the *Charlotte* in for a landing near the former US Navy flying boat station. Turning off the magnetos he locks the propeller and coasts the seaplane towards a small private hangar where Walden Wilson waits. A burly, buzz-cut native with chestnut skin roasted by the sun, Wilson snags the propeller and pushes the seaplane rearward into the hangar. "Ahoy!"

"Ahoy, Waldy! Sorry for the short notice."

"That's what you always say."

"Well, they don't call me Paine for nothing."

"That's the truth." Waldy ties the *Charlotte* to the pier. "She's secure. Come on out, White family."

Wilson watches the seaplane's door open and his godson Quetelet Edison Dalton White rush out. Sprouting tall like his father with his mother's red sand hair, the eleven year old is all knees and elbows as he shouts, "Ahoy, Waldy!"

"Ahoy, Q.E.D.!" He hugs the boy off his feet. "What say you ditch this trip and stay and help me? I'm diving on the *Resa Jane* tomorrow."

"You found her?"

"Thanks to that new side-scan sonar your mom and granddad have me testing out. Would you believe that old brig lies no more than five miles from here?"

"I can help, too!" shouts Xami Zoey Tauri, Peregrine's niece and goddaughter. Ten years old and tawny with chocolate hair and eyes, Zoey favors her father, Adeem, an archaeologist, more than her mother Kestrel, an intellectual historian. Waldy hugs her like he did Dalton and tells her, "Who says you can't, X.Z?" To the *Charlotte*, "How about it, Peregrine? Heck, just sell me the ragamuffins. I'll make you a good offer."

"Maybe I'll just give them to you, seeing how much they want to spend time with me." Next off of the plane is his best friend's better half. Five feet five inches, robust, and nearly ten years younger than her husband, Dr. Peregrine White, FRM, MD, DSc, etc., is bobbysoxer beautiful with an obdurate intelligence to her face and indefatigable brilliance in her eyes. Most folks often doubted and worried when they were confronted by the mysteries of the universe, but Peregrine embraced its enigmas with a wonder and an acceptance that there will always be something new and incredible to discover but not all of it will be pleasant.

The same could be said of her father, who follows Peregrine off. The grandson of Scotch-Irish immigrants, a Georgia native, and a graduate of the Sorbonne, Dr. Linn is large in height and girth with a voracious appetite for knowledge, discovery, and American Southern cuisine. Short on patience but big on loyalty, he is a white-haired Southern variation of Professor George Edward Challenger, and in a blustery voice he chides, "What sort of gratitude is this? Abandoning your parents and I at such a time!"

Dalton says, "Waldy was just asking for some help, Grandpa. That's all."

"Don't I need help? Who's going to arrange my socks and iron my shirt collars? Young people today have no respect for their elders."

Last to deplane is White, who locks the *Charlotte* and tosses Wilson the keys. "What's this I hear about a mutiny?"

"If I can seed some dissent during the day I sleep good at night."

"I wouldn't mind helping myself if you've really located the *Resa Jane*."

Peregrine taps her foot. "Fine. Who needs you? Dad and I will go by ourselves."

"How? Neither of you are pilots."

"We'll manage. How hard can it be if you can do it?"

Waldy and Zoey laugh as Dalton snickers, "She got you good, Dad."

"And I guess you never want to ride co-pilot again, eh, brat-face?"

Dalton blanches as Linn interrupts, "This is all very entertaining but we're expected elsewhere."

"You're right, Duck. Family, grab your gear and let's roll out."

Fifteen minutes later the *Falco* takes off. A Dassault-Breguet *Mystère 20* converted into an airborne caravan, workshop, and research lab, its first stop is Atlanta where the jet will refuel before flying to North Platte.

Regardless of White's threat Dalton sits in the second seat, reading out instruments as the *Falco* levels off.

"Good job," White compliments. "You'll be ready to learn avigation soon."

"What about taking the controls?"

"You can't fly until you know how to get where you're going."

Peregrine enters the cockpit and ruffles Dalton's hair. "And maybe not crash in the flight simulator."

"I'm getting better."

"'Better' doesn't pay the hospital bills. Now scoot so I can jaw with your father."

"Yes, ma'am." Dalton reluctantly leaves to join his grandfather and cousin.

"Most fathers teach their sons how to throw a baseball."

"We're not most families."

"That's a point." Peregrine settles into the co-pilot seat. "How's the weather?"

"Clear sailing, but you knew that." White glances her way. "Something on your mind, pet?"

"Just thinking."

"About what?"

"Maybe the kids should have stayed with Waldy."

"We're a family. We stay together. That's our way."

"And normally I'm fine with that."

"You think hiking around a prairie is more dangerous than diving on a shipwreck?"

"Six men are dead and cause of death is unknown."

"I thought the meteorite caused it."

"We don't even know if we're dealing with a meteorite. Until it's located it's technically an unidentified flying object, emphasis on 'unidentified.' And even if it turns out to be a meteorite… well… we've read 'The Colour Out of Space.'"

"We also read *The Little Prince* and Captain Ruppelt's UFO report. What's happened? You were excited on Lost Key."

"I'm worried I let my enthusiasm blind me to my motherly obligations."

White nods. "Do you want to turn back?"

"Could we err on the side of caution?"

"You mean have Duck watch the kids in a nearby town until you know what we're dealing with?"

Peregrine smiles.

"I'm okay with that but Duck won't like it."

"I'll handle my father."

"That's my S.O.P." Short for 'standard operating procedure.'

Peregrine smiles. "I love you, P."

White takes her hand and kisses her fingers. "I love you more, P."

5:21 AM CST. Nebraska Highway 47 North.

Jennie Banks feels grouchy as she drives home from Gothenburg.

It is taking longer than usual because the Brady-Moorefield crossing is closed and after pulling a double shift at Arneson & Gygax Feeding Company she is weary, sweaty, and smells like a half ton of soybean and cereal grain. The extra money is nice since a dry July and first half of August pared the number of bushels she and her husband Noah had been expecting from this year's corn crop, but that is the way it goes in farming and all Jennie wants right now is to make sure Noah has something more than coffee for breakfast and then hit the sheets. So instead of staying on the Highway 47 North detour Jennie takes a backroad to County Road 773. It is longer but devoid of traffic so faster.

When Jennie reaches the 773 intersection she turns west and switches off the cattlemen report on the radio, and as she scuttles down the two-lane gravel road two-striped and red-legged grasshoppers leap willy-nilly in the high beams of her '57 Chevy 3800. Then as she approaches an intersection Jennie spies what looks like someone's blurry silhouette in the ground mist on the Lindberg Cemetery side of the crossroad. If this was January Jennie would offer whoever it is a ride. That is what you do in the valley when the weather turns frigid and blustery. But it is warm and dewy this morning and it has not been long enough since Charlie Starkweather's bloody spree that Jennie feels comfortable picking up strangers if she doesn't have to, so she keeps her eyes on the road and crosses the intersection.

Here County Road 773 becomes East Fairview Road, which means Jennie is less than two miles from home, but before she drives another hundred yards Jennie sees another blurry silhouette alongside the road. No doubt this is weird so she passes the figure without looking or slowing down, but before she goes another hundred yards Jennie sees yet another silhouette.

"What's going on?"

Jennie exhilarates. Home is over the next rise and in the distance she can make out that the kitchen lights are on. She takes comfort knowing Noah is waiting there for her, but then the blurry silhouette appears again and floats into the middle of the road. It begins to glow but Jennie never hits the brakes. Not even when the radiant image glides towards the truck, slips through the windshield like an apparition, and glares at her with an unhuman face.

Jennie loses control of the Chevy and it swerves off the road.

Skips over a ditch.

Bounds over a stretch of fallow ground and tumbles into a small canyon.

There it settles, high beams buried in the earth, casting an eerie light around the hood as an even eerier light envelopes the cab and swallows Jennie Banks.

"Cassavius!"

That moment. Dismal Tributary Base Camp.

The contingency operation was set up as soon as support personnel arrived from Offutt AFB, and once Joseph could reasonably confirm it was safe to venture to the west bank the five bodies were collected and transported to the Armed Forces Medical Examiner System. The shop van was also retrieved and assigned to the captain, who is startled awake by the Geiger counter crackling.

Joseph jumps off her cot and grabs the instrument. It is detecting long range alpha particles, indicating the presence of cosmic rays, but the count rate is low and swiftly declining. Bolting outside she waves the instrument's pancake probe and just before the crackling fades out pinpoints the origin of the alpha particles is in the direction of the spring pool.

She hurries to the camp's management center where Way has set up his bunk but the colonel is not there. She finds him in the operations center conferring with his signal officer and provost marshal. Before Joseph can report Way informs her, "Dr. White's team has landed and should be here within the hour."

"The Geiger counter just detected alpha particles on the west bank, which makes no sense to me."

"Are they dangerous?"

"Not really and they're gone now, but I have no clue what triggered them. Hopefully Dr. White will. Have there been any updates from AFMES?"

"I was about to follow up with them when we found an intruder within our perimeter."

"A gawker?"

"All we know so far is he lives in the next nearest town, Svea-Dal."

"What's he doing out here at this hour?"

"He says a dream made him come out here to look for something hidden in the ground but he doesn't know what it is or where it's at."

Joseph lets her expression communicate her bewilderment.

"It's got me puzzled, too, captain. Like you just said, hopefully the good doctor can help make sense of this when she gets here."

That moment. Lee Bird Field, North Platte, Nebr.

The *Falco* is met by a USAF G-506 truck and two M151 personnel transport jeeps. Peregrine supervises the transfer of equipment from jet to truck and then rides in the cargo bed while White follows in one jeep and the children and Linn follow in the other.

At the Svea-Dal exit the second jeep turns off and its occupants are taken to the Anderson Motel, a bitty two-suite adobe structure on Main Street. Staying with them as an attaché is the driver, Staff Sergeant Anthony Barrett. Meanwhile the truck and first jeep continue to the base camp where Joseph and Way present Peregrine a full report while the provost marshal, Lieutenant Ted Nichols, approaches White. "I've been told you were a top-notch interrogator in the MRP."

"I was an SIB investigator but I did interrogate suspects or prisoners when there was a need."

"Well, I have a need for a second opinion." Nichols, a well-proportioned man in his middle thirties, hands White a sky blue file with the word CLASSIFIED embossed in red on the flap. "We picked an interloper up this morning and identified him as Ralph Wingate from Svea-Dal. Served in the First World War. Clean record there and no police record as a civilian except for a couple of disturbance calls."

"Lovely." White scans the pages and frowns. "The man sounds like a loon."

"He does, but assuming he just happened to go off the rails at this particular moment may be negligent."

"Louie, you and I think alike." White smirks. "Let's go chat up your trespasser."

Meanwhile Peregrine, Joseph, and Way have a teleconference in the operations center with Linn at the Anderson Motel and Curtain in Washington DC. Peregrine asks Curtain, "Does AFMES have any theories about what triggered the rapid progeria in Captain Lynch and the others?"

"We're still waiting on their postmortem reports."

Joseph asks, "Does that word the corporals shouted mean anything?"

"'Cassavius' is not a known word. Could they have shouted

something else?"

Joseph and Way both seem certain they heard correctly.

"Then we'll keep researching. Peregrine, how do you want to proceed?"

"Carefully without delay."

"What about those long range alpha particles? Couldn't that have indicated the presence of some sort of ternary fission?"

Way asks, "What is that?"

"A form of nuclear fission."

"You mean like an atom bomb?"

Linn, always ready to play the role of teacher, explains, "Atomic bombs are fission bombs; however nuclear fission can be employed beneficially, most notably in power reactors for a generating station or the power system of a vessel such as a submarine. But power reactors emit a steady stream of particles, so it seems more likely that the particles were – for lack of a better word – a telltale of a shower of secondary particles produced by cosmic rays, a common natural event."

Peregrine tells Curtain, "I've brought along one of the remotely controlled ground-penetrating radars I developed for the Army and Navy's explosive ordnance disposal corps. Even if the source was some sort of power reactor the electromagnetic energy my GPR uses wouldn't even tickle it."

"Give it a try. But like you said… carefully."

It takes Peregrine and Joseph twenty minutes to set up the GPR, which resembles a lawnmower designed by Kenneth Strickfaden. At Way's insistence the women wear NBC (nuclear, biological, chemical) suits while on the west bank. Back on the east bank Peregrine drives the GPR in a search grid pattern starting at the edge of the spring pool. Roving at a speed of one mile per hour while emitting cone-shaped pulses into the ground the GPR – nicknamed Babs by Dalton and Zoey after their languid but nosey great aunt – makes slow but steady progress and after approximately thirty minutes it registers a diffractor in the quicksand. Staring at the cathode ray tube receiving feedback from the GPR Peregrine says, "That hyperbola appears to roughly be about the size and shape of a pineapple."

Joseph agrees. "If it is a meteorite it's a class 4, but it looks extremely smooth."

"It also has more than the usual metal content and it's not iron-nickel."

"Maybe it's oldhamite. It's rare on earth but sometimes found in meteorites."

Way asks, "Should we salvage it?"

"That would probably be wise with the aquifer," Peregrine answers.

"What do you mean?"

"The Ogallala Aquifer underlies approximately 174,000 square miles in Nebraska and seven other states, and is not only the primary water source for crop irrigation but provides drinking water for over one million people."

Way's eyes widen. "Oh Lord."

"The object is about six feet down. My husband often helps the Navy's salvage department so I suggest we ask his advice on how to recover it."

White is not happy when Way pulls him from the interrogation, but simmers down as Peregrine explains the situation. "Well, people are so much lighter than quicksand it's impossible to dive in it, and even if you could submerge there would be no visibility below the surface. I would contact the nearest roads department or construction company and have them bring out a steam shovel or an excavator. Have them park on the overpass and reach the pool from there. Then use the GPR to guide the operator where to scoop. Also have them bring a dirt sifter if they have one. The kind used for sifting backfill."

Way and Joseph leave to requisition the equipment but Peregrine hangs back. "You never cease to amaze me, Paine White."

He pretends to blush. "Me? You're the genius, Peregrine White."

"And you're the jack of all trades and master of most. Speaking of which, how's it going with the trespasser?"

A queer expression dawns over White's face. "Oh, yeah, I best get back to Nichols and the medic."

"Medic? Is the man sick?"

"Maybe in a *Shadow Out of Time*-y kind of way."

"Pardon?"

"He claims a nightmare compelled him to come here to search for something in the ground."

"That's a coincidence."

"Isn't it? He also claims that ever since he had the dream he's been sharing his brain with some sort of greater intelligence."

"Grandiose delusions?"

"All I know he has yet to make an inconsistent or contradictory statement. Lieutenant Nichols also hasn't found anything that links him to Quite Bird. So we asked and he's agreed to a lie detector test."

"Do you have a polygraph?"

"No, but he's okay with us using truth serum instead."

"Hence the medic. You are aware that such psychoactive drugs are not one hundred percent reliable."

"I am. All we can do is try it and see what happens."

11:45 AM CST. The Hitchin' Post Restaurant, Svea-Dal.

The only establishment in town to grab a bite, the Hitchin' Post is four doors down from the Anderson on the opposite side of the crossroads that makes up Svea-Dal's miniscule business district. Today is a football Saturday with the Cornhuskers playing South Dakota so the restaurant is filling up with locals, but Linn, the cousins, and Barrett find a booth in a back corner. Plenty of eyes follow as they wade through the crowd and after the foursome orders four runzas a farmer asks Barrett, "You with that bunch that closed down Brady-Moorefield?"

"I wouldn't know anything about that."

"So what's going on out there?"

"I couldn't say."

"Does it have anything to do with those three boys that went missing? Word is you found their Willys. It's painted all kinds of different colors."

Before Barrett can toss out another deflection a second farmer comments, "Them boys aren't the only ones missing. The State Patrol is searching for Jennie Banks. She took Highway 13 out of Gothenburg this morning and no one's seen her since."

A third farmer adds, "I heard the State Patrol is looking for her and Noah's half out of his mind."

The conversation develops a life of its own and makes the rounds of the patrons while Dalton quietly inquires of his grandfather, "Should we tell Mom about the missing lady? It might have something to do with… you know."

"The State Patrol is coordinating with the Air Force, QED, so I'm sure she is aware of the situation."

Dalton drops the subject and glances at Zoey: *Are you thinking what I'm thinking?*

When their lunch arrives the children quietly but deliberately eat while Linn and Barrett engage in a friendly debate over the superiority of the runza or the pork tenderloin sandwich. When the game comes on the two men start watching and the children get Linn's permission to go to the Brady Elementary School playground. On the way out Dalton waits while Zoey detours towards the ladies' room but slips into a phone booth. She finds the Banks' address in the directory and the children leave. Stopping at the M151 they borrow the Nebraska Official State Highway map and the Rand McNally Nebraska map from the glove box and take them into their hotel room.

"You know," Zoey says as she examines the State Highway map, "we should assume the State Patrol has searched the surrounding highways and all country roads by now."

"Yes, but look at all the links and spurs and recreation roads. There are all kinds of places to search."

"Not if we eliminate the unlikeliest routes a person traveling from Gothenburg to the Banks' farm would have driven."

"I thought we were already looking for unlikely routes."

"We are. I said 'unlikeliest.'"

"Oh." Some silence, and then Dalton cheers, "I think this might be it!"

Zoey looks at a thin black line Dalton is pointing at. "That doesn't appear on my map. What is that?"

"There's no designation. I bet it's an old farm road. But look! It connects Highway 47 to Country Road 773 which turns into East Fairview Road where the Banks live."

"That way is longer than if she stayed on Highway 47."

"But it would have been quicker because there would be a bunch more cars on the highway from the detour."

"Maybe." Zoey muses on this possibility. "How do we find out?"

Dalton grins a mischievous grin and Zoey recalls her Plato: "Of all the animals the boy is the most unmanageable."

Thirty minutes later Dalton parks the M151 on the side of East Fairview Road across from a white clapboard two-story farmhouse with a covered front porch. "There is the Banks house."

Zoey sits in the passenger seat consulting the Rand McNally map. "In two miles this turns into County Road 773 and then in another half-mile it meets your farm road." The two pause to listen to a transistor radio in Zoey's lap. The football game is playing and Nebraska is ahead 6-0 in the first quarter.

"We still have a couple of hours." Dalton puts the jeep into gear and drives slowly. "If we don't find anything by the middle of the third quarter we turn back. Agreed?"

"Agreed. I just hope we're not spotted by the police."

"So what if we are? This is farm country. It's no big deal for kids to drive around here."

"This isn't a tractor. It's a military vehicle. Which we hotwired."

"You worry too much."

"And you don't worry enough."

This is a familiar back-and-forth between the cousins and as usual neither speaks to the other for several minutes afterwards.

That moment. Dismal Tributary Base Camp.

An excavator and dirt sifter from the Lincoln County Roads Department has arrived and work is under way. In quick order the "pineapple" is strained from the colloid and although smeared with sand and dirt Peregrine can make out that, "It almost looks like a mock-up for some sort of aerodynamic submersible, especially with these spiral striations. I suggest we take it to the *Falco* and clean and examine it in my laboratory."

Way disagrees. "I can't authorize this thing leaving the base. Besides we should tell our superiors what we've found."

"But they will want to know if this thing is responsible for the deaths of Captain Lynch and the others and we don't know yet. We can't even say if this is the product of some foreign power's military program or if it is of extraterrestrial origin."

Joseph asks, "Can we keep a lid on this until the captain and I conduct a prelim in the shop van?"

"How long will that take?"

Realizing time is of the essence Peregrine estimates, "One hour but two would be better."

Way respects White's reputation and Joseph's professionalism but has to weigh this request against the logistics of maintaining a communication blackout for one hundred and twenty minutes and his responsibilities to the chain of command. He decides: "Two hours. No longer. And if you can finish sooner—"

"Understood."

That moment. East Fairview Road.

The cousins pull up behind a state patrol car parked a couple of hundred feet from the 773 intersection. Zoey switches off the transistor as Dalton cautiously parks beside the vehicle and says, "I don't see anyone."

"Why would he leave his car along the side of the road?"

"Probably because he found what we're looking for."

Zoey exits the jeep to peer through the patrol car's windows. Seeing nothing helpful inside she climbs on the trunk and scampers onto the roof to look around. "Oh my gosh!"

"What?"

"Tire tracks! Some vehicle jumped this ditch and landed in the field! The tracks are all wonky."

"Where do they go?"

"The far end of the field."

"Let's have a look-see." Dalton disconnects the ignition and the power wires to stop the engine and the cousins proceed towards the field.

"What if we run into the patrolman?"

"We'll ask him if we can help."

As they walk Zoey marvels at the patchwork expanse encompassed by rolling yellow swells that spreads out around them: dozens of emerald cookie-cutter spheres of cropland framed by dirt roads, each section tenanted by a center pivot irrigator, their steel dazzlingly reflecting the late summer sun. "You can see for miles."

"Sure can." Dalton is unimpressed.

"It's like a sea, desolate but beautiful."

"It's boring. Everything is so fla-a-A-H-T!"

Zoey snags Dalton before he tumbles into a canyon, his cry echoing down the depression only to be supplanted by someone shouting up, "What are you doing here?" The cousins spot the patrolman clambering towards the wreckage of a pickup with its front end buried in the ground.

"We saw your squad car," Dalton says and Zoey asks, "Do you need help?"

"It's not a squad car and you shouldn't be here. Go home."

The patrolman reaches the pickup and cups his hands around his eyes as he squints through the driver-side window, but the sun is shining into the cab through the back window so neither he nor the cousins notice a strange glittering beginning to glimmer within the truck.

That moment. The shop van.

Peregrine finds herself missing the *Falco's* potable water system as she uses a water bucket and a brush to wash the "pineapple" and scrub corrosion off its shell. She would have also preferred her lab's adjustable overhead lighting and HVAC to the fluorescent lamp, fan, and heater installed in the watertight shop's ceiling. Built for conducting maintenance, not research, the cramped space is resourcefully furnished with benches, supply lockers, a worktable with mounted tabletop tools, and a controller box for the electrical equipment. Placing the "pineapple" on a lab scale borrowed from the military treatment facility, she tells Joseph, "Whatever this hunk is I bet it ranks 10 on the Mohs." A magnet test proved it is not a ferrous metal and the women plan on giving it a spark test after this measurement. "Four grams per milliliter. No wonder it didn't float in the quicksand."

"So is it a mock-up or a wodge?"

"Impossible to say without taking an x-ray, but somehow this has been honed and polished into a perfect tear-shape with precise striations." Peregrine pauses to ponder. "It's hardly an elegant compromise but maybe we could risk boring—"

The Geiger counter suddenly crackles and Joseph grabs it. "Alpha particles. Stronger than this morning. Maybe because this thing is no longer submerged."

And then the "pineapple" wobbles.

It rocks a few more times and then the crackling decrescendos as the swaying subsides until both noise and motion ceases.

Joseph stutters, "Is… something… alive in there?"

Peregrine is likewise flabbergasted. "I don't know, but just in case… " She places the "pineapple" inside the portable biosafety cabinet brought from the *Falco*. Then Peregrine pauses again. "It exhibited no animation prior to the Geiger counter going off… but what could be the connection?" Peregrine is stumped but then remembers the trespasser who was looking for something in the ground. "Perhaps there is someone we can ask."

A few moments earlier. The interrogation tent.

Captain Yeakel Benneville, general medical officer and twenty year veteran, is monitoring Wingate's vitals. The subject has been in a hypnagogic state for several minutes but so far has only given the same answers to White and Nichols's questions as he did before the injection. Then Wingate intones, "Someone's looking through the window."

Nichols swivels his head around to make sure the window flaps are all still closed. "Which window?"

"The driver's window." Wingate points at the air in front of him.

"Where are you?"

"Inside someone's truck."

White asks Benneville, "Is he trance channeling?"

Benneville frowns as he shines his ophthalmoscope's light into Wingate's eyes. "More likely it's hallucinatory palinopsia elicited by the drugs."

Nevertheless White asks Wingate, "Who do you see?"

Wingate leans forward. Squints. "Looks like a highway patrolman." Abruptly jerks back. "There's a dead woman in here! She looks older than Methuselah!"

White asks Nichols, "How old is that missing woman? And what was she driving?"

"Jennie Banks? In her late thirties and she was in her pickup. But you don't think he's really—"

Wingate stammers, "There's a light! There's someone… some thing… in the light!"

White: "Describe who you're seeing."

Wingate's face contorts with disgust. "It looks like he's been gassed. All withered and pruny and skinnier than a skeleton. Now it's reaching… oh Lordy."

The next moment the cousins scream as black smoke pours through the window glass to cover the patrolman like a powder snow avalanche. Glowings and gloomings whirl within its billows and then the children hear a cry: "Cassavius!" The miasma grows quiet and motionless but only briefly before it begins drifting up the canyon wall, leaving behind a very old man's corpse dressed in the patrolman's uniform.

In the interrogation tent Wingate tells White, "It's not working."

"What's not working?"

"Wait—now its's heading towards those kids."

"What kids?" When Wingate describes the boy and girl he sees White presses the two-way button on his watch and calls, "Dalton!"

No reply.

"Answer me Dalton!"

"Dad!"

White can hear that his son is outside, running, and scared. "Where are you?"

"East Fairview Road near County Road 773!"

"Is Zoey there?"

The girl answers. "Yes! We just saw—"

"How did you get out there?"

"We took Sergeant Barrett's jeep! We wanted—"

"Get in that jeep and drive here to the base. Can you do that?"

Dalton answers, "As soon as we get back to it!"

"How far away are you?"

"Not far."

"All right. I'll meet you on the way here." White asks Nichols, "Motorpool?"

A woman's voice says, "I'll show you." The men turn to see a wan and rattled Peregrine standing inside the tent's door. Joseph, beside her, continues, "And I'll go with you. I familiarized myself with the roads."

"Thank you." White looks at his wife. "Are you coming?"

She wants to more than anything but, "I can be more useful here. Hurry, Paine."

"I'll call you when I have them."

Peregrine asks Nichols to fetch Way and then asks Benneville for his patient's name. Then, doing her best to concentrate, Peregrine asks the dosed man, "Mr. Wingate, can you still see the children? Are they safe?"

"Yes. They're running way up ahead."

Peregrine sighs. "All right. Are you still having those strange thoughts?"

"Yes."

"Can you describe them to me?"

"It's gobbledygook."

"I see." Peregrine murmurs, "If you're not pretending I'd give anything to tap into your head right now."

As if in response Wingate's eyes glaze blank and sightless, his skin assumes a cadaverous hue, and in a glutinous timbre he says, "Wingate does not pretend."

Peregrine trades confounded gawks with Benneville, who rechecks the subject's vitals and verifies, "Mr. Wingate is physically fine."

"I am not Wingate. He is my channel and substitute."

Peregrine cocks her head. "Who are you then?"

"Cassavius of Malpertuis."

Cocks her head the other way. "Is that another planet?"

"If you wish to call it that."

Dozens of wondrous questions buzz in Peregrine's mind but she stays on point: "We found an object in the quicksand by the river. Is that what Wingate came here to find?"

"Describe it." Peregrine does. "Yes."

"Why?"

"What I was is in it."

"Are you trapped? Is it a spacecraft?"

"It is my barge and its mission must end lest I forever be spectra and lemure."

"What mission? Why did you come to Earth, Cassavius? What do you want?"

"To return to Malpertuis but I cannot."

"Why?"

"Death is not permitted in Malpertuis and I am beyond rescue. I am dead."

The cousins jump into the jeep before Dalton dares to peek back to see how close the miasma is, but, "It's gone!"

Zoey looks. "Where is it?"

"I don't know and I'm not going back to look!" Dalton starts the engine. "Let's go!" Taking off, he points ahead. "We can look from that high ground by the crossroads!"

The girl scrunches her face. "That's a cemetery!"

"Who cares? Call my Dad and let him know we're stopping there."

Ten minutes later White skids his borrowed M38A1 jeep to a stop behind the M151 parked in front of the Lindberg Cemetery sign. He tosses his dive watch to Joseph before dashing into the graveyard where he hugs his son and niece, paddles them once, and hugs them again. Meanwhile the captain updates Peregrine and the mother's relief is palpable through the speaker. "Are you heading back?"

White takes his watch and tells Peregrine, "You better call Hoyt. We can see the black cloud thing that got the airmen and it's heading west but it moves herky-jerky quick. It jumps ahead dozens of yards or more at a time faster than the eye can blink."

"In intermittent spurts?"

"Yes. It jumps, rests, then jumps again. It is traveling parallel to East Fairview Road so if it stays on its present course it will be in Svea-Dal in at most fifteen minutes."

Peregrine gasps, "Dad!"

"I know. Call and warn him. And you better have Way tell the town's civil defense to start evacuations toot sweet."

Nichols has returned to the tent with the colonel, who says, "Will do."

"In the meantime Captain Joseph is going to bring the kids to the base while I try to get ahead of this thing and play Paul Revere with any farms along its path."

Way adds, "And I'll see if we can track down the phone numbers to those farms and warn them to get out." To which Peregrine adds, "Thank you, captain. And Paine, be careful."

"Always." White slips his watch back on and tells Dalton and Zoey, "Behave and do what you're told. And when this is over you are going to apologize to your grandfather and Sergeant Barrett."

The discomfited cousins answer in union: "Yes, sir."

The fourth quarter is about to begin with the Cornhuskers ahead 43-0 when Peregrine calls her father. The Hitchin' Post is still packed so Linn and Barrett step outside to hear better and Peregrine barely finishes explaining the situation before the town's tornado sirens commence wailing.

Barrett scowls, "That's only going to drive everybody into shelters."

"Then," Linn counters, "we will have to try to keep them outside until the warden arrives."

Peregrine says, "Do your best but stay clear of that thing. Be careful."

As Linn disconnects patrons start sauntering out of the Hitchin' Post to see what triggered the sirens on a clear blue day. People in houses do likewise, pulling back curtains to peer out or stepping outside onto their porches.

Barrett asks, "So what do we tell them?"

"I say we tell them the warden will be giving away tickets to the next Cornhusker game to anyone who gathers in the town square. He can take it from there when he arrives."

A few minutes later Peregrine answers a call from White: "Every time I gain on this jack-o'-lantern it springs ahead. I can't even get near enough to try to lure it away."

"Has it come across any people?"

"No, thank God, but Svea-Dal is about a mile off. How goes the EVAC?"

"To quote my father: 'Glacial.'"

White slaps the steering wheel in frustration. "Then I'm going to have to follow it into town and try to help out any way I can there. And, yes, I'll be careful."

"You better." The Whites disconnect as Way points to Wingate and asks, "Hasn't he said anything that might be helpful?"

Benneville: "The last thing he told us was that he's dead."

Way frowns. "'Dead'?"

Peregrine: "If Cassavius is an extraterrestrial using Wingate as a communication channel, his true meaning could be getting lost in translation. English may not have equivalent words for what he is trying to describe. He also called the object we salvaged a 'barge' and referred to himself as 'spectra and lemure.'"

"What are those?"

"Troublesome and wandering ghosts."

Way's frown deepens. "Well I don't believe in ghosts. Of course I used to not believe in little green men but now I'm not so sure."

From the tent's door Joseph comments, "At least when it comes to extraterrestrials you have the Drake equation to fall back on. And Dr. White? Those two people you're expecting are here."

Peregrine tears up, runs outside, and wraps her arms around Dalton and Zoey. "Oh I'm so glad you're okay! Don't ever do that again!"

"We just wanted to help like you and Dad do," Dalton mumbles through the embrace while Zoey adds, "But that poor patrolman—"

"I know, sweetie, I know."

Joseph gives the family a couple more seconds before inquiring, "Any updates?"

Peregrine shakes her head as she keeps on hugging.

"What was that just now about ghosts?"

Zoey looks at her aunt oddly. "You don't believe in ghosts."

"No, I don't." Peregrine tells Joseph, "My sister and Zoey's mom is a spiritualist. I'll tell her she's being irrational but then she'll tell me I'm too rational and all my phantoms are manufactured by Westinghouse. It's a little back and forth we—" Inspiration kindles in Peregrine's eyes. "I think that's it!"

Joseph says, "What is it?"

"I'll explain on the way. I need back in the shop van."

"Yes, ma'am." Joseph orders one of the sentries posted outside the interrogation tent to watch the children while Peregrine kisses the cousins and instructs them, "Do as you're told."

As the women rush to the van Peregrine slaps her forehead. "I was so frightened about Dalton and Zoey that I let myself get lost in what Cassavius was saying instead of what he was trying to tell us."

"Which is what?"

"Cassavius said he is unable to return to his world because he is dead and death is not permitted in Malpertuis. What if his race obtained something akin to bio-indefinite mortality and now it shuns any reminder of death, like the victims of fatal injury or disease? If I'm right then I think Cassavius's 'barge' is more like a funerary probe."

Joseph scrunches her face. "You mean a space coffin?"

"That and more. Cassavius said the probe has a mission. It appears to be attempting to reanimate Cassavius by some predatory method that generates a photonic vapor that somehow accelerates cellular senescence in the beings it contacts and transmits the resultant bioenergy to the probe via alpha particles. The problem is the bioenergy can't reanimate Cassavius because he is, in his words, 'beyond rescue,' but until the probe ceases in its attempts he retains some semblance of his living consciousness."

"Or maybe he's not technically deceased but in some form of stasis. But what made you even think of this?"

"Westinghouse phantoms! 'Ghost" can refer to a faint secondary image on optical systems caused by mismatched impedance, and we may be dealing with something like that only way more advanced."

Reaching the shop van Joseph waves at two Air Policemen standing guard, unlocks the back panel doors, and follows Peregrine inside. "So what do we do? Crack open the pineapple and try to switch off the reanimator before the dark cloud reaches Svea-Dal?"

"Not 'we.' Me." Peregrine grabs an NBC suit from a locker. "If I open the probe and let loose anything uncontrollable or hazardous in here then you'll have to drive the van towards the nearest quicksand and sink it."

"I can't do that!"

"There's no time to argue about it!"

"But think about your family!"

"They'll understand. My husband is racing to join my father in Svea-Dal and Dalton and Zoey tried to help in their own way. This is who we are, Jean. This is what we do."

"But—"

"Please!"

Joseph begrudgingly nods and exits.

Peregrine bolts the doors, sets her watch and the biosafety cabinet on the workbench, takes a heavy duty pistol-grip drill from a tool locker, and wriggles into the NBC suit except for the hood. Then she calls White, who says, "Tell me you have good news."

"The kids are here and I have an idea. But it's risky."

"How risky?"

"I'll know in a minute. Do I have that long?"

"Just about that."

"Stay on the line and keep me posted on what that thing is doing. And, yes, I'll be careful."

"You better."

Peregrine slips on the snug hood, opens the cabinet, and prepares to begin boring. "Okay, here goes."

"What did you say? You came through muffled."

Peregrine tries to yank the hood up enough to expose her mouth but the rubber fabric constricts around her head like a finger trap.

"It's one spurt from town! Can you hear me?"

"Yes!" Peregrine hollers, hoping White understood her. Selecting an insertion spot she presses the drill tip against the shell but then the striations and the concept behind a finger trap's weave construction triggers a notion. Trading the drill for the probe Peregrine grasps it by the ends and twists her hands in opposite directions.

At that instant Wingate violently shudders and yells, "Possible breach imminent! Vacuum is threatened!"

Meanwhile White watches the thing appear to cavitate and implode. "It's gone! It must have jumped into town!"

"It's here!" Peregrine screams as the dark glittering cloud forms from nowhere over the shop's floor.

It stops after blanketing half of the floor and Peregrine figures the thing is recuperating after the lengthier-than-normal spurt back to the probe. Not knowing how long this reprieve will last she slams the shell against the tabletop hoping to bust any remaining corrosion and then desperately grits her teeth, grunts, and twists the shell again and again.

Suddenly there is a loud *pop* as the shell unravels like a ribbon of peeled apple skin followed by a *whoosh* as a sudden suck of air fills the probe's interior. At the same time an object flops out of the probe and into the cabinet like a carp dropped into a cooler and Peregrine finds herself looking at her very first extraterrestrial.

At least she assumes it is an alien based upon its eidonomy, which is instantly imprinted in Peregrine's memory: its face, so redolent of *Synanceia horrida*; its fibrous and corrugated skin; and its macilent – spindly really – extremities with elongated hindlegs and triangular or leafy feet and hands. Just as memorable is its swift decomposition after being exposed to the air after who knows how long, the bizarre carcass shrinking and rotting and crumbling into a loathsome mass of dust.

Tossing the uncoiled pineapple back into the cabinet, Peregrine slams shut the lid.

In the interrogation tent Wingate regains his color and in a normal voice declares, "They're gone."

"What's gone?" Benneville asks as he rechecks Wingate's vitals.

"All those weird thoughts are out of my head."

Way leans forward and asks, "What do you see?"

"Just you right now." Wingate squints at the colonel. "Who are you, anyway?"

In the shop van the dark vapor fades away.

Peregrine checks the NBC's monitoring badges and seeing normal readings she peels off the hood, grabs her watch, and plops on a bench. White is calling her name and she tells him, "I'm okay. It's over."

"What happened?"

Peregrine opens her mouth but realizes she has no definite answer. "I'm not sure. I'll try to explain later. You check on Dad. I'll check on the kids." But first Peregrine leans against the wall behind the bench to catch her breath.

The following night, 20:16 AST. Kepler Cove, Lost Key.

"So Aunt Peregrine, was it really a ghost?"

Peregrine is walking from Linndorsa to the dock carrying a pitcher of lemon tea and some glasses. Zoey and Dalton are lying on blankets, Linn is sitting in a folding chair, and White, sitting cross-legged, asks her, "How did things go with Hoyt?"

"He is still disappointed about what happened to the probe and the carcass, but he also wants me to come to DC to oversee SPUR's investigation of them."

"How soon?" White asks.

Peregrine smiles as she sits next to him. "I told him I'd have to get back to him. We just got home."

White smiles back and winks as Zoey repeats her question.

"You're guess is as good as mine, sweetie." Peregrine beings pouring tea for everyone.

"Tut-tut," Linn utters. "Certainly you have some theories."

"Not yet. You're the one who taught me that theorizing before one has data is a capital mistake since one may twist facts to suit theories." Peregrine winks at Zoey. "Like rather or not ghosts are real."

Dalton stares up at the night and asks, "So how many of those probes do you think may be shooting around the universe?"

"I couldn't even guess, honey."

"Why do you think Cassavius chose Mr. Wingate to communicate through?"

"Again, I couldn't guess. Not when we still know next to nothing about Cassavius' people or their technology."

"I'm afraid she's right, QED," Linn tells his grandson. "It is the scientist's fate to meticulously disengage the truth from the snares of misdirection no matter how long it takes."

White says, "One thing I'd like to learn is how did Dalton plan on explaining the missing gas in Sergeant Barrett's jeep after his and Zoey's little joyride."

Zoey sighs, "He would have thought of something. He always does."

Dalton says nothing, only grins.

White laughs. "So another adventure and another bunch of unanswered questions."

"For now," Peregrine agrees, a glint of anticipatory wonder in her eyes. "But that's the biz."

THE AMAZING ADVENTURES OF BOOM JACKSON

By Tony Jones

Gordon Stadium, State University, late afternoon

A LATE SEPTEMBER BREEZE SWEPT across the field. Cooling players, coaches, fans, and cheerleaders alike, it carried the scents of approaching autumn. Henry Jackson ignored it. Henry Jackson was ready. Third and inches, deep into the fourth quarter, the game poised 28-28, throwing into the wind and almost the full length of the field from the opponent's end. Cheerleaders rallied their team for one last miracle. Jackson smiled — miracles were his stock in trade. He readied the ball as fans screamed his name. One last glance at the cheerleaders and he glimpsed Cassie. For a moment he thought about his plans for later. Only a moment. He refocused on the game.

Then, from high in the sky, a lambent purple beam struck. It grew in intensity until all present were forced to close their eyes and shield them with their hands.

Fans screamed even louder. For a moment Jackson went to make the play, then stopped as two of his own team ran for him, grunting and howling. Across the field he saw players and officials tearing into each other — flesh ripping, screaming faces and oozing blood all lit in the evil purple light. Three cheerleaders attacked a coach, tearing at his throat and reveling as blood spurted across their faces. The others joined the general melee of mindless violence.

Cassie screamed loudest of all as she squeezed the eyeballs from the head of an opposing cheerleader. Her elegantly manicured nails made the perfect tools for popping. Not that she cared about nails or anything but the joy of death.

On the field turned battlefield, Jackson looked for a way to escape. As his sanity deserted him, he was reminded of the zombie movie he and his pals had seen on fake IDs a few weeks back, except these zombies were his team-mates. His best friend jumped him from behind. Dropping the ball, Jackson rolled and clawed his friend's throat, no recognition in their vacant eyes. Warm blood spurted onto Jackson's face, his eyes, his nose, his mouth. The taste filled him with a vicious vitality. He remembered nothing else…

#   #   #

State Hospital, 6am the next morning

Pete Jackson was buying yet one more coffee from the new machine at the end of hospital corridor. The previous two he'd left unfinished as he spent his time fidgeting, pacing, pestering the nursing staff and all the while no news. The coffee wasn't even that good, as bad as the base coffee, and that took some doing.

The latest nurse on duty had suggested the 24-hour diner across the block, but he didn't want to miss anything. It didn't help he was just one of dozens of people desperately waiting to hear about loved ones struck down in the *football frenzy* as the local radio had decided to call it. Some frenzy, he thought, given the number of police involved something more had happened than just a brawl between rival colleges. Something much bigger.

He decided to check with the nurse one more time, entirely forgetting about his latest drink as he strode back towards the desk.

As he approached, he saw she had a telephone receiver pressed firmly to one ear while she talked to two other, younger nurses. All three looked tense, all three looked as though they'd had as little sleep as he had.

'Peter Jackson?' a woman's voice asked from behind.

He turned quickly, hoping to see a doctor, though he'd not seen any women doctors since arriving. He had no problem with women doctors, some of the most capable medics in Korea had been female.

He saw a tall redhead, late-20s and not wearing a white coat. Not a doctor. Another day he might have thought she was pretty, might even have used the Air Force test pilot charm on her. Not today. Instead of a stethoscope or medical records, she held a small pocketbook in her left hand, a slim blue pen in her right.

'Peter Jackson? My name's Vale Ashdown. I'm a freelance reporter,' she continued.

'I'd guessed as much. If you want a story, go ask someone else. I thought Press weren't allowed on the wards.'

'I have my ways. I don't need your story either, I need your help.'

He shook his head.

'Please, just leave me alone,' he said and started to turn to walk back to the coffee machine.

Vale put the cap back on her pen, closed her notebook and put both away in her coat. She reached out her now empty right hand.

'My name's Vale Ashdown. You're Peter Jackson the test pilot. Your brother Henry was one of several dozen badly injured people brought into the hospital yesterday evening. As many more died on or around the football pitch. Am I close?'

He turned back to face her, taking in pale green eyes and steely, determined half-smile.

'Go on.'

Vale continued without seeming to draw breath.

'I've asked around. They triaged everyone who came in. Most urgent cases are in surgery or have already been operated on and are in recuperation. Those who can wait have been stabilized as far as possible. Others have been made comfortable and relatives contacted.'

'Others?' Jackson asked, dreading the answer. 'What others?'

Vale looked him straight in the eyes.

'Not everyone can be saved,' she answered without hesitation. 'Where possible they've been sedated, and relatives contacted.'

'And is Henry one of them?'

'As far as I can find out all their relatives have been contacted by the police. The hospital knows you're here, and they'd have spoken to you.'

Jackson released a breath he didn't realize he was holding. 'So where is he?' he asked.

Vale was about to answer when they were interrupted by yet another duty nurse.

'Mr. Jackson?' she asked.

He nodded.

'Can you come with me please? I'd like to give you an update on your brother.'

'Just tell me. Is he… OK?'

The nurse, and older woman in her early fifties with a trace of an Irish accent, looked at the clipboard she was carrying.

'Compared to most survivors he was lucky.'

'That's great news! When can I see him?'

'I said *compared to the others*. He didn't need surgery, but has multiple wounds, contusions, cracked ribs and a broken collar bone. Several deep scratched on his face, but we think his eyes are OK. He's been sent to St. Benedict's — we've no space here. They'll stitch him up and set him up in a ward.'

'How far is St. Benedicts?' Jackson asked.

'The ambulance only left 20 minutes ago. It will be at least three hours before he can be seen, and everyone involved is unconscious. Not quite a coma, but something similar. I suggest you take some time to freshen up. There's a diner two blocks away if you want some food.'

Without waiting for more questions, the nurse turned away.

'I tell you what,' Vale said putting away her notebook and pen, 'why don't you buy me breakfast and I'll explain how you can help me. Then you can go see if they'll let you visit your brother.'

Like the nurse, Vale Arden didn't wait for him to respond. Instead, she linked her arm through his and led him away…

# # #

10,000 feet above Washington the following afternoon

At the controls of his plane, Pete Jackson felt at peace. From this height the world seemed serene, the few clouds scattered around merely part of the scenery. Focus brought him relief from anxious fear about his brother and allowed him to put Vale Arden out of his thoughts as he concentrated on dials and gauges.

'No sign of any gremlins!' he said.

Beside him in the plane's other seat, Vale scowled.

'When you said you'd take me up, I thought we'd be in a jet, not some noisy relic from the war,' Vale shouted over the sound of the plane's engine.

'Relic!' Jackson exclaimed. 'I'll have you know the *Bird Dog* here is a highly tuned version of the original Cessna, with thousands of flying hours to its credit.'

He patted the dashboard.

'Don't listen to her,' he said.

Vale poked him in the arm.

'How high are we?' she asked.

Jackson indicated the dashboard.

'A little over ten thousand feet. We can go higher if you'd like, but from here we get a good view of Metropolitan University. Not that there's any sign of your mysterious light!'

'And what's your theory?' she said raising her voice. 'Why else do these awful events only happen at universities: State, Harvard, the Sorbonne in Paris, France as well as Oxford, England?'

'I get it,' Jackson said. 'And yes, it matches your list of missing scientists, but what are you suggesting? What do you think is happening? What does this light do?'

'I don't know about the light,' Vale answered, 'but at least five different sources reported seeing something bright in both the Paris event and Moscow.'

Jackson interrupted. 'And you've got sources in Moscow?'

Vale didn't answer. Puzzled, Jackson realized her attention was focused on a large, grey shape high above them. It had no wings. No propeller. It resembled a large tin can with gouts of dark smoke shooting from behind. It was like nothing he'd ever seen.

'Let's take a closer look,' he said working the controls. He flicked a switch and spoke into a radio microphone.

'This is Bird Dog 7 alpha 7 to control, come in control.' He waited. 'Control, Bird Dog 7 alpha 7, do you read me. Over.'

He flicked more controls and was greeted with nothing but static.

'Problem?' Vale asked.

'Radio's not working. Maybe we should return to the field.'

'And miss the story of a lifetime?'

'It's no story if you can't call it in.'

As they argued, the plane flew higher, and the mysterious craft above changed course.

'That's it,' Jackson said. 'They're coming our way; I'm getting out of here.'

As he yanked at controls, the strange vessel drew nearer. He pulled, twisted, and cussed, but nearer they came.

'If we'd used one of your jets, we'd have no problem. You could do one of your famous *sonic booms*. That is what they call you *Boom* Jackson?'

Too busy to respond, Boom Jackson tried to dive as fast as the carburetor would allow without stalling. From outside a red glow illuminated the cockpit, the engine cut out and the electrical systems all stopped. Instead of falling to their deaths, the plane hung in the sky as a dark shadow moved above them. Boom and Vale watched powerless as they were drawn into a cargo bay in the sinister ship. Heavy metal doors clunked shut.

Boom and Vale looked at each other.

'I guess we'd better meet our captors,' Vale said.

'I guess you're right,' Jackson said as he took a handgun from a compartment, checked the ammunition, and placed it in his pocket.

They undid their belts and left the plane. As they walked out into the metal deck, a door opened....

#   #   #

Jackson held up a hand and gestured towards the shadow of the plane.

As he and Vale hid, a group of people in full-body, black leather armor came in. Each was perhaps eight inches shorter than Jackson, each carried a metal baton perhaps 18 inches long. Their faces were all covered, and they made no effort to look for occupants of the plane.

As Jackson and Vale watched, the newcomers formed a guard either side of the door and stood to attention. Through the door came a woman, dressed in silks and putting Jackson in mind of a picture of Queen Cleopatra he'd seen in a museum. The woman was several inches taller than her entourage and had a dark yet frightening beauty. Jackson felt she was more likely to go biting snakes than the other way round.

The woman strode forward.

'Come forward,' she called, gazing directly at where Jackson and Vale were crouching.

Jackson stood and moved a pace forward, Vale stood just behind. He reached into his pocket and felt the comforting metal of his gun.

'Who are you, and why have you captured us? We're United States citizens.'

The woman laughed; a sound capable of curdling milk from twenty paces. Vale shuddered.

'I am Countess Halo. Now come here so my men can take you prisoner.'

Jackson yanked the gun from his pocket and pointed it at the Countess.

'Not so fast,' he said. 'We demand an explanation.'

The Countess smiled. 'It's quite simple. Even Earthmen can understand. I've been testing my father's modified Z-Ray.'

'Z-Ray?' Vale asked. 'Is that what's been terrorizing our colleges?'

'Terrorizing? You mean testing. The Zombie Ray is how we conquer the galaxy. Once adjusted for your metabolisms, we shall use it to decimate the Earth's population and add your planet's wealth to our own.'

As she spoke, she smiled. When she finished, she made a gesture and her soldiers moved forward.

Jackson fired his pistol, hitting one of the soldiers in the arm. Three others moved in and beat him with their batons, knocking the pistol to the ground. Vale dived to grab it, but she too was attacked. Moments later the two were dragged forward to the Countess.

She stepped to within inches of Jackson. 'What do I call you?' she asked.

'Everyone calls me Boom.'

She moved even closer then ran a finger down the side of his face.

'We have a few hours before we get to my father's planet, perhaps you'd like to keep my company in my cabin?'

'I'd sooner kiss a rattlesnake.'

'Pity. Never mind, a few days in my father's mines on Rondor will no doubt change your mind. If you survive.'

He struggled briefly, the Countess ignoring him as she moved over to Vale. Jackson watched as she stroked the woman's face the same way she'd stroked his.

'How about you,' the Countess asked.

Vale glared.

'Oh well,' the Countess said, moving back to the door. 'I'm sure my father will have no trouble working his charms on you.'

She called to her men.

'Lock them up.'

Jackson tried again to struggle, but it was no use. With half-a-dozen attackers, it wasn't long before he was knocked unconscious…

# # #

Several days later in the mines underneath Rondor City

Boom Jackson had seen war and hardship firsthand, kept in good physical shape and passed every test the Department of Defense could devise. Nothing prepared him for slavery in the mines of planet Rondor.

They consisted of a simple network of tunnels stretching for miles. Slaves were not mistreated, there was no need. Each was equipped with a small pick and a wheeled metal basket. They were to descend the mines and dig for a dark orange mineral found in small nodules in the rock. The mineral, Rogonite, had a mild glow, which Boom was sure was radioactive. The least of his problems. More important were food and escape. At the end of shift, workers brought everything they'd dug back to the central area. Machines weighed the Rogonite ore and dispensed food. Food was a generous description for the grey, metallic tasting gloop the machine dispensed. No digging, no Rogonite, no food.

On the first day, Boom was ignored by the other slaves. Nobody explained the system and he spent hours trying to find ways to escape, to be ignored. When weighing time came, the other slaves ate their gloop in silence, ignoring him as he starved. On the second day he followed them, tried to make conversation but was rebuffed by their leader who called himself Duke Octarion of the Neptune Men. He was allowed to observe, but none of the dozen or so other slaves was to talk to him.

At the end of the shift, he'd gather a substantial quantity of Rogonite and, as he tried to eat his large portion of gloop, heard mutterings about the giant. The Neptune men were even shorter than Countess Halo's soldiers.

When he wasn't eating, digging, or looking for ways to escape, his mind was full of images of the depravities Emperor Rogon might be inflicting upon Vale. While the Neptune men had no interest in helping him escape, they'd wasting no time in suggesting what might be happening to Vale. Boom regretted telling them about her, but he'd been trying to gain their help to rescue her. Instead, he'd given them leverage to torment him for fun. There was no other entertainment in the mine....

#   #   #

On the fifth day Boom was digging a seam with no luck. Two hours, and all he had to show were a handful of Rogonite fragments. He heard a crash. Then shouting.

He ran to the source of the disturbance and saw Octarion and two other Neptune Men trying to move a rockfall lying across a several of their fellow slaves. Without hesitation he lent his strength to the challenge, and together they were soon able to free the trapped Neptune Men. Two had already died, and their bodies were moved to one side.

'I thank you,' Octarion said. 'Without your help, my son Nonarion might have perished along with the others.'

'No need,' Boon replied. 'I just did what was right,'

Octarion looked hard at him a moment, then moved to help his son walk back to the central area. There Octarion operated a speaking device in the wall and asked for medical treatment.

Ten minutes later a group of guards exited a steel door, behind them a man carrying a small bag. The man gestured to Octarion and the others to bring the wounded forward. The guards made a show of pointing their guns to reinforce the point.

The man examined the first of the wounded.

'This one will survive. He can't dig for two days but after that he will be fine.'

He moved to the next. This one had lost consciousness as he'd been carried. The examination looked at the damage to the man's leg.

'Broken,' he said. He gestured to a guard, who came across, pointed his weapon and shot. Once.

Boom couldn't believe what he was seeing. He moved to protest, but Octarion stooped him.

'If he can't dig, he's no use in the mines. Emperor Rogon has strict rules,' Octarion said.

Next was Octarion's son. The examination took longer. While Nonarion's legs were undamaged, his ribs had taken the weight of several rocks. The examiner shook his head. As he gestured to the guard, Octarion screamed and leapt forward. The rest of the Neptune Men joined in. Boom rushed the nearest guard, grabbed his weapon, and used it knock him unconscious. Moments later the guards lay on the ground, while the Neptune Men forced open the steel door.

Octarion and another helped Nonarion stand.

'Thank you for your help, Earth Man,' Octarion said. 'We're off to the Rocket Bay. I suggest you do the same.'

Escape was tempting, but he had to find out what had happened to Vale.

'Thank you, but I must rescue Vale.'

Octarion pointed at the unconscious guards.

'You might find some of their uniforms fit you well enough to move around undiscovered,' he said. 'Good luck!'

Boom pieced together a cloak from one guard and pants from another. The disguise wasn't perfect but would have to do. He began to explore the vast buildings above the mines.

#   #   #

At first, Boom found it easy to wander the brightly lit yet barely used corridors. He saw no more guards, just serious looking people making going about their business. There were no maps on display. Through windows he caught site of numerous other buildings, like some vast alien version of New York City, complete with flying cars silhouetted against am ominous red sky.

Then an alarm sounded. A shrill klaxon blasting from all corners. People rushed to their destinations and Boom noticed a group of guards coming his way from a stairwell. He ducked through the nearest door.

Inside a room as large as an aircraft hangar with ceiling some fifty or sixty feet above, a group of men and women operated the controls of vast machines beyond Boom's understanding.

The room's occupants ignored him completely. While the klaxon was still clearly audible, they continued to work various controls and check switches and dials. An ozone smell reach Boom's nose, and he noticed the hairs on his arms were all standing up. Beneath the klaxon there was also an ominous low hum emanating from huge steel coils twenty feet in the air.

Boom walked toward the nearest machine. It's operator, a woman in her fifties, with glasses and short hair ignored him. He saw she wore a thin metallic band in her hair, with circular pads pressed into her temples. Looking round he saw everyone had the same alien devices. He reached out to remove the band.

The woman screamed then collapsed. Boom tried to revive her with no success. Everyone else carried on with their mysterious tasks. Everyone except a bearded man in the far corner who seemed to be watching Boom while still working his machine.

Boom walked across the room. At first the man seemed oblivious to him, but then waved Boom closer.

'My name's Jackson, Pete Jackson, but everyone calls me *Boom*.'

The man raised an eyebrow, then reached out a hand.

'Very pleased to meet you Mr. Boom Jackson. My name is Professor Krakov. I'm from the Moscow Institute of science.'

Boom shock the man's hand. He'd heard of the Moscow Institute but couldn't remember why.

'What's going on here?' Boom asked.

Before answering, Krakov removed his headband.

'We were all captured from Earth and made to work these infernal machines. For some reason the mind control didn't work on me, so I adjusted my headband to make sure.'

He put the band back around his head.

'What are all these machines?' Boom asked.

'This is a control center for Emperor Rogon's Z-Ray machines. We've been tuning them to work on people from Earth. We have more resistance than most races. We're preparing them for a celebration later today.'

'So, you're a traitor,' Boom said.

The man shook his head vigorously.

'Quite the contrary, I've arranged a surprise for when the machines are turned to full power during the celebrations.'

'I've just thought,' Boom said. 'There've been several incidents on Earth. My brother was caught by some ray playing college football. Was that you?'

Krakov's shoulders slumped.

'We've been made to test the machine on the very universities we were kidnapped from. Everyday Rogon comes to torment us. He turns off the mind control bands just to see how we suffer under the knowledge of what we are doing for him. I only stayed to learn how they work so I could sabotage them.'

'Vale was right,' Boom said. 'There was a connection between the disappearances and the Z-Ray.'

'Vale? You know Vale?'

Boom nodded.

'I've bad news for you,' Krakov said. 'Today's celebrations… they're for Rogon's wedding… to Vale.'

'Wedding?!'

Before Boom could continue a group of guards burst into the room. Krakov turned to his machine.

By the time the guards grabbed Boom, Krakov again looked every inch the mindless slave. Only a quick wink proved otherwise.

#   #   #

In a cage opening out into an arena

Boom grabbed the cage bars but even his human strength wasn't enough to open a gap. He'd been told he was to provide entertainment for Rogon's wedding. A duel to the death. As he'd been thrown in the cage a short sword was thrown after him. Perhaps the length of his forearm, it was blunt and didn't look strong enough to force the cage door.

A cacophony of atonal sound boomed from above the arena. An unpleasant mix of trumpet and church organ, it could hardly be described as music. What seemed to be dozens of drummers began to play a slow march. On cue people began filling seats above the arena pit. Boom could see only a small portion of the seating, but still looked for Vale. There was no sign.

The drumming stopped.

The cage door facing the arena opened. The side of the cage behind began to move. inwards. Boom had no choice but to enter the arena — being crushed to death wasn't high on his list.

As he got his bearings, he scanned for Vale. This was yet another huge room, with a vast vaulted ceiling made of some glassy crystal, through which Boom could glimpse that awful red sky. He looked down.

On one side he saw a platform. Two seated figures were flanked with guards. From the placing, this would be where the Emperor would sit. The distance was too far to be certain, but squinting Boom could see one figure sat in a throne, gesturing for the show to begin. The other was red-haired. Was it Vale?

The figure in the throne stood and raised an arm.

'Begin,' a commanding voice rang out.

Despite the distance, the man's voice was loud and clear. It had no expression. This must be Emperor Rogon. Rogon lowered his arm and sat.

From the other side of the arena pit, Boom heard another cage door opening. Into the arena strode a shorter man, wielding a sword identical to Boom's, but with a confidence suggesting years of familiarity. It was Octarion.

Octarion approached cautiously, blade poised. The crowd roared.

'I have no quarrel with you,' Boom shouted over the noise.

'Nor I, you,' Octarion replied. 'I have no choice — fight or my son dies. Kill you or I die. That's the way of ceremonial weddings. We fight to the death.'

As he finished speaking, Octarion lunged. Boom waved his own sword and blocked the blow. Octarion spun and caught Boom a glancing blow on the rub cage. Boom reached with his free hand and felt blood.

For several minutes they sparred, Boom doing his best to deflect Octarion's sword and make some foray of his own. He didn't want to hurt the other man, but maybe he could wear him down or find a way to knock him out?

The crowd grew restless. Octarion feinted, Boom followed with a block as Octarion spun again and knocked the sword from Boom's hand. As Boom rushed to grab the weapon, Octarion tripped him. Boom lay sprawled and winded as Octarion raised his sword for the death dealing blow.

Boom tensed.

Octarion looked towards the Emperor. Once more the Emperor's voice rang out.

'You fought well, Octarion. Despite their physical strength, these humans have no skill when it comes to fighting. Conquest of their planet will be easy, particularly now the Z-ray is ready.'

Boom tried reach for his sword, but Octarion kicked the blade further away all the while watching Boom as an eagle might watch a wounded animal.

'Before you dispatch this Earthman, let him witness the death of millions of his kind. FIRE THE Z-RAY!'

Through the glassy ceiling high above, Boom saw shafts of violet spring from hellish generators deep in the bowels of the city. They merged into a single spear of light blasting out into the heavens. They grew brighter and harsher. The crowd cheered. Octarion flexed his wrist.

Then the rays grey brighter still. Too bright. A vast explosion rocked the building, and the rays were extinguished. People panicked. The lights failed; smoke began to billow in from all sides. Guards tried to keep order but were overwhelmed as more explosions rocked the arena.

Octarion stumbled. Boom stood, grabbed his own sword, and pointed at the cage doors.

'I don't want to fight you,' Boom said. 'The explosion opened the cages, you can escape.'

Octarion nodded and stood.

'Head for the Rocket Bay,' he said.

'I've just some unfinished business, see you soon.'

Boom raced to a set of steps carved in the arena wall. A guard tried to stop him, but Boom had no time to waste and cut the man down with one savage sweep of his sword. He raced across to the platform where he saw two people. One a tall man dressed all in black — boots, clothes, cloak, his skin pale, his physique thin to the point of emaciation. He had no visible hair. The other was Vale.

'So,' Rogon said. 'You can fight after all.'

Boom made to approach Rogon, but four guards blocked his way. As he weighed his chances, he glanced at Vale. She sat motionless, on her head a band like those he'd seen in Krakov's control room. She appeared calm and untroubled and was dressed in only a few wispy layers of silks doing little to hide the contours of her body.

'No,' Rogon said. 'I will deal with this one myself.' He pointed at one of the guards. 'You. Prepare my personal rocketship. I have a honeymoon to go to. This palace is but one of many. We can build other Z-rays.'

He turned to face Boom, pulling a long black dagger from his belt with a thin, ring adorned hand. Boom's arena sword was easily twice the length.

'This is for Vale!' Boom shouted and lunged.

Rogon barely moved, but Boom's attack missed completely. As Boom swung back, Rogon caught the edge of the sword with his dagger. The sword sheared into two pieces. Boom moved back.

He realized the dagger would be quite capable of slicing through bone as easily as butter, and, like Octarion, it seemed Rogon was more than skilled with the weapon.

Boom threw his broken sword at Rogon's face and rushed forward to grab the dagger arm using all his close combat training. He might be one of the world's best test pilots, but he'd also done plenty of hand-to-hand fighting for Uncle Sam. Twisting and forcing his thumbs into Rogon's sinews the Emperor released the dagger and staggered back.

'No matter. I have other means.' As Rogon spoke, he twisted a ruby ring one quarter counterclockwise.

A vivid red beam struck Boom and brought a searing fire to his every fiber of flesh. Try as he might he could only just stop from screaming with pain.

Rogon twisted the ruby again. The pain flared. Boom struggled to maintain his sanity. His heart raced and threated to burst through his ribs. His vision began to fail, then all went dark.

The pain stopped.

Taking a deep breath, Boom opened his eyes and saw Rogon staggering back. Beside him stood Vale. She held the Emperor's dagger in both hands, a look of horror on her face. On the ground was the lower portion of Rogon's arm, carved away like a turkey breast on Thanksgiving. Boom looked again at Rogon. Black blood spurted from his mortal wound. His knees buckled.

'Thus end all tyrants,' Boom said as he lashed out with his booted foot, knocking the evil monster to the ground to die as he deserved.

'Is he dead?' Vale asked.

Boom turned to see she'd grabbed a shawl and wrapped it around her shoulders to cover her torso and restore some modesty.

'When he used his ring on you it released me from his bonds,' Vale said. 'I had to take my chance. I had to....'

'It's OK,' Boom said. 'He got what he deserved.'

Another explosion rocked the room and cracks opened in the crystal dome as shards of the glassy substance fell to the ground, one narrowly missing Vale.

'Come on,' Boon said. 'Let's get out of here. I think I can figure out the way to the Rocket Bay.'

# # #

In the Rocket Bay

With only a couple of false turns, and ignored by the few panicking people they encountered, Boom and Vale entered Rogon's Rocket Bay, beneath the fast-disintegrating palace. Another large and well-lit cavern, some dozen rocketships identical to the one they'd been captured by occupied the space.

Unsure which to take, Boom noticed a figure outside a rocketship to the left. He thought he recognised him. As they approached, he saw it was Professor Krakov. He was disconnected a pipe Boom assumed provided some kind of fuel.

Hearing their approach Krakov turned.

'Boom Jackson,' he shouted. 'Welcome, welcome. Did you like my surprise? The explosions were more magnificent than I expected.'

Beside Krakov an open door led into the rocketship.

'Come,' Krakov said, pointing. 'You go inside, I'll just finish here then we can be off.'

Boom and Vale went into the rocketship and made their way to the front. Amidst the controls he saw another familiar figure, this one sat at what he took to be the steering controls. It was Countess Halo.

'You!' Boom exclaimed.

The Countess turned, recognised them, and smiled.

'Thank you,' she said. 'My father needed killing for a long time. Now I'm in charge of the Empire. We will take this rocketship back to Mars where I have my own Z-ray towers.'

'You'd better think again,' Boom said. 'I'm sure I can fly this thing. We're going back to Earth.'

The unmistakable sound of a weapon being readied came from behind.

'I think it's you who had better think again,' Krakov said, holding a gun pointed directly at Boom. 'For too long the Countess and I have planned this. We won't let you spoil our victory. Who wants to go back to Earth when the Galaxy awaits!'

The Countess flicked several switches and the rocketship lifted from the cavern floor and moved slowly forward. As the exit doors approached, she pulled a lever, and the ship began to accelerate. Just as they cleared the Rocket Bay, another explosion sent a cloud of smoke out into the lurid sky and the shock wave knocked them violently from side to side.

Taking advantage of the distraction, Boom landed a punch on Krakov's jaw, knocking him to the ground. Taking the gun made it easy for Boom and Vale to lock the Countess and the unconscious Krakov in a side room, tying them securely to chairs. Back at the controls it seemed the Countess had already set course for Mars.

'I think I can figure these controls out, but it might take some time.'

'I'm sure we can think of something to do,' Vale said from just behind him.

Boom scratched his chin nervously. He wanted to ask Vale how she was, wanted to ask what Rogon had done to her, but dreaded hearing the answer.

Vale moved forward and faced him, blocking his view of the controls. She slowly straddled his legs and sat facing him, her face inches from his own. Despite the ordeals she must have suffered, Boom thought she looked more beautiful than any woman he'd ever seen. He noticed her cloak had slipped to the floor, leaving her barely covered.

'It's time for your reward,' she said.

A searing pair tore through Boom's stomach. He looked down in horror to see Vale had stabbed him with Rogon's dagger, his blood running over her hand. She twisted the blade as she ripped from side to side.

'Who wants to go to Earth? With Rogon dead, my unborn child is the next Emperor of the Galaxy, Until he or she reaches age, that leaves me in charge.'

She leant forward and kissed Boon once on the forehead.

'Rest in Peace,' she said, gouging the dagger through more of his internal organs until he slumped back quite dead.

She cleaned the worst of the blood on her silky blouse and smiled. ♜

ACT OF GOD

By Heath W. Shelby

Saturday, November 5, 2022
12:05pm
Main Street
Grubbs, Arkansas

JOSH KINARD OPENED HIS EYES to complete and utter darkness. Ringing filled Josh's ears and the distinct coppery smell of blood made his heart beat faster. Josh attempted to rub his eyes, in the hopes of seeing something…anything other than darkness. Josh quickly discovered his right arm was pinned under something. Josh was immobile and true panic began to take over.

"HELP!!!"

The sound of his own terrified voice didn't make Josh feel any better about his situation.

What happened?

The last thing Josh remembered was sitting in his recliner. Josh had just finished watching *Championship Wrestling* with the kids and was about to get ready for the Arkansas Razorback football team's game against the Liberty Flames. There was an…explosion?

The kids!

"HELP! Someone get me out of here!"

"…Josh? Is that you?…"

From somewhere in the darkness above him, Josh heard the worried voice of his wife.

"Brooke?! I'm here! I'm stuck! I need help!"

"Hang on, Josh! Help is here!"

From the darkness above, Josh heard the sound of shifting timbers. Suddenly, a beam of sunlight filled Josh's eyes.

"Josh?! Buddy, are you okay?!"

Josh squinted as his eyes adjusted to the bright light.

"Justin?!"

The brightness of the sunlight was replaced by the silhouette of Josh's next door neighbor, Justin Simpson.

"Hang on, buddy! We'll get you outta there!"

"Justin…are the kids…"

"They're fine."

Justin hollered over his shoulder, "Kaydence! Get over here, girl! I need your help!"

Kaydence Simpson rushed to her dad's side and together they began to lift heavy timbers and other debris off of their trapped neighbor.

"Josh, grab my hand and we'll get you out of there!"

With his arm finally freed, Josh reached up and took hold of the outstretched hand of his neighbor.

"What happened?"

"I guess it was a tornado."

Justin and Kaydence helped Josh to his unsteady feet.

"A tornado? But there wasn't a cloud in the sky…"

"Josh!"

With tears steaming down her face, Brooke Kinard rushed over to embrace her husband.

"I thought…we…had…lost you…"

Josh kissed his sobbing wife's forehead.

"Honey, I'm okay…but you're gonna have to let me go. You're

crushing me."

Brooke quickly released her husband, stepped back and wiped away the tears streaming down her now blushing face.

"Honey, where are the twins?"

"Josh, I have the boys."

Josh turned to see his neighbor's wife, Phyllisha Simpson, leading his sons around the corner of what was left of their family home.

"Dad! Dad!"

Carter and Carsen ran into their father's waiting arms and the three broke into tears. Brooke's attempt to wipe the tears from her face failed miserably as she watched the reunion of the three most important guys in her life.

Phyllisha walked over to her husband and wrapped her arm around his waist.

"Justin, honey…what happened here?"

"Phyllisha, I don't know…"

Justin walked to the front of the yard and looked up and down Main Street of his hometown of Grubbs, Arkansas. From what Justin could see, it appeared that the path of the storm had traveled directly - almost too directly - down the highway from north of town, and then ventured off the road when the twister arrived at Butch's Barber Shop, laying waste to the business, wiping out the Grubbs Volunteer Fire Department Fire Station and then laying waste to Josh's house.

"Hmmm…"

"What is it, honey?"

Justin pointed down the highway.

"Have you ever seen anything like that?"

"Like what?"

"The path of that tornado…it traveled straight down the road…and, look! The road is all torn up…but the houses and the businesses on each side of the road…they are fine! When have you seen a tornado that small? And the tornado traveled straight down the highway…and only left the road when it got right here…almost like it was…"

"Like it was what?"

Justin shook his head and said, "Nothing…that would be crazy."

"CADE!! CADE!! Has anyone seen my son?!"

Everyone's attention shifted across Main Street to the Grubbs City Hall. A wide-eyed lady frantically ran across the parking lot into the middle of the street.

Justin rushed to meet the panicked woman.

"Mayor Carlton? Angie…what's wrong?"

Angie Carlton wasn't the mayor of Grubbs at the moment. Angie was just a terrified mom.

"I can't find my son…"

Angie walked past Justin to the other side of Main Street to what remained of Butch's Barber Shop. The small rock building was nothing but rubble. Parked next to the rubble was an unscathed red Ford F350.

"We came to town so Cade could get a haircut at Dad's…and I just went across the street to finish up some work…and…what happened?!"

"It was a tornado…I think…"

"And where's Dad?!"

"…mom…"

"Cade?!"

Angie looked beneath her dad's Ford and tears of joy filled her eyes. Between the pickup's back tires, Angie found her son safe and sound.

"Mom? What happened…"

Angie grabbed her son by his arms and pulled him from beneath her father's truck. Before Cade could object, Angie wrapped her son in a smothering embrace.

"I thought I lost you! What happened?!"

Cade pulled away from his mom and began to dust himself off.

"When you dropped me off, I was going to go into Poppy's to get a haircut, but he was busy…someone was in the chair…I told Poppy I was going to wait outside…I closed the door…and I heard…"

"A howling."

Cade turned to see a newly-bandaged Josh Kinard walking down the sidewalk toward him.

"Yeah…and screaming…"

Angie grabbed her son by his shoulders and looked desperately into his eyes.

"Cade! Where's Poppy?!"

Cade's eyes went wide with panic as he broke free from his mom's grasp and rushed to the rubble of his grandfather's barber shop. Cade dropped to his knees and began to fling rocks and timber to either side of him.

"Poppy!"

Angie joined her son, and was quickly joined by Josh, Justin, Phyllisha and Kaydence as they frantically searched for the town's barber.

"Over here! I've got him!"

Josh waved the searchers over to where he was holding the hand of Butch Williams.

"Mr. Butch, hang on! We're gonna get you out of there!"

As Josh and Justin helped Butch to his feet, Angie ran to her dad's side.

"Dad! Are you okay?!"

"Yeah…just got my bell rung…"

Angie helped her father over to his undamaged pickup truck, opened the driver's door and helped him climb in and sit down. Butch leaned back in the driver's seat, surveyed what was left of his business and let out a defeated sigh.

"It's…all gone…"

"It's okay, Dad. All that matters is that you are alright."

Butch suddenly sat up straight and his eyes went wide.

"What is it, Dad?"

"John!"

"John? John, who?"

Butch climbed out of his truck and walked back to the rubble of his barber shop.

"John Ivy. He was in the chair when…this happened…"

Justin gestured to his wife and Josh. "Guys, get over here and let's try to find John."

Butch shook his head. "Y'all won't find him…"

Undaunted, Josh dropped to his knees and began to move rocks and broken timber. "Sure we will, Mr. Butch. We just have to -"

"No. John is gone."

Hearing the finality in Butch's voice, the gathered crowd stopped what they were doing and looked to the clearly emotional barber.

"John just came in and asked for a little off the top…next thing I know, there was the horrible noise…and the ceiling…the entire roof…just disappeared. And then John…"

Butch closed his eyes as if he was trying to remember details of the traumatic moment.

"Dad? What is it?"

"Something…grabbed John…"

"Dad, I am sure the tornado just picked him up and carried him away. We're lucky the wind didn't get you, too."

Butch waved his hands and shook his head. "No, no, no. You don't understand. It wasn't the wind that grabbed John. There was…something in that funnel cloud…I saw…something…"

The crowd looked at Butch in stunned silence.

"Dad, you're just in shock right now. Cade, call your Nanny and let her know what has happened here and let her know that Poppy is okay. Also, see if your dad is still at her house. Ask him to get over here and help us."

Cade fished his iPhone out of the back pocket of his jeans and pulled up his grandmother's phone number. A confused, worried look settled across Cade's face.

"Cade? What's wrong?"

"I don't have a signal. Do you?"

Angie looked at her phone. "I don't either. Does anyone have a signal?"

Everyone gathered around the remains of the storm's path checked their phones, only to discover there was no signal to be found on any cell phone.

"Let me run over to City Hall. Maybe the land line is working. Cade, stay here with Poppy."

As the Angie ran across the street to the Grubbs City Hall, the crowd's attention was suddenly diverted by the sound of a motorcycle approaching from the intersection at the end of Main Street.

12:47pm
Main Street
Grubbs

Rick Jordan (RJ to his friends and listeners) rode his Harley Davidson into Grubbs after his Saturday morning shift on KOKR in nearby Newport. As he turned onto Main Street, RJ was stunned to see a trail of destruction leading from Butch's Barber Shop to his across-the-street neighbor's house.

RJ parked his bike in his front yard, removed his mirrored shades and ran across the street to the gathered crowd.

"Josh? What in the world happened here?!"

"You tell me, RJ. You have all those fancy weather radars at the radio station…what did the National Weather Service say about this?!"

RJ looked at Josh, feeling like his neighbor was somehow blaming him for this disaster.

"The weather forecast isn't calling for rain for the next 10 days…"

RJ looked up and down what remained of Main Street and a look of confusion swept across his face.

"Did y'all hear anything before the tornado hit?"

"Yeah, there was a roaring, screaming sound -"

"No, no. What I meant is did anyone hear the tornado siren? Jackson County Emergency Management sets off the sirens countywide when a twister is spotted."

"I didn't…did anyone else?"

The storm victims settled their eyes on Josh and they all slowly shook their heads.

12:52pm
Main Street
Grubbs, Arkansas

Angie Carlton burst out of the front door of the Grubbs City Hall. "The land line isn't working! And I can't raise anyone on the emergency radio!"

"Mom…what are we supposed to do?"

Angie fished her car key fob from her pocket and tossed it to her son. "Cade, take the car, drive down to Nanny's house and pick up your dad."

Cade looked hesitantly at his mom. "Are you sure…"

"Go. Take Poppy with you. And be careful. The road out of town should be fine."

12:55pm
Highway 18 East

Cade Carlton felt a great sense of relief as the chaos of Grubbs disappeared in the rear view mirror of his mom's Nissan Altima.

"Poppy? Are you okay?"

Butch Williams rubbed his aching head and replied, "Yeah, I'm just still a little shook up…"

"Do you mind if I turn on some music?"

"Nothing too loud…my head is killin' me."

Cade turned on Garth Brooks' "The Thunder Rolls" and adjusted the car stereo's volume to 5.

"There. That's an appropriate song for -"

"Watch out!"

Cade stepped on the car's brake pedal with both feet and skidded to a halt mere feet from a huge crevice that stretched across the highway. Cade shifted the transmission into "park" and looked to his grandfather for an answer.

"What is that?"

"I don't know…this wasn't here when I came to work this morning… let's get out so I can look at it."

Butch exited the car and walked to the edge of the hole in the ground, which was actually what appeared to be a canyon. At least three car lengths across, the crevice was so deep that Butch couldn't see the bottom of the newly-appeared canyon.

As his grandson joined him at the edge of the immense hole in the ground, Butch pointed to his left and then to his right.

"Would you look at that?"

"What is it, Poppy?"

"As far as I can see…in both directions…I don't see an end to this hole in the ground…"

Cade looked in both directions and realized his grandfather was right. The canyon seemed to have no end as far as the eye could see.

"It's almost as if…we are being cut off…"

"Poppy? What do we do?"

Butch turned and looked back towards Grubbs. "Well, the highway north of town was destroyed, so that just leaves the highway going west toward Newport. Let's head that way and…"

Butch trailed off as he noticed something strange south of town in the middle of the wooded Cache River bottoms. A dark funnel cloud rose up from the woods and proceeded to travel west.

"That can't be right…"

"What is it, Poppy?"

"That's not how funnel clouds work…"

"What do you mean?"

Butch pointed to the twister that was now picking up speed. "Funnel clouds drop down from the sky…they don't develop on the ground like that and then climb up to the sky…that's not a normal tornado…"

Grandfather and grandson watched the twister uproot trees as it cut a path through the Cache River bottoms, making a beeline toward the southern part of Grubbs.

"Cade, get in the car. We need to head back to town. They're gonna need some help."

1:11pm
Gum Street
South Grubbs

"Belle! Belle!! Where are you, girl?!"

Shea Vines was trying to help his parents get safely into their storm cellar when he was distracted by the cries of his next door neighbor, Karen Cragg.

"Mom…Dad…y'all get down in the storm cellar. I'm going to go see what's wrong with Karen."

Alvin and Sandy Vines reluctantly descended the stairs into the dank storm cellar. Sandy paused, turned around and looked at her son. "Shea, you hurry up. I'm gonna wait right here and keep this door open until you come back."

"Okay, Mom. I'll be right back!"

Shea ran around the corner of his parents' house and saw Karen walking down the middle of Gum Street with a panicked look on her face.

"Karen! What are you doing?! Get in the cellar with us!"

"Shea! You have to help me! My dog…I can't find Belle!"

Shea ran to Karen's side, grabbed her arm and tried to direct her to safety.

"Karen! We've got to get into the storm cellar! Look!"

Shea pointed to the south end of town, where a twister was on the ground and quickly heading their way. The wind picked up, debris began to blow down the street and a deafening roaring, screaming sound filled the air.

"arf…arf…arf…"

In the midst of the approaching storm, Karen could hear her lost dog somewhere close by.

"Shea! Belle is under the porch of your parents' house! Belle! Come here, girl!"

Belle sprinted from beneath the porch and ran right into Karen's waiting arms.

"Karen! We've got to go!"

Before Shea could lead Karen to safety, a tree fell from the sky, landing on top of the storm cellar.

"Mom! Dad!"

"Shea! We've got to find cover!"

Shea looked around the yard as the wind increased and more debris swirled around them.

"Get under my Humvee!"

Karen and Shea ran as quick as they could toward the Humvee parked in the driveway. Belle tried to jump out of Karen's arms as the storm closed in.

"Shea! Get under the truck and I'll hand Belle to you! I can't hold onto her!"

Shea crawled under the Humvee and reached for Belle. Just as Shea grabbed the terrified dog, Karen was snatched away by the roaring, screaming cyclone. Shea held Belle tightly and closed his eyes as his Humvee rocked up and down. The sound of the storm was ear shattering…until it suddenly stopped.

An eerie silence surrounded Shea, as he slowly opened his eyes and looked out from beneath his Humvee. Shea started to climb out from beneath the vehicle when suddenly the silence was broken.

"FUMP!"

Something landed on the top of Shea's Humvee.

"Fump, fump, fump, fump, fump…"

Shea could hear something rolling down the hood of the Humvee. Shea glanced to the front of the vehicle as the object rolled off the hood, landed on the ground, rolled under the Humvee and stopped a foot from where he was crouched, holding Belle. Shock swept over Shea as Belle squirmed free and ran to lick the blood from the face of her master's severed head.

1:12 pm
Highway 18
Cook's Cafe
Grubbs

"You hear that?"

John Allen Miser dropped his spatula beside the grill and ran from behind the counter to the front window of Cook's Cafe.

"What is it?"

John Allen looked back at his wife as he opened the front door.

"Shane…we're going to have to get out of here…"

Shane ran to her husband's side.

"John Allen, what is it?! You're scaring me!"

John Allen pointed to the south end of town at a cloud of swirling debris, powered by roaring tornado.

"It's another tornado! It's heading this way! We've got to go!"

John Allen grabbed his wife's hand and pulled Shane toward the back door of the cafe.

"Wait! Wait! Wait!!"

Shane pulled free from her husband's grasp and looked frantically around the cafe that had been in her family's name since her grandfather opened the establishment in the 1970s.

"We can't just leave it -"

John Allen grabbed his wife by the shoulders and looked her in the eyes.

"Shane. If we have to, we can rebuild. I love you…but if we don't get out of here now…"

Shane nodded as tears rolled down her cheeks. John Allen took his wife by the hand and led her out the back door of the cafe.

"Hey! Come on! Y'all get in here!"

Stephanie Smith ran across the back parking lot of Cook's Cafe, pointing at an open storm cellar in a yard behind her.

"Come on! I've got the grandkids in there! There's plenty of room! Hurry! It's coming!"

Stephanie ran to the storm cellar, opened the door and turned back to see death and destruction making its way from the southern part of town right toward them.

"Shane! John Allen! Run!!"

Shane and John Allen couldn't hear Stephanie's pleas over the roaring of the approaching storm. The couple raced toward the storm cellar as swirling debris clouded their vision.

KAREESHHHHH!

Just as Shane reached the storm cellar, the windows of the cafe and the surrounding homes and buildings exploded. Shane dropped to her knees from the sharp pain of glass that had ripped through her shirt and jeans and buried itself in her skin.

"Shane! Come on!"

Stephanie had left the safety of the storm cellar to help Shane to her feet.

"Where's John Allen?!"

Stephanie helped Shane to her feet as the wind suddenly dissipated and the sky cleared. Shane could see her husband standing in Stephanie's backyard.

"John Allen?"

Shane began to walk toward her husband as John Allen dropped to his knees and fell on his face. The last thing Shane saw before she fainted was the handle of John Allen's spatula protruding from the back of her dead husband's skull.

1:35 pm
Highway 18 West
Grubbs

"Don't turn here. Keep driving."

Butch Williams pointed down the highway as his grandson slowed to turn at the intersection of Highway 18 and Main Street.

"Look at all the glass! There's been another storm here. It looks like it hit the cafe…Let's head on to Newport and see if we can get some help."

Cade Carlton re-accelerated and sped through Grubbs. As they left the city limits, Cade began to slow down again.

"Poppy! Look!"

Cade stopped the car and pointed off into the distance to his left. Another twister rose from the ground just outside of town, picked up speed, traveled across the highway and headed north of Grubbs. A cloud of debris encircled the tornado, making it clear to Butch and his grandson that this path, just like the highway to the east, was now impassable and Grubbs was effectively cut off from the outside world and any would be help.

1:45 pm
Highway 18
West of Grubbs

Jackson County Sheriff Kevin Whaley was spending his Saturday afternoon like he spent many a Saturday afternoon: taking a patrol out to his old hometown of Grubbs to check on his parents. This Saturday felt a little different for Sheriff Whaley because he wasn't able to get either his mom or dad to answer their cellphones. And, now that he got closer to Grubbs, Sheriff Whaley became more concerned because his cellphone had no service at all.

As he drove past OK Flying Service and rounded the corner leading into Grubbs, Sheriff Whaley's blood ran cold. Sheriff Whaley parked his cruiser, exited the vehicle and tried to make sense of what he was seeing.

The highway leading into Grubbs was destroyed. A giant crevice was cut across the highway and appeared to circumnavigate the entire town. Off in the distance to the north of Grubbs, Sheriff Whaley could make out what appeared to be a tornado, churning up even more destruction in its wake.

Sheriff Whaley reached into his cruiser and grabbed his emergency radio. "Dispatch, this is Sheriff Whaley! We need some help out here in Grubbs! Grubbs has been hit by a tornado! I repeat, Grubbs has been hit by a tornado! Mobilize the National Guard! Now! NOW!"

1:59 pm
Guffey Street
Northeast Grubbs

"Mom! Come on!"

Jason Blackford had successfully managed to get his grandmother into the storm cellar behind their house, but he couldn't get his mother to understand the urgency of their current situation.

"MOM?!"

"Jason, I will be there as soon as I get my shoes on."

Jason ran back into the house and found his mother slowly putting on her Nike Cortez shoes.

"Mom! Really?! We've got to get into the storm cellar!"

Jodi Blackford looked up at her panicked son and tried to calm him with just a look.

"Jason, it's going to be okay. Where is Mom?"

"I've already got Gran down in the storm cellar. We are just waiting on you!"

Jason helped his mother to her feet and walked her to the front door, where he saw something that stopped him in his tracks: a tornado was heading directly toward their house.

Strong winds greeted Jason and Jodi as they stepped outside. The swirling winds carried leaves and other debris around their house, as mother and son tried to make their way to the backyard and the safety of their storm cellar. Absolute panic sat in as the winds were accompanied by a deafening roaring, screeching sound.

Jason opened the solid steel door of the storm cellar and turned back toward his mother.

"Mom! Come on! Get in!"

Jodi ran toward the safety of the storm cellar and was stopped short in her tracks. Something had a hold of her.

"Mom? What's wrong?! Come on!"

Jodi's eyes went wide as she tried to take a step forward and discovered she couldn't move. Jodi tried to step forward again and felt searing pain sink into her back as if knives…lots of knives had suddenly slid into her back around her spine.

"Jason! Get in the cellar with Gran! NOW!"

"Mom?!"

"Now, Jason! Get in -"

Right before Jason's eyes, his mother was yanked up into the sky and into the approaching twister.

"Mom!!!"

Jason felt a hand on his shoulder and turned to see his terrified grandmother.

"Jason, we've got to get in the cellar! Come on! Get in and close the door!"

Ann Tapp led her shell shocked grandson down the steps of the storm cellar, reached behind her and closed the heavy steel door.

"Gran…Mom is gone…"

Ann hugged her grandson and tried to comfort him, as well as herself.

"I know, Jason…As soon as the storm blows over, we'll go out and look for your mother."

Grandmother and grandson huddled together in the dark, dank storm cellar and listened as the wind and debris pounded on the steel door. Suddenly, the sounds of the wind and falling debris disappeared and was replaced by the sound of raindrops on the steel door.

"Jason, it sounds like the storm's blown over. Open the door and let's go look for your mother."

Hesitantly, Jason climbed the stairs, pushed open the steel door and stepped out into what remained of their backyard. Jason wiped the rain from his eyes as he tried to see any sign of his mother.

"Jason…"

Jason turned to see what his grandmother wanted and wiped more of the falling rain from his eyes.

"Gran, stay in the storm cellar. It's raining -"

"Jason!"

"What is it, Gran?"

"That's not rain…look…"

Jason looked at his hands and noticed they were completely red. Jason wiped his eyes again and looked at both his hands, realizing they - like he - were completely covered in blood.

"Gran..."

WHAM!!

Something fell from the sky and landed on the now open steel door of the storm cellar. Jason slowly looked to his right to see what the object was. Laying at the bottom of the steel door was one of his mother's Nike Cortez shoes, still attached to her left foot and what remained of her left calf.

2:24 pm
West of Grubbs

United States Army Spec 4 Danny Baty had planned on spending the afternoon catfishing on the White River, but he just happened to be at the Newport Air Base when a call for assistance went out for the National Guard. Now, Danny found himself flying a Huey helicopter loaded with a couple of doctors and other Army personnel into Grubbs, which apparently was now a disaster site.

From what he had heard, the rescue mission was the result of tornadoes, but Danny hadn't seen a cloud in the sky the entire day in nearby Newport.

"Do you have an idea of what we are flying into?"

Danny looked over his right shoulder at Dr. Shelly Churchwell, adjusted the microphone on his headset and shook his head.

"No, ma'am. All I know is that Grubbs has been hit by some kind of storm, the roads are out and there may be several wounded. We're supposed to fly you and Dr. Lunday in here to take care of those wounded, while the rest of us drop off some supplies and assess the situation."

Shelly looked over at Dr. Lori Lunday and tried to give her coworker a reassuring look. Shelly knew her friend didn't like to fly and neither one of them had planned to spend their Saturday shift in a helicopter on its way to a disaster site.

"You okay?"

Lori shook her head, raised the microphone on her headset and held her right hand over her mouth.

Shelly reached into the backpack at her feet, found a paper bag and handed it to her nauseated friend. Lori started to reach for the bag, paused and held up her left hand.

"Lori, take it. You're pale as a sheet."

Lori readjusted the microphone on her headset as she shook her head.

"It's fine. It's fine. It's fine."

Shelly wasn't sure if Lori was actually okay, or if her friend was simply trying to convince herself that she was fine.

"Heads up!"

The helicopter copilot, Warrant Officer Dave Doggett, was pointing off into the distance at a funnel cloud that was traveling just northeast of Grubbs. The twister dissipated, not up into a cloud, but it appeared that the cloud disappeared into the ground.

"Danny…you ever seen anything like that?"

"No…I can't say I have…"

2:32 pm
Main Street
Grubbs

As he parked his mom's car at the Grubbs City Hall, Cade Carlton noticed that there were fewer people gathered around the destruction on Main Street. Cade got out of the car and was immediately swept up into his mother's arms.

"It's about time y'all got back! I have been worried sick! There's been more tornadoes around town since you've been gone!"

Cade pulled away from his mother's frantic embrace and asked her, "Mom, where is everyone? Did one of the tornadoes…"

"No, no…we got some folks into the safe room in the basement of City Hall. Josh and Brooke took their kids down there. Phyllisha and Kaydence just took some bottled water down there."

"Angie, we've got some bad news."

"Dad, what is it?"

Butch Williams walked over to his daughter with a look of defeat on his face.

"We drove both east and west…both ends of the highway are completely cut off…and gone…the only other way out of town is Highway 37 north toward Ballew's Chapel. If we can somehow get a vehicle up -"

"I don't think that's going to work, Dad. While y'all were gone, another tornado cut across the road and ended up somewhere on the northeast side of town."

"Do y'all hear that?!"

Everyone turned to see what RJ Jordan was excited about.

Whoop…whoop…whoop…whoop…whoop…

Somewhere west of Grubbs was the sound of help in the form of an approaching helicopter.

RJ pointed over the tree line behind what was left of Butch's Barber Shop and the Grubbs Volunteer Fire Department.

"There!"

In the distance, the survivors could see a helicopter on a direct flight path towards Grubbs.

A wave of relief washed over RJ's face as he turned back to his neighbors. "Help is on the way!"

"I wouldn't be so sure of that…"

Justin Simpson grabbed RJ by the shoulder, turned him and pointed to the north of town where another funnel cloud rose up from the ground and began traveling west…right toward the approaching helicopter.

2:52 pm
West of Grubbs

"Danny…are you seeing what I see…"

United States Army Spec 4 Danny Baty looked to his left to see what Warrant Officer Dave Doggett was pointing at. Northwest of Grubbs a funnel cloud was tearing through open fields as it followed a path that appeared to be leading it on a collision course with their helicopter.

Danny looked over at his copilot with concern on his face, and then turned back to address their passengers.

"Docs, y'all need to hang on. It's about to get rough."

Doctors Lori Lunday and Shelly Churchwell strained in their seats to see what had their pilot so worried.

"Is that a…"

Lori looked at Shelly with terror in her eyes.

"That's a tornado!"

Danny banked the chopper toward the right and was shocked to see the funnel cloud pick up speed and correct its course in order to follow the aircraft.

"What the -"

"Danny, that thing is following us!"

"Dave, hang on! I'm going to turn around and head back to the airport! This ain't natural…something is -"

"Danny, look out!"

Danny banked the helicopter hard right as a telephone pole flew from the funnel cloud toward their aircraft.

"That was close! Dave, we've got to get out of here! Now!"

As Danny turned the helicopter back toward the Newport Air Base, a second telephone pole zipped past the aircraft to his right.

"Danny, that was way too close for comfort!"

"Dave, take a look behind us…how close is that funnel cloud?"

Dave looked over his right shoulder and was shocked to see the funnel cloud was closing in quick on the helicopter. Before he could warn his pilot, Dave saw three telephone poles launch from inside the funnel cloud, almost as if they were thrown right into the direction of the helicopter.

"Danny…we've gotta -"

Before Dave could warn his pilot and their passengers, a pair of telephone poles struck the helicopter, igniting the fuel tank and lighting up the skies west of Grubbs.

2:59 pm
Main Street
Grubbs

BOOM!!!

The survivors congregated on Main Street, who were minutes ago excited about the prospect of rescue, now looked on in horrific disbelief as the helicopter west of Grubbs exploded in a ball of flame.

Justin Simpson looked at his neighbors, hoping someone had an answer.

"What…what are we supposed to do…now?"

Josh Kinard slowly shook his head. "I...don't know..."

Phyllisha Simpson ran out of the Grubbs City Hall screaming at her husband, "Justin! What was that noise?!"

"Honey, a helicopter just blew up...west of town..."

Angie Carlton pointed south toward the end of Main Street.

"Tornado!!"

A funnel cloud rose up from the ground at the end of Main Street and began heading north toward the gathered survivors.

"Everyone! Get in the safe room in City Hall now! Go! Go! Go!"

Before the crowd could get across the street, a large tree dropped from the sky and landed on top of City Hall, collapsing the entire structure.

"Everyone! Over here! Get in the storm cellar in my backyard!"

The survivors turned to follow RJ Jordan across Main Street, but came to a halt when RJ's motorcycle was snatched up by the powerful winds.

"Come on -"

RJ's plea was cut short when his motorcycle whirled through the air, obliterating his head in a mist of blood and bone as the cycle passed through RJ and landed into the wall of his home.

"STOP IT!!! JUST STOP IT!!! DEAR GOD WE'VE HAD ENOUGH!!!"

Angie's screams echoed over the roar of the storm...and it seemed as if the storm had heard her plea. The winds began to die down and the roar of the storm ceased to exist.

The survivors huddled in the middle of Main Street and watched as the funnel cloud that was in the middle of the road shrunk back to the ground. In the midst of the dissipating cloud of dust, a figure appeared...some type of creature...

"What is that..."

Josh stepped toward the mysterious being and stopped as he heard a chilling, guttural growl emanating from the creature.

"RRRAAAWWWWWRRR..."

The creature stepped forward on two legs and the survivors could see the source of the growl and all of the destruction in and around their town. The creature stood about four feet tall and was covered in brown hair over the majority of its body, with off white hair covering its jaws and stomach.

It's large mouth was full of long, sharp fangs that appeared to have bits of bloody meat stuck between them. The beast's black eyeballs exuded anger and hatred as the creature surveyed the frightened survivors.

The beast slowly walked toward its would be victims and drool streamed from its mouth.

"RRRRRAWWWWRRRR!!!"

Blood, spittle and rancid breath spewed from the beast's mouth as it let out another chilling growl.

The beast took two more steps forward and its large mouth appeared to turn up into an evil grin. The beast stretched a clawed hand toward its victims and appeared to grin even more.

BLAM! BLAM! BLAM!

The beast flinched as three shots struck its hairy body. The beast turned and looked to the south end of Main Street and was greeted by two more gunshots.

BLAM! BLAM!

The gunshots struck the beast in its chest. The beast looked down at its chest, rubbed its mussed up hair and released another angry growl.

"RRRRAAAAWWWWWRRRR!!!"

The creature began running in circles until it picked up enough speed to produce a funnel cloud and then it sped off east through what remained of Grubbs.

As the cloud of dust and debris began to disappear, a man walked up Main Street toward the baffled survivors. The man stood barely five foot tall, even taller with his 10 gallon cowboy hat. The man settled a pair of revolvers into the gun holster around his waist and reached up to twirl his long red mustache.

"You folks okay?"

Angie stepped forward and nodded at the stranger.

"We will be…Mister?"

"It don't matter who I am, missus! I was down around Estico doing me some rabbit hunting when I heard all the commotion up here, so I decided to see what in the tarnation was going on."

"Mister…what was that thing?"

"Ma'am, that thing there is an absolute devil! I've ran into that ole galoot many times before. That beast will eat anything and everything, especially ducks and rabbits. Y'all got off lucky!"

Angie looked around her town and into the terrified faces of the survivors gathered around her.

"Mister…we don't feel too lucky right now…do you…think that…thing…will come back?"

The stranger pulled the pistols from his holster, turned and began walking in the direction the beast had gone.

"You don't worry, little missy. I'm the fastest gun north, south, east and west of the Pecos. That varmint had better say its prayers. Dead devils tell no tales."

CLOSE YOUR EYES
AND MAKE BELIEVE

By Bryan Young

IN JAMES'S IMAGINATION, HE WAS always a little green frog, and not at all timid or shy like he felt. In his world of make-believe, the other kids in his class wanted to play with him and follow him wherever he went. Miss Nana always told them how important it was to be brave and to do scary things, but that was never at the top of James's list.

He didn't like leaving his mother at the door every day when she dropped him off. He didn't like having to leave the classroom, either. Being home at night was something he didn't like because he didn't like it when his father came home smelling like beer.

Once he was settled in at class, he felt content enough to forget about all of the horrible things he had to endure and feel safe.

Safe.

"Come along, children," Miss Nana said, leading James and the rest of the class through the hallway, back to their nursery. Spending time in the gymnasium, tumbling on the mats and pretending they were dodging giant boulders and stealing fabulous treasures was fun, but it didn't feel the same as the comfort of their classroom.

When the alarms sounded, loud and shrieking, James wished he was that little green frog and could just hop away to be safe.

"What's going on, Miss Nana?" One of the other kids, Eleanor, asked.

"It sounds like a drill," she said, but the waver in her voice troubled James. It sounded just like his mom when she told him that things would be alright when dad got home.

"Like a fire drill?" Ralph asked. "Are we going out to the field?"

"No," Miss Nana said over the alarms. "Not a fire drill. "We need to get to the classroom. Now."

Another sound could be heard over the announcements and the alarms, and James likened it to firecrackers going off and that didn't bode well for James. He was afraid of fireworks. They were loud and bright and they scared him because he never knew what to expect and any time his parents used fireworks, that usually meant his dad's friends came over and that always meant more beer.

Miss Nana started jogging toward the classroom and the children followed. James tried to ignore everything else, the alarm, the fireworks, everything, just focusing in on Miss Nana's green-and-white striped socks as they headed for the classroom.

That little frog inside of James, the one who felt like he could be the leader, insisted that he lag behind the rest of the class. He wanted to herd his friends into the classroom from the rear and ensure they all got to safety.

Their teacher opened the door to their classroom and stood at it, ushering the rest of the children in, James doing his best to hold down the back of the line.

"Miss Nana," James asked when he reached the door, "What's going on?"

"Just go inside James," she said, then she turned around to see something coming toward her. "James. Inside," she said.

But James wanted to see, too. He stepped back out into the hallway and saw a flash married to the sound of the fireworks, but much, much louder. Miss Nana shoved him into the classroom, but then she fell herself.

James's eyes widened to the size of ping pong balls and he wished he really was a frog, able to slink away onto a lily pad.

Blood pooled beneath Miss Nana, lying there in the hallway and James wanted to believe it was nothing more than a bottle of broken raspberry syrup. The door slowly closed and another shot rang out in James's ears. Thinking fast, he pulled the door shut and locked it.

Turning around, his back against the door, James looked to the rest of the kids on the other side of the room.

"Where's Miss Nana?" one of the twins asked, pushing her glasses back up the bridge of her nose.

"She had to go," James said, thinking quickly.

"What's that red on your face?" Ralph asked.

"Raspberry syrup. Miss Nana dropped it." James wiped his face with his sleeve, hoping he could get it all. He didn't want to worry any of the other kids.

"What are we supposed to do now?" Eleanor said. "Miss Nana doesn't usually leave us alone like this."

"Uh," James said. The sound of more fireworks on the other side of the door caused him to flinch. They were getting closer. Maybe even right outside. "She said to play hide and seek. We need to find our best hiding spots until she comes back."

"Hide and seek," Ralph said, groaning. "I want to play a real game."

"What if..." James flinched at the sounds of more fireworks outside. "... we were hiding from a monster. A great big terrible monster that was trying to find us and eat us?"

"Yeah!" the other twin said, pushing his glasses up on his nose, just the same as his sister. "That sounds like fun. Can I be the monster?"

"I think we should all be running from the monster," James said. "We just have to find our hiding spots, quick."

"No, someone has to be the monster," Ralph said. "I'll do it."

"Okay," James said. "What kind of monster are you?"

"I'm seven feet tall," Ralph said, "with brown fur and floppy ears and big white teeth. Roar!"

The rest of the kids scattered as Ralph stomped around the room, making noise.

"Maybe he should be a silent monster, Ralph," James suggested, still listening for the sounds outside the door and any sign the terror had stopped.

All James heard was indistinct shouting beyond the door, further down the hallway. He hoped to hear Miss Nana's voice again, but after what happened, he didn't know if that would ever happen again.

"Roar," Ralph whispered. "How's that?"

"Better," James whispered back. "But what if I took a turn and you went to hide?"

James didn't want anything to happen to any of the others. Ralph especially, so he raised his arms and mouthed a silent roar, growing three sizes into a giant frog monster, with bulbous eyes and slimy skin. "Hide," he whispered, "or I'll eat you whole!"

Ralph's dog monster shrunk in size, back to that of a kid, and he scrambled away, looking for a hiding spot amongst the other kids. First, he tried beneath the sand table, but Eleanor was already there. "Beat it, Ralph," she told him.

James followed behind him, finally leaving the door behind, hoping it wouldn't open and a real monster would walk in.

Ralph moved to the nap mats, looking for somewhere to hide behind them, but John was already there. He didn't talk much, so it was no surprise when he growled and barked at Ralph, letting him know he'd need to find another spot.

James roared quietly once more, hoping that Ralph could find a hiding spot of his own and quickly.

Behind Miss Nana's desk they went, only to find the twins hiding beneath it. "Find somewhere else, Ralph," one of them said.

"Yeah," said the other.

"Where am I going to hide?" Ralph complained.

"You better hurry," James said.

That's when the sirens sounded. Distant at first.

"They're coming to get me!" James said, a little louder this time, hoping that it would all be over soon.

It was all he could do to keep the fear at bay.

He wanted to feel safe again.

He thought about not wanting to leave his mom and hoped he'd be able to see her again.

He thought about what it would be like if he couldn't, and the tears leaked from his eyes. He did his best to ignore them, though, because he had to stay strong and brave for the rest. At least that's what the little green frog in his imagination told him to do.

That little green frog told him that it would be okay. That none of this was real. That he would see his mom again. All he had to do was keep all the other weirdos in the class safe.

James looked out the window--a massive round one at the back of the classroom--as the sirens drew closer. The police cars bathed the classroom in blue and red flashing lights and James imagined they were the army coming to get his big green lizard frog.

"They're getting closer," James told the rest of the children. "You only have to hide from me a little longer and the army will fix it all."

Eleanor snorted from her hiding place. James couldn't tell if that was her stifling a laugh or a cry. He didn't think any of the other kids had seen what he'd seen, so he wasn't sure how scared they were. Maybe they were just as scared as he was. Maybe they saw Miss Nana. If they hadn't yet, maybe they would.

The sound of the doorknob froze James in place.

Someone tried opening the door from the outside.

"What's that?" one of the twins asked.

"Shhh!" James whispered harshly, "Stay hidden, it's the real monster!"

He hoped he'd locked the door right. He couldn't always push the button the right way when they'd done drills about hiding inside the classroom. It didn't always stay locked, the button would push in all the way. His hands were small. But Miss Nana had always been there to make sure it had locked properly.

Frozen, he stared at the door.

The knob twisted, and the lock popped.

"Oh no," James said.

He couldn't move, he had to know what was on the other side of the door.

It opened slowly and the monster stepped inside.

To James, the monster looked like nothing he'd ever seen. Dripping red, it might have crawled from the swamp. Instead of hands, it had a metal arm, smoking at the tip. Curiously, the monster wore a hat, bright red to match the syrup. It had words on it, but the syrup had obscured them, making it impossible for James to read.

James gulped.

The look on the monster's face was mute. It held neither rage nor hate. Empty, vacant like a lot.

To James, if he had to describe it, he would say it didn't look like anyone was home inside the monster.

James blinked.

And the monster locked eyes with him.

James didn't know what to do. He didn't want anything bad to happen.

He just wanted to be safe.

That's all he wanted.

To feel loved.

And cared for.

And he didn't always get that.

The monster made a noise, but James couldn't understand him. It was like he spoke an entirely different language.

Then, the monster shifted its stance and James realized that he didn't have metal hands, but was holding something metal. The monster reached up to its face and wiped so much of the syrup from it and took a closer look at James.

"Freeze!" someone shouted from the hallway.

The monster looked away, out toward the voices, then back at James.

The face of the monster transformed and he roared, just like Ralph had been doing. He aimed his metal hands at James and there was a flash of light and pop like a firework.

James didn't feel anything. His whole body went cold and numb like he was frozen in a block of ice.

The monster, though, the monster's head exploded like a jar of raspberry syrup, and for James, that's exactly what he saw. It shattered against the door and the syrup ran down the side of it, pouring over the heap of the monster like a stack of pancakes. Behind him, James saw another stack, with the green-and-white striped socks coming out the bottom of them, just like the wicked witch of the east.

James blinked again, then looked down and felt like he was a stack of pancakes, too.

"It's okay, everybody," James said weakly. He tried to smile. "They got the monster..."

James collapsed with a smile.

And the little green frog smiled back at him. "See? We can do anything if we put our minds to it..." ♜

THE SHADOWS UNDER MARIANA BASE

By Scott Pearson

CAPTAIN K. C. STEPHENSON LOOKED UP from a seismic report on her desk monitor as Jeri Dexter, just back from a dive to Challenger Deep, stepped over the bulkhead of the open door to her office. Mariana Base was about five thousand meters underwater; the Deep went down another five thousand plus, deeper than Everest was tall. Stephenson tilted her head to one side. She felt her thick braid of gray hair shift across the back of her blue jumpsuit. The captain didn't like the look on Dexter's face.

"What's wrong?" Stephenson said. Her senior submersible pilot plopped down in the chair across from her.

Dexter shook her head. Her hair didn't move. Although a civilian—no one on Mariana Base was on active duty—her ginger hair was high and tight. "I finally got a glimpse of one of those drones. Sort of."

For the last few months, DiluviTech, a multinational marine technology company that was their largest corporate funder, had been testing autonomous drones in the Deep. While Mariana Base was expected to update all their funders on any scientific discovery, it wasn't a two-way street. DiluviTech hadn't answered a single query about the drones.

"What do you mean, 'sort of'?"

"By the time I got it in our lights, the thing was underground!"

"In a cave?"

"No, the drone buried itself, like a crab. Which explains why it's been so hard to find the buggers." Dexter got up and stepped around the corner of the desk, gesturing to the keyboard. After a nod from Stephenson, Dexter brought up a short clip on the monitor. A quick motion at the edge of the floodlights left an oblong shape in the silt at the bottom of the Deep, so subtle you could miss it and the small diaphanous clouds rising from the seafloor like steam from a kettle. "Look at the heat it's throwing off! What's it doing, drilling into the rock beneath?" Dexter returned to her seat.

Stephenson leaned back in her chair. "Why would they do that?"

"I don't know, I'm just the pilot," Dexter said.

For nothing good, Stephenson was certain. DiluviTech wasn't interested in the pure science coming out of the permanently staffed ocean base overlooking the Mariana Trench. Their brochures were all about luxury underwater hotels, but what they really wanted were tech breakthroughs that could be used for secret listening posts in international waters and who knew what other unsavory military applications. Stephenson didn't like them, but she just ran the base, not the coffers that kept the base active.

"Did you install a camera to monitor that spot?"

"The bad news is I didn't have a spare with me. Before I went chasing drones, Shell got some great footage of a bunch of those spongy-looking things, xenophyophores."

"What's Bill say?" Dr. William Shabalala was the base's specialist on deep-sea life; Michelle Jeong was their documentarian.

"He did a little happy dance. He's never seen so many so close together, practically like a colony, and never such big ones, at least thirty centimeters across. So the good news is that's where I put the only camera I had, mounted and wired to the hub." To get live feeds, all their cameras were connected to a hub in the Deep from which a single fiber-optic cable ran all the way back to the base.

"No wonder you were down there so long. Great job."

"Yeah." But Dexter didn't sound satisfied. She remained seated, staring off at a wall monitor displaying a retro aquarium screensaver.

"Was there something else?" Stephenson said.

Dexter turned away from the monitor, facing the captain, her expression serious. "I'm... not sure it's worth reporting."

After some silence, Stephenson leaned forward, elbows on her desk. "Well, just tell me." She smiled and added, "Then I'll decide if you shouldn't have told me."

That seemed to help Dexter relax. "Okay. On the way back, after the drone. I didn't see anything, not directly in the lights. But around the edges... I don't know. Shadows? How can there be shadows outside the light?" She folded her arms across her chest. "Maybe those crab drones hiding underground in the Deep creeped me out. Not exactly scientific, I admit."

Stephenson just nodded, unsure what to do about someone feeling spooked, but reluctant to shrug it off when that person was as experienced as Dexter. There had been a few small quakes centered down in the trench the last couple weeks, which always put people on edge, but not Dexter. It took a special kind of calm to pilot a submersible beneath ten thousand meters of water crushing down on you, and Stephenson had never seen Dexter rattled, even during the rare base emergency. The growing silence was broken by an eerie whale song reverberating through the small office.

Both women couldn't help but laugh at the perfectly timed sound punctuating the mood, and it broke the tension.

Stephenson said, "No telling ghost stories. Just show Malai the clip of the—"

She was cut off by the intercom. "Bridge to Captain Stephenson."

Stephenson gestured for Dexter to stay and thumbed the desk intercom. "Stephenson."

It was David Thomas, her second-in-command. A former astronaut, he'd served on the ISS. When he'd been told he was too old to go to Mars, he'd decided if he couldn't go further from Earth, he'd "go closer." He'd resigned his commission and applied to Mariana Base. She was glad to have him here at the bottom of the world.

"Cap, we've got an unidentified personnel submersible heading toward us."

Stephenson frowned. "I don't recall expecting anyone."

"Nope, nothing scheduled. Silence on the UT so far."

"On my way."

\#   \#   \#

Stephenson stepped over the bulkhead onto the bridge. Dexter, trailing behind her, made a beeline to Malai Watana, their lead tech specialist, to play her the clip that almost showed the drone.

The bridge was small, just four multipurpose workstations and a wall of monitors. There were only a few actual ports in the whole station, backups in case the exterior cameras were down. No big windows at five thousand meters deep, and generally not a whole lot to see out there anyway, even with the floodlights on. Though once a sperm whale had swum around the base for several minutes checking them out, which had the crew running from port to port to watch it directly.

Omari Nichols, their communications and sonar specialist, was just putting down the mic for the underwater telephone. Thomas stood next to him, his frown softened by his neatly trimmed salt-and-pepper beard.

Stephenson took in his expression and reluctantly said, "News?"

Thomas leaned his lanky frame against Nichols's station. "Sub's from DiluviTech."

Stephenson glanced over at Dexter standing behind Watana at the tech's workstation. A surprise visit from a DiluviTech rep right after Dexter had almost seen one of their drones? It had to be a coincidence, given how long dives to and from the base took, not to mention that there was no way the footage could have made it to anyone above the water. Still, it was a little unnerving.

Dexter said, "Is it too late to turn off the lights and pretend nobody's home?"

Nichols swiveled his chair to face her. "Sorry, Dex, I already responded to him."

"You gave us away? That'll cost you two dessert rations."

Light laughter in the small room was cut off by a yelp from Watana. She was staring intently at her desk monitor. She noticed everyone looking at her. Embarrassed, she said, "Sorry, something on the new camera startled me.”

“What?” Stephenson said.

“Just some movement at the edge of the light. But it was too fast, it had to be some sort of digital artifact. I’ll see if I can enhance it.”

“Okay,” Stephenson said, acting as if all the unusual things happening at once were not all happening at once. The last thing she needed was a jumpy crew in front of some corporate rep. “Well, it’s almost time to welcome our unexpected guest.”

“Uninvited guest,” Dexter muttered, an edge in her voice.

Stephenson chose to not hear that and added, “Dave, round up Anne and meet me in the docking bay.” Dr. Anne Martin was their specialist in seismology. She’d been busy lately and could use a break.

The astronaut turned aquanaut gave a boy scout salute and followed Stephenson off the bridge.

#   #   #

By the time Thomas and Martin stepped up beside Stephenson in the docking bay, the disconcerting grinding and clanking sounds of the automated docking procedure were echoing through the room. The deck of the bay featured three docking hatches, two for their regular submersibles, *Seaquest* and *Seaview*, and a third for supplies and personnel from the surface: visitor parking. The far wall had a series of doors into escape pods, though in cases of extreme emergency, the entire base could jettison from the seafloor and rise to the surface.

Stephenson glanced at Thomas, who nodded toward Martin with a concerned expression. Stephenson turned to face the scientist and saw why. It was only four in the afternoon, but Martin looked exhausted. “You okay?”

Martin rubbed at her eyes, then pushed a stray lock of blond hair behind her right ear. “Sorry, boss, I haven’t been sleeping well. I’ve been obsessing over the seismic readings of the last couple weeks.”

“Get some proper sleep tonight, grab something from the infirmary if you need to.”

“Will do.”

With a final clank, the handwheel atop the visitor hatch spun around and the hatch opened. A brown duffle bag popped up, like an earthworm coming out of the ground, followed by a slender man in a green jumpsuit. He climbed out, staggered to his feet, and spread his arms, swaying a bit from side to side on the deck.

"Whoa, sorry, solid ground again." He ran a hand through his disheveled brown hair, which left it equally disheveled in a different direction, and looked around the docking bay.

Stephenson stepped forward, but before she could say anything, the man's eyes settled on something over her shoulder.

"Welcome to Mariana Base, Gateway to Challenger Deep," he read aloud.

That's what the sign hanging on the wall behind Stephenson said. Her grandkids had made it and decorated it with glitter, so it was the official motto as far as she was concerned.

"You stole my line," Stephenson said, and stuck out her hand. "Captain K. C. Stephenson."

"Love it!" he said. "Phil Reid." He reached out but quickly pulled his hand back. "Oh, sorry, I should warn you." He held his hand up, displaying black-smudged fingers. "I'm a sketcher. Charcoal mostly." When Stephenson kept her hand extended, he grasped it firmly. Then he turned to Thomas and pointed at him. "David Thomas. You've been in freakin' outer space!"

Thomas, still looking cranky about the surprise visit, chuckled in spite of himself. "Indeed I have. Welcome to under space."

"Hah! I see what you did there." Reid turned toward Martin and tilted his head to the side. "You look as tired as I feel." At Martin's awkward silence, Reid looked aghast. "Sorry, that was rude. I'm just... well, I took off from Newark at the ass crack of dawn Wednesday on the twenty-three-hour flight to Guam. Hotel lost my reservation, but finally got me a room where I managed to get a little shuteye over the sounds of the couple next door arguing all night, then I hauled my sleep-deprived butt onto the boat six this morning. Started the long dive down here at three. My first solo. So here I am, jet-lagged and running on fumes. I apologize again."

Martin shrugged. "It's okay. I *am* tired. I've been listening to seismic sounds for so long, I almost think they're talking to me!"

"Sounds like we both need a nap." He shook Martin's hand and turned back to Stephenson. "Captain, I know you must have a boatload of questions, but would you mind if I just went straight to the guest quarters and, what do you say down here, hit the rack? Give me just an hour or so, and then I can get you up to speed?"

Stephenson was still annoyed that a corporate rep showed up unannounced, but it was a reasonable request. "Sure, that's fine."

Martin said, "I'm heading back to my quarters, Captain, I can drop him off on the way."

"Great, thanks," said Reid. He picked up his duffle, then dropped it back to the deck. "Oh, I almost forgot." He stepped back to the open hatch to his submersible. Dropping to the floor, he reached down into the sub and pulled out a small canvas cooler. He got up and presented it to Stephenson. "I brought some tinala' katni and fina'denne' from the island. Should be enough for everyone."

"Thanks," said Stephenson, taking the cooler.

With a smile and a nod at her and Thomas, Reid scooped up his duffle and followed Martin out of the docking bay, making small talk as they went.

"Dammit," Stephenson said after they disappeared through the door.

"What?" said Thomas.

"I kind of like this corporate guy."

"I know." Thomas scratched at his beard. "It's annoying."

Feeling a bit better about the visit, Stephenson headed out of the bay while Thomas went to dog the hatch to Reid's sub. She stopped as the voice of Watana came over the intercom. "Bridge to Captain Stephenson."

Stephenson could usually go days without being paged by the bridge, and now she was getting her second in under an hour. She stepped over to the bay's control station, which was a touchscreen monitor on the wall, and tabbed open the intercom, keeping a casual tone in her voice. "Stephenson."

"Something weird. Best see for yourself. And you should bring Shabalala."

# # #

Stephenson and Shabalala joined Watana at her workstation. The young woman looked grim and was tugging on her long black ponytail. As Thomas squeezed in beside them, Stephenson noticed the odd expression on his face. She just raised her eyebrows at him.

"Later," he said, leaning toward Watana.

Stephenson gave him a small nod and also focused on the seated technician. "What's up?"

Watana let go of her hair and tapped at her keyboard. "We lost the feed on the new camera."

Shabalala's shoulders slumped. "Not the one by the xenophyophores?"

"Yes."

Thomas frowned. "Dex only placed that, what, four hours ago?"

Stephenson knew where he was going, because it was her first thought as well. "Was it defective?"

"No, that's what I'm about to show you." Watana gestured to one of the monitors on the wall. "A few minutes ago, there was a... commotion. It triggered the camera and we got this."

At first the monitor was just black, only a time stamp displayed in the lower right corner. Then the camera's floodlight came on, illuminating the cluster of big xenophyophores, spread several feet across the seafloor and a little way up a nearby cliff face. Each of them looked like a cross between coral and a sponge. Beyond that superficial comparison, no two of them looked at all similar, unlike what you'd expect from a group of them in close quarters.

Before Stephenson could think much about that, a motion at the edge of frame caught her eye. Then a creature lunged across the xenophyophores, like some sort of giant centipede, with multiple eyestalks, its body segments a riot of baroque colors. It moved faster than anything she'd seen at that depth and tore into the xenophyophores like a shark in a feeding frenzy. Someone gasped, and she realized that everyone on the bridge had pulled back upon seeing the creature and its carnage, especially as more and more of it snaked into frame, with no tail end of its undulating body yet in sight. Suddenly another, even longer version of the thing burst forth from the darkness and attacked the first one, ripping it in two with a single bite.

The water clouded with green ooze seeping from both still-writhing parts of the smaller beast, which seemed to quickly attract a swarm of the things, surging into frame, snapping and tearing at each other as much as at the remaining xenophyophores. The churning mass then exploded directly toward the camera. There was a short, blurry moment before the autofocus kicked in, and they saw a flurry of entangled legs and mouth parts, a hellish kaleidoscope of colors and motion, then snow. After a few seconds, Watana turned off the monitor.

The bridge was deathly quiet except for the occasional electronic tone signifying something functioning as it should. Next came the soft sounds of people letting out held breaths and looking around at their crewmates.

Stephenson turned toward Shabalala, who looked both exhilarated and horrified. "What the hell were those?" she said, louder than she'd intended.

Shabalala swallowed audibly. "I... wow." He shook his head. "Malai, can you bring up a still frame?"

Watana answered with a clattering of keys, then moused around until she had a clear image of one of the creatures. "That's what startled me earlier, barely beyond the range of the light. I couldn't believe my eyes then, but..." There was no need to finish the sentence.

Shabalala ran a hand over his close-shorn hair. "They look like some kind of annelid worm, but they have attributes from a variety of polychaete species and are much larger—frightfully so. Some polychaetes do get a few meters long, but they're usually quite small around, like a finger width or so. Those look..." He stepped closer to the monitor. "Comparing them to the xenophyophores, I'd guess some were as big around as a grapefruit and several meters long. It barely seems physiologically possible. The only previously recorded polychaete specimens in Challenger Deep were just a few centimeters long."

He stared closely at the monitor without speaking, then turned back to everyone else. "First the big xenophyophores and now these giant polychaetes—or whatever they are—this turns our entire understanding of the Challenger Deep biome upside down. We've got to get another camera down there."

"Yes, we do." Stephenson smiled, displacing the unnerved look she'd felt on her face while watching the bloodbath. Nature's violence aside, this was what drove her down here, the otherworldly environment. Short of inventing warp drive, the deep sea was the closest she'd ever get to another world. Unless they built a base beneath the ice on Europa anytime soon. Part of Mariana Base's mission was researching the kind of life that might be found in similar extraterrestrial environments, within the solar system or beyond.

Stephenson leaned against the workstation. "Can we tell if the camera was destroyed or if the cable just broke?"

Watana shook her head. "Not for certain. But it's more likely the cable was severed. The camera housings are pretty tough."

Stephenson stood up straight. "Omar, tell Jeff to prep the *Seaquest*, he's going down there ASAP." Jeff Ford was her other pilot, second to Dexter only by seniority.

"Dex won't like that," Nichols mumbled as he slipped his earbud in.

"She knows the rules," Thomas said.

Nichols grimaced at himself. "Yes, sir. Sorry, sir."

Stephenson patted Watana on the shoulder. "Get another camera ready, just in case. Make sure Jeff has everything he might need to make the repairs. Better yet, why don't you go with him."

"Will do!" Watana leaped to her feet and hurried out the door. It had been a while since she'd been to the Deep, and she was clearly excited to go.

Stephenson sat in the chair Watana had vacated and looked up at Thomas. "So why the weird look before?"

He shrugged. "I don't want to make too much of it." Unzipping a pocket on his jumpsuit, he pulled out a folded piece of paper and handed it to his captain.

Stephenson could see dark smudges peeking out from the folds. "Let me guess. Our corporate sketch artist?"

"Mm-hmm. Found the thing when I was dogging the hatch. I shouldn't poke into personal belongings, but I wanted to see if he was any good."

She unfolded the paper, careful not to get any charcoal on her uniform. The thing staring back at her from the paper was all mismatched eyes, writhing tentacles, and the hint of an amorphous body, mostly captured in charcoal, but with an occasional watercolor highlight in blood red or putrescent green. Almost forgetting to blink, she stared at it until it seemed like it moved.

Stephenson folded it back up. "Well, that's the stuff of nightmares."

"And makes your therapist review your meds."

She tucked it into one of her own pockets as she shook her head. "Not fair. My youngest nephew is a big horror fan. Clive Barker, gory movies. He'd love this."

"Okay, I'll grant you that. I guess it's just so... incongruous."

"What did you expect? He's a corporate type, so he only draws, what, filing cabinets?"

"No. Not just." Thomas waited a beat. "Maybe cubicles too. A break room to liven things up."

She rolled her eyes at him then stood. "I'm going back to my office. Send Reid my way when he's up."

# # #

"You know the rules," Stephenson said without looking up from her monitor. She could tell by the footsteps it was Dexter who had just stomped through her open door, and she knew why the pilot was there.

"But I know right where the camera was. I should be the one—"

"I don't have pilots deep dive twice in a row and you know it." Stephenson took off her reading glasses and put her monitor to sleep so Dexter wouldn't notice the brief report she'd just received from Watana, Shabalala, and Dr. Ross Lozano, their environmental specialist. Dexter was upset enough already; she hadn't brought up the drone she'd encountered, but Stephenson knew that rankled the pilot. "Jeff has the coordinates, and he's already on the way down."

Dexter slumped like a pouty child into the chair in front of Stephenson's desk. "At least tell me he took the *Seaquest*."

"That's what I assigned him." A couple weeks earlier, Ford had scraped the side of the *Seaquest* against a cliff face, and Dexter had told everyone that he was never again allowed to touch "her" *Seaview*.

There was a knock on the bulkhead beside her open door. Stephenson

194

and Dexter both looked up. Reid stood there, looking puzzled. "Did I hear you talking about a dive? This isn't a regular dive time."

Stephenson didn't appreciate his tone, especially with what she knew. And to think she'd been starting to like the guy. "I didn't realize you tracked our schedule that closely. But I order supplementary dives whenever we need them."

"Of course. Sorry for interrupting."

The apology sounded sincere, but she didn't buy it. With a meaningful look at Dexter, Stephenson waved Reid in. Dexter stood and gave voice to Stephenson's suspicions.

"What he means, Captain, is they're sending another of their mystery drones down the Deep around now, and we might get a close peek if we're down there too."

Reid hesitated for a second, one foot in Stephenson's office, one outside, then smiled and brought his trailing foot over the bulkhead. "Okay, you caught me: corporate lackey." He extended a charcoal-smudged hand toward Dexter. "Phil Reid. You must be Jeri Dexter. I wouldn't mind getting some piloting pointers from you. You've got more hours logged down there than anyone."

Dexter glanced at Stephenson with an expression that said she saw right through his flattery. She shook his hand, then rubbed at the charcoal that had ended up on her own fingers. Stephenson appreciated how Dexter hadn't let on that they'd already gotten a glimpse of a drone, which made her regret that she hadn't updated the pilot.

Dexter gave Reid the squint eye for a little longer then said, "Right, I'm going up to the bridge to keep an eye on the hot-rodder." She never was going to let Ford off the hook. Gesturing at the now-vacant chair, she said, "Have a seat."

"Nice to meet you," Reid called after her as she disappeared around a bend in the corridor. He settled into the chair and glanced around the office. "Well. I feel a little like I'm in the principal's office."

Stephenson leaned back in her chair. "That sounds about right, Mr. Reid."

His usual genial expression hardened for a split second, then returned.

"If I'm getting detention, I want—"

Her intercom buzzed to life. "Case, it's Anne."

Stephenson held up her index finger toward Reid and tabbed the intercom with her other hand. "I'm in a meeting, and you're supposed to be sleeping."

"Can't sleep." Her voice was shaky. "These seismic readings. He's coming."

Stephenson frowned. She was staring down at her desk but noticed Reid lean closer. "Who's coming?"

"These readings are telling me—"

"But who's coming?" Stephenson glanced up at Reid. He shrugged.

Martin didn't respond for a while. Finally, she said, "Who?"

"*You* said '*He's* coming.' I'm asking—"

"Sorry, sorry, meant *it's* coming."

"What is?"

More silence.

"Anne?"

"It could just be a big quake."

Stephenson rubbed her eyes. "I'll meet you in the lab in a few minutes."

"I'll be waiting."

After Martin clicked off, Stephenson texted Dr. Kelly Barrett, their physician, to immediately check in on Martin. Next, she got up to pour a glass of water, mostly so she could turn her back on Reid and take a calming breath.

"If you want to go see Anne," said Reid from behind her, "we can talk later."

Stephenson really did want to check on Martin, but she had to deal with this DiluviTech situation as well, and Martin was in good hands with Barrett. She took a sip of water and turned around, pointedly not offering him a glass. "Why the surprise visit?"

He grinned. "Straight to the meal, no apéritif?"

She was tired of his overly pleasant demeanor. "No alcohol allowed on the base."

"Of course." He apparently took the hint, his grin fading to a kind of neutral smile. "As you know, we've been testing some drones over the last month or so."

She dropped into her chair. "More like three months. What are these drones doing?"

"They're separate from our partnership with Mariana Base." His soft smile remained, though his eyes seemed to harden.

Stephenson pointed at her monitor. "Well, your last drone came down closer to Dex than you realize. My scientists just sent me a theory about the amount of heat it was giving off even after descending through thousands of meters of water just above freezing. They hypothesize that it was carrying spent nuclear fuel."

Reid's smile was frozen on his face like a mask. "As I said, *separate* from our partnership."

"Were all the drones dumping nuclear waste in contravention of international treaties?"

"I can tell you that our tests are complete."

Stephenson folded her hands together so that she wouldn't make them into fists. "The only explanation my team could imagine is that you're trying to embed nuclear waste into the Pacific Plate so that it will slowly be subducted below the crust, deep beneath the trench. A concept I'm told is problematic, at best, on several levels."

"I'm just here for the final step."

"They also wondered if other hazardous waste was involved in these tests. Anything that might have affected the local wildlife."

"All I need is room and board." He casually drummed the fingers of his left hand on the arm of the chair.

She leaned forward. "I have the authority to put you off this base."

Something flashed across Reid's face, gone so fast she couldn't be sure, but she thought it was fear. He got up, moved to the side table, and poured himself a glass of water. She wondered if he had done so to hide his face for a moment, much as she had done.

Reid took a drink and returned to his seat, setting his glass on the edge of her desk. His expression was composed and cold. "You could do that, but then I doubt things would go well for the program at the next board meeting."

And there it was. The sword always dangling above from corporate funding. If she didn't play the game, the base could be shut down. She rationalized that there wasn't much they could do about what had already happened, and if the drone tests really were done, the best thing might be to retreat for now and be able to fight back later. She unclenched her hands and forced a polite expression onto her face. "So what do you have left to do?"

Reid smiled at her capitulation, and that burned in her gut. He slouched in his chair, relaxing in his win. "Just work in my quarters. Maybe take my submersible to the Deep."

Stephenson realized she'd begun fidgeting with her braid, stopped, and tossed it back behind her. If she was stuck with him, she should try to keep things amicable. The image of his charcoal sketch flashed in her mind's eye, which drew her gaze to his darkened right hand. "I thought you were going to get some rest. Looks like you were drawing more instead."

He held up his hand and wiggled his fingers in the air, smiling as if the last few minutes hadn't happened. "I couldn't sleep, too excited to be here. But drawing relaxes me."

"What do you draw?" She took another sip of water, found herself wondering if anyone had something stronger stashed somewhere on the base.

Reid looked away from her. "Oh, this and that. You probably wouldn't like it."

"How do you know?" She reached into a pocket on her jumpsuit, pulled out the folded sketch, and opened it up flat on her desk, exposing the bloated body, its coiling, knotting tentacles, all the unmatching eyes staring in different directions, the hints of bloody, decomposing gore. "You left this in your sub. Gruesome, but quite evocative..."

She trailed off as she glimpsed something in Reid's expression, something dark. She'd been expecting him to lap up the compliment, but instead his look sent a chill through her. Then just as quickly it was gone—like the hint of fear earlier—and he casually reached across the desk for the paper.

"What, this old thing?" he said dismissively. "I've done better." He crumpled it into a ball.

Stephenson just stared at him. The sketch obviously wasn't an old, discarded piece; she guessed he'd sketched on the way down in the submersible. She could not figure this guy out.

Reid stood up and tossed the ball of paper onto her desk. "Well, now that you're up to speed, I better let you go."

Stephenson watched him go without responding. She had a feeling that she was far from up to speed.

#   #   #

The lab was a shared space with four multipurpose workstations and a couple large tables. The only light in the room at the moment was from active monitors on desks and several more around the walls—some displayed charts, others active readouts that were continually updating. Lozano's work was visible on a desk monitor, as was material related to Shabalala's studies. Martin's seismic data was displayed across a few wall screens in multiple formats. Martin and Barrett were sitting across from each other at a table littered with printouts and handwritten notes. The doctor looked professionally calm. Martin looked defensive, like she kept the table between them for protection and might bolt from her chair at any second.

Stephenson had been in here just a few days earlier and everything had seemed fine; now she felt guilt wash over her. The well-being of her crew was her responsibility as much as Barrett's. Clearly Martin had been struggling longer than Stephenson or Barrett had realized, and she'd reached a tipping point.

"Good, you're finally here," Martin said, keeping her eyes on Barrett. "Will you please tell the doctor the importance of my findings?"

Stephenson glanced at Barrett who, with a subtle look, encouraged the captain to reply.

"Of course. But just to make sure I explain things correctly, could you give me an update?"

Martin grabbed a handful of papers from the table and waved them in the air. "It's all here in black and white. All you have to do is listen."

"I'm not sure I—"

Martin threw the papers at a monitor with active seismic readings.

"Look! Can't you hear that?" The papers fluttered to the deck.

"Hear...?"

Martin stomped closer to the monitor. She stabbed at the readings with her right index finger, impacting the screen so hard it left a visible dent of pixels that stopped displaying the right colors. "The words are clear as day. He whispers, but I hear." She spun back around to face them. "Can't *you* hear? He's coming."

Stephenson exchanged a worried look with Barrett. The doctor gestured to keep Martin talking. Stephenson took a few steps toward the seismologist. She remembered that in the docking bay Martin had said the seismic sounds she'd been listening to were talking to her, or something like that. At the time, Stephenson thought it was a figure of speech. But just a few minutes ago on the intercom she'd also said, "He's coming," though she'd quickly walked it back.

"Who's coming?"

"Don't you hear him?" She tilted her head and pointed, waving her arm around in multiple directions. The fingernail on her right index finger was bleeding, partially torn away from the skin. "The whispering prisoner." She started poking herself in the temple, hard, with her bloody finger. "The dead dreamer. He shall rise from the deeps if we call him. He wants us to. But I won't. I won't call him!"

"Anne, please—" Stephenson froze as Barrett suddenly darted toward Martin, a jet injector in her outstretched hand.

Martin flinched backward, but the injector hissed against her arm. "What—?" She rubbed at the injection point. "What'd you do? I'm trying to save us..." But already her head was lolling, her eyelids fluttering.

Barrett spoke for the first time since Stephenson had arrived. "Help me, Captain."

Stephenson and Barrett each took an arm, supporting the swaying woman between them as they headed for the infirmary. Martin mumbled a word here and there, barely audible.

"What happened, Kelly?" Stephenson said.

"I don't know. Yet."

"I knew she was overworking herself. I should have—"

"We all had extensive psych evals before coming down here." Barrett paused as they maneuvered Martin through the door of the infirmary and onto a bed. "None of us could've guessed this could happen. And so quickly."

"I suppose you're right." Stephenson was glad they hadn't passed anyone in the corridor on the way here. When Martin recovered, this was all going to be embarrassing for her. The fewer people who saw her like this the better.

"Of course I'm right. I'm the doctor."

They exchanged only slightly forced smiles.

#   #   #

After Stephenson had helped Barrett get Martin settled, she made her way up the curving ramp to the bridge. Thomas was there, pacing, while Shabalala, Lozano, Nichols, and Dexter each sat at a workstation. Jeong stood in a corner. Thomas stopped walking, shifting a bit to one side to make room for Stephenson.

She'd updated Thomas from the infirmary about Martin's condition and her meeting with Reid and told him to relay the DiluviTech situation to the rest of the crew. He'd filled her in on the *Seaquest* dive. A lot of things were going wrong at once. "When it rains..." Thomas said quietly.

Stephenson shook her head. "Not a metaphor I want to use under five thousand meters of water."

He shrugged. "If the sub fits."

Nichols said, "Here we go, *Seaquest* has patched in." There were places all along their fiber-optic cables where a submersible could plug in for live video communication with the base. He gestured toward two of the wall monitors as Ford and Watana each appeared on a separate screen.

"How's it look down there?" Stephenson said, her tone growing more serious as she took in their expressions. Ford was focused, Watana a little rattled.

Watana leaned closer to her video pickup. "The camera's missing, along with a couple of meters of cable. No sign of it—or the creepy-crawlies—in a ten-meter radius. Like they dragged it away with them."

Stephenson tapped Shabalala on the shoulder. "What do you think?"

"Their size combined with the aggressive behavior... it's possible they inadvertently carried it away in their frenzy."

Watana said, "We could lay new cable from the last junction—"

"What do you mean 'we'?" Ford interrupted.

"All right," Watana continued, smirking, "*Jeff* could lay new cable with his amazing robot-arm skills."

"I could peel a hard-boiled egg with those things," he drawled.

"Then we could run it back to where the xenophyophores were, but they're gone too."

"Gone?" Shabalala blurted.

"Let me just show you," said Watana. "I'm turning on the starboard camera..." She was looking off frame and tapping at her controls. Nichols joined in on his keyboard and another wall monitor flared to life.

The giant polychaetes had wiped out the entire xenophyophore colony, leaving behind only bits and pieces littering the seafloor. Shrimp-like amphipods—normal sized, about five centimeters long—were picking through the remains. The polychaetes had also done a number on themselves; there were still a few big chunks of the worms floating around, greenish haze oozing from the ends. The larger, longer pieces occasionally twitched and spasmed, as if trying to swim. The bridge went quiet.

"Are they still alive?" Stephenson asked.

"Possibly," said Shabalala, barely above a whisper. "Normal-sized polychaetes, like many worms, can grow back whatever is lost. Cut one in half, you end up with two."

"Yikes," Dexter said.

Watana turned back to face them. "Under the circumstances, I didn't know if you wanted the camera replaced or not."

Shabalala rubbed his chin and glanced toward Stephenson.

"Your call," she said with a shrug.

"No, I guess not. Maybe you can find where the polychaetes—"

"Whoa, hold the phone. Look at this." Ford was maneuvering the sub, then switched to a feed from his front camera. At a glance, the seafloor looked like sand, but it was actually a layer of silt and detritus that had sunk to the bottom from ten thousand meters of water above. The barren, gray wasteland was lit only by the floodlights on the *Seaquest*. Across that wasteland were several deep furrows, as if something had been dragged—or had crawled—along the bottom. A sea cucumber in the middle of one of the furrows gave a sense of scale. Whatever had made those furrows had been large. Very large.

Once again the bridge went quiet. Shabalala slowly glanced around, realizing everyone was looking at him. He raised both hands in the air palm up. "I'm at a loss. Maybe the polychaete swarm made those furrows somehow, but to be honest, I'm afraid there's something much bigger down there we haven't seen yet."

Everyone's attention was drawn back to the monitors as Watana shouted, "What was that?"

"What?" said Ford. "I didn't see anything."

"Malai, what did you see?" Stephenson said, willing her voice to stay calm.

"Shadows. Moving just beyond the light."

Stephenson exchanged looks with Dexter; that's what she'd seen too.

Ford was peering from side to side, obviously checking his feeds from the submersible's cameras. "Yeah, I see it now too. Maybe just silt in a weird current? Barely shows up. Let me just—"

All the feeds from the sub went to snow.

"Omari?" said Stephenson, an edge of worry in her voice.

Nichols was tapping away at his controls. "They disconnected from the feed, Captain. I might be able to spot them from another camera... there."

Nichols looked up to the wall monitors, and everyone followed his lead. Four of them came on, the live feed distributed across all four in one big, grainy image. The *Seaquest* was at the edge of the camera's floodlight; Nichols had cranked the light as high as it could go, zoomed in as much as the camera was able. The submersible was listing a little to port. The seafloor beneath it was a boiling swarm of polychaetes, many of them larger than seen in the previous frenzy. Beyond the sub, barely discernible, was a hint of movement, darkest-black tentacles against the dark black of the Deep, more shadowy than substantial, more rumor than reality.

Dexter was out of her seat like a shot, leaping through the bridge door and racing down the ramp.

"Dex!" called Thomas.

"There'll be no stopping her," Stephenson said. "Go with."

"It'll take an hour and a half to get to them—at least three round trip." He used his rational, matter-of-fact astronaut voice, a port in a storm.

"We have to try. But I don't trust her alone." Stephenson felt her stomach roil. She could be sending out a rescue mission... or initiating another disaster.

Thomas simply gave her a little salute and trotted off calmly, as if he was just late to dinner. She watched him go for a few seconds, then turned to the rest of the crew on the bridge. They all looked back at her, nervous, confused, wide-eyed. Everything happening was unprecedented. She looked back at them steadily. They were all professionals, cross-trained for a variety of emergency situations. They'd passed their drills with high marks. They were ready for this. She nodded at them confidently.

"Okay, everyone, let's get busy. Omari, launch a comms relay to the surface then help Shell get every camera feed up and running. Use every wall and desk monitor, we need full coverage. Ross, launch our camera drone to the hub and coordinate with Shell. We need eyes on what the hell is going on down there after our subs come back. Bill, get down to Kelly and prep for the return of the subs." She turned to leave the bridge.

"Cap, where're you going?' said Nichols.

She'd gotten so focused, she'd forgotten to tell them. "I'm going to see if Reid has the guts or the heart to assist with this rescue mission."

#   #   #

The corridors were quiet as Stephenson jogged down to the guest quarters. As she got nearer, it seemed even quieter, more than it should be; there were always subtle sounds of computers and air vents and heaters and such in the background, random metallic pings in the superstructure, the occasional whale song echoing through the base. For a moment, there seemed to be an unnatural absence of sound, as if in a vacuum, but then she heard something humming, not any electronic equipment, but organic... a person lowly murmuring?

It was coming from the guest quarters. Reid was singing to himself. She had to force herself to remember he likely knew nothing about what was happening in the Deep, to not snap at him when she needed his help, when she was already on thin ice with him. While she paused to compose herself, she couldn't help but try to hear what song he was singing. Whatever it was, it wasn't pleasant, more of a guttural chant, and in a language she didn't recognize... or perhaps just nonsense sounds strung together for effect. Either way, it sent a shiver through her as she reached for the chime.

After she pressed the button, the room beyond went quiet. Or at least the chanting stopped, leaving a soft scratching in its absence. She knew, rationally, that it was the sound of charcoal dragging across a surface, but for a second she imagined that it was exactly the scratching noise the polychaetes would make if they were inside and scrabbling across the deck. She actually jerked her head left and right, then up to the ceiling, half expecting to see the hellish creatures descending upon her. She shook the image out her mind.

"Reid!" She pounded on the door. "There's an emergency."

The door swung open suddenly and she jumped back as Reid stepped quickly over the bulkhead, slamming the door shut behind him. Both his hands were black with charcoal, and he had a dazed and excited expression on his face, as if he'd just been in the front row watching his favorite band play his favorite song.

"What emergency?" He looked up and down the corridor, as if everything must be fine if there weren't any flames visible.

"Something's happened to one of the submersibles. I've sent our other one down—"

"And you want to know if I'll join this likely impossible rescue attempt." He said it without malice, but detached, like it was an interesting hypothetical.

"Yes. Look, I know we don't see eye to eye, but—"

"Don't worry. I was on my way down shortly anyway."

"You... were?" This guy was always wrong-footing her. Then he started past her, heading for the docking bay. She turned and hurried to follow him.

"I told you in your office I might need to go down the Deep as part of the final step. I've been training for this for a long time."

Did he have emergency training? "Training for what?"

He turned and smiled at her; it was disconcerting in a way she couldn't put her finger on. "The final step," he said, his simple statement underscored by the soft rumble of a quake down in the trench.

#   #   #

It was the longest three and a half hours of her life. There was little to do but wait and watch while the *Seaview* made the slow dive down to the *Seaquest*. When the comms relay reached the surface, she requested an emergency ship with a chopper be sent to them, just in case. Their support team in Guam was hampered by bad weather, but they would launch when they could. Then she just watched along with the rest of the crew.

Watched as the *Seaview* approached the drifting *Seaquest*, Reid's submersible not far behind. Luckily, there were no frenzied polychaetes nearby, none of the nearly transparent black tentacles. The *Seaquest* looked undamaged. The *Seaview* locked on to its sister ship with its robotic arms. They were probably able to patch into the drifting sub's comm system, but Dexter and Thomas wasted no time connecting to the hub and headed back to base as fast as possible. Stephenson would not know what had happened until they were back.

The strangest twist was noticed by Jeong, who had been scanning every feed while Stephenson and everyone else became focused on the two submersibles rising toward the base. "Captain, monitor five."

Stephenson scanned across the wall until she found the specified feed. There was Reid's submersible, holding position, not following the others back. "What the hell's he up to?" she said. But her attention was drawn back to her own submersibles, her own people. She didn't much care what the strange corporate rep was doing. Another deep rumble ran through the station.

#   #   #

Omari got through to the *Seaview* on the UT when they were five minutes out from the base.

"We talked to Malai briefly," Thomas reported. Stephenson had never been so happy to hear someone's voice. "She was in a panic, almost incoherent. Seems Jeff is dead, though the details were... unbelievable. She hasn't spoken for the last twenty minutes, but I can still hear her moving."

Stephenson leaned close to the mic at the workstation where she sat. "What did she say?"

A telling pause. "I'd rather not repeat any of it. Just be in the bay when we get there."

"I'm on my way now." She told Jeong to keep an eye on Reid, and everyone else to stay on the bridge. She didn't want a crowd in the bay. Barrett and Shabalala were there already, emergency medical gear at the ready. She told them Ford might be dead, and Watana likely in shock. She walked briskly down the ramp.

Everyone on the base was jittery, full of adrenalin, and no one had eaten properly in nearly four hours. The three of them in the bay fidgeted, looking back and forth at the three interior hatches. When the clunks and clangs of the docking process started, they raced to the middle hatch. Dexter and Thomas would have maneuvered the *Seaquest* into dock first, so they were less than a minute away from finding out what had happened to Ford and Watana.

Finally a green telltale lit up, and Shabalala spun the wheel on the interior hatch and threw it open. No sounds emanated from the *Seaquest*; Watana wasn't opening the hatch. Shabalala reached down to open the submersible. As he did so, the sounds of the *Seaview* docking echoed through the bay.

Shabalala got the hatch open then scrambled backward with a shout, falling on his ass. Watana burst up out of the hatch covered in blood, eyes closed. When her eyes snapped open, she started screaming. Stephenson and Barrett both froze for a moment, overwhelmed by the sight and the stench of death wafting from the open hatch.

As Shabalala scrambled back to his feet, Stephenson and Barrett shook off their shock and went into action. Barrett and Shabalala grabbed Watana while Stephenson started down into the *Seaquest*. Stephenson stopped, recoiling from the sight of Ford somehow torn limb from limb within an undamaged submersible, blood and tissue everywhere. Thomas and Dexter rushed up as she slumped to the deck beside the open hatch. She tried to wave them back, but they both peered down into the *Seaquest*. Dexter went pale and turned away. Watana, in Barrett's arms, had quieted to a whimper. Shabalala leaned against a bulkhead, staring down at the blood and tissue transferred to his jumpsuit from Watana. A quake shook the bay enough that the open hatches fell shut with hard clangs, the harsh metallic sound echoing sharply in Stephenson's ears, then all was quiet again. Stephenson and Thomas looked at each other, speechless.

The silence was broken by Jeong's quavering voice loud over the intercom. "Captain, you need to get back here!"

#   #   #

Running back up to the bridge, Thomas right behind her, Stephenson was winded like she'd never be able to catch her breath. Their echoing footsteps were joined by a now almost constant subsonic rumbling in the deck. What she'd seen in the bay—Ford's gruesome remains, Barrett and Shabalala leading the near catatonic, blood-soaked Watana to the infirmary— was a surreal blur.

Everything came into sharp focus, like waking from a dream, as she stumbled over the bulkhead onto the bridge: the frightened chatter of her crew, Nichols talking to the surface, Jeong's head snapping back and forth as she monitored all the feeds.

"What the fuck!" Thomas shouted behind her.

She'd never heard him raise his voice or swear, not on duty. Turning in surprise, she saw that he was staring past her at the monitors. She spun back around. Entering the bridge, she'd thought the monitors were all blank, but she saw now that Jeong had synced them to display a single feed across the whole wall. In the center of the blackness was a spot of light. Reid's submersible still down in the Deep.

Then she saw the shades of black. Moving. Like the tentacles glimpsed earlier. But on a more massive scale. She couldn't figure out how such semitransparent blackness could even register on their cameras, but she couldn't deny what she was seeing, as much as she wanted to, because everyone was staring at the monitors, their matching dumbfounded expressions evidence that they were all seeing the same thing. A colossal humanoid shape in the Deep, its disproportionately huge head a mass of writhing tentacles, like a misshapen octopus on its neck. The submersible was dwarfed by the thing's face, from which glared two black orbs each wider than the sub was long.

Another quake, accompanied by a groan from the station's superstructure, shook her attention away from the monitors and she moved to the central workstation, to a control panel beneath a plexiglass cover—the emergency release that would blow the base from its moorings. Engines would kick in, controlling the ascent, keeping them level during the long rise to the surface.

Stephenson called out, "Dave!" He tore his eyes from the monitors and saw where she was. He moved beside her as she cracked the seal on the cover and threw it open. She dug at her collar to withdraw a key on a chain around her neck. Thomas mimicked her motions. As they inserted the keys that would arm the system, the intercom blared to life.

Barrett, who likely wasn't watching the thing in the Deep on a monitor, yelled, "Need help. Anne—"

Another channel cut in, Martin also yelling, but controlled, focused. "He's coming! Those drones weren't dumping, they were delivering *offerings.*"

Stephenson suddenly understood two things: Martin had been right all along, and the strange smile Reid had given her on the way to the docking bay had been the beatific expression of a fanatic. The revelations, too late, seemed pointless. She nodded at Thomas as they turned the keys simultaneously. The red button between the keys, beneath another protective cover, started flashing. Thomas flipped open the cover and held his hand over the button. On the monitors, the horrific colossus looked more solid. Something else moved behind it... no, not something else, more of the same. The thing spread vast wings, which were growing more opaque as they opened.

Martin was shouting again. "Someone help me in Reid's quarters!"

Stephenson had a gut feeling—she had to listen to Martin. She pointed at Thomas's finger poised above the flashing button. "Not until I say so!" And she ran from the bridge, his shocked expression at the order frozen in her mind. This would either be the best intuitive leap she'd ever made, or the worst decision of her life.

#   #   #

Stephenson rounded a corner, nearly falling as a quake again shook the base. She kept her feet under her, however, and sprinted the final meters to the guest quarters. The door was already open, with sounds of a struggle coming from within. She dashed through the door and skidded to a stop as she took in the room. Nearly every surface was covered with charcoal scribblings. Words in mismatched sizes and languages, arcane symbols, obscure drawings scrawled across the floor, up the walls, and across the ceiling. Strange perspectives that seemed impossible to draw and made her dizzy. In the center of the room Martin and Barrett struggled with each other; Barrett held a jet injector.

"Stand down, Doctor!" Stephenson said, rushing toward them. She grabbed the doctor's arm.

Barrett froze, confused. "Captain?"

"Kelly—trust me." Stephenson pushed the two women apart and turned to Martin. "What do we do?"

With a wave of her arm to indicate the whole room, she said, "These are incantations. Summonings. Dark spells to break barriers between worlds." She dropped to her hands and knees and started smearing the charcoal. Stephenson stared. Could it be that easy?

The room shook, the biggest quake yet. Thomas's voice came across the intercom, echoing across the base. "Captain!"

Stephenson jumped to the wall intercom to respond. "Don't push that button! Activate fire suppression in the guest quarters."

"What?"

"Do it!" She grabbed the hands of the two other women and rushed them out the door.

Seconds later, nozzles popped out of the ceiling and sprayed suppressant throughout the room. The white foam turned gray as it absorbed the charcoal. It ran down the walls and dripped from the ceiling, forming a dark sludge on the floor.

Stephenson let go of Martin's and Barrett's hands and ran for the nearest monitor. Switching it on, she called up the feed from the bridge, just in time to see the nightmare colossus shudder, its wings drooping, its body appearing less substantial as it started sinking. It fixed its malevolent gaze upon the submersible and its tentacles stretched forward, snaring Reid's submersible. The tentacles clenched like a fist, and as the colossus continued to fade away, so did any remains of the submersible. Soon the quakes, the colossus, and Reid were all no more.

#   #   #

"That's what it was," Watana said, speaking quietly from her bed in the infirmary. She'd suffered only a broken leg and dislocated shoulder—at least, those were her only physical injuries. She had turned down the chance to be airlifted to Guam; she wasn't ready to get back in a submersible yet. Or to leave her crewmates. She handed the uncrumpled charcoal drawing back to Stephenson, who sat beside her. "It appeared right after the shadow tentacles outside grabbed us."

Stephenson nodded. "Pulling you away from the communication port. That's when we lost your video feed."

Watana closed her eyes. "At first it was just like a sheer, billowing cloth. If I'd been alone, I'd've thought I was hallucinating. Then the details started filling in. That's when Jeff noticed it between us. We just watched, couldn't believe it." She opened her eyes, staring at the ceiling, tears streaming down her cheeks. "When it was solid, it attacked Jeff. It was howling. Jeff cried out once, but... the sounds."

Stephenson dropped the sketch and took Watana's hands in hers. "You don't have to tell me any more. Just rest."

"The blood and everything. Everywhere like rain, like sleet, coming down on me, in my mouth. I was screaming long before I realized I was. The howling thing never stopped to breathe, the howling never stopped. All the while it was on Jeff, the eyes all over it were staring at me, like a snake at a mouse. Then it was on me, I was kicking it, and it yanked me close, I thought it was going to rip my arm from my body, tear me up like Jeff. Then it was gone." Watana turned toward her captain. "Why? Why did it leave me?"

Stephenson shook her head and squeezed Watana's hands. "We'll never know."

Thomas joined them on the other side of the bed. As Watana turned to look up at him, he put his hand lightly on her head, like a worried father. "The only person who might have known is gone. Straight to hell, is my guess." He moved his hand from her head to the bed rail. He looked from Watana to Stephenson. "DiluviTech says they fired Reid over a week ago. I don't buy it."

Stephenson clenched her jaw. She didn't trust herself to speak without flying into a rage. On the way to the infirmary, she'd swung by the mess to dispose of the food Reid had brought from the surface; she wouldn't have been surprised if he'd drugged it.

Martin spoke up from where she was resting in the next bed. "No more shadows? I haven't felt any quakes."

"All quiet," Thomas said. "So far."

Martin sat up. "That thing's thoughts were transmitting like seismic waves. I could hear them in the quakes. Understand them. I can't explain it. It's just a feeling, a presence. Like when people say, 'There's just something in the air.'"

Stephenson found her voice. "But now... there's just something in the water." And she was sure the shadows were still there. Somewhere in the Deep. ♜

THE LUCK OF BIG RED

By Will McDermott

JEROD FOUND HIM LYING IN his own filth surrounded by a half-dozen empty bottles of booze behind a dumpster while emptying the backstage trash. He thought about leaving him there.

"I'm no humanitarian," Jerod mumbled to himself. "I got enough troubles. Can't go saving every bum on the street. Just too many. Gotta look out for number one, right?"

But something about the pale figure made Jerod pause before heading inside and closing the theater door on the poor schlub in the muck. And it wasn't that the drunk figure was a rabbit. That was part of it, certainly, but even that hadn't truly fazed Jerod.

It could have been the look of desperation on the creature's face or the black circle around his eye that caught the janitor's attention. It might have been the matted fur on his legs or the giant number seven on his back paw that piqued his interest

Maybe, just maybe, Jerod the janitor felt the tiniest twinge of pity, or even guilt, over the state of this down-on-his-luck rabbit. The creature obviously had no one left in this rotten world to care for him and nothing to his name. Yet, despite all that, this dirty, reeking rabbit still clutched a severed rabbit's paw tight against his chest, as if his life depended on not losing it.

Later on, though, Jerod would admit to himself that even facing that pitiful, furry face seeking the smallest bit of empathy from another lost soul in this world, he would have left that dirty, old rabbit to rot in the gutter if it hadn't glanced up into Jerod's eyes and said, "Brother, can you spare a dime?"

Jerod had heard the stories of the dancing and singing rabbit, but he'd never seen him perform. And even though the pitiful creature looked like he'd be worth more in a pot with some stew vegetables at this point than on stage bringing the house down, Jerod immediately saw dollar signs dancing in his head So, he bundled the rabbit under his arm and took him inside to sit by the furnace.

After the rabbit, whom the world had known as Big Red, warmed up and sobered up a bit over a cup of joe, he told this story.

#   #   #

I remember where it all began to go wrong. We'd been on the top of the world for what seemed like forever. My luck had rocketed us from the side streets of Reno to the center stage in Vegas. We were the talk of the town, and everyone wanted to see our show. We packed them in night after night until that fateful Sunday matinee. It all started just like any other night.

"Ladies and Gentlemen, The Sands is proud to present, for a sixth consecutive week, The Great Mortoni and the most magical rabbit on the Las Vegas Strip — Big Red!"

Applause erupted throughout the 2,000-seat auditorium as I danced my way onto stage. My long ears skimmed the boards with every cartwheel and back-flip. The applause grew stronger and louder, and the crowd jumped to their feet and cheered as I launched into my final, spinning, triple-flip.

I landed in a four-legged crouch, posing briefly as a normal bunny before leaping back into the air, kicking my legs over my ears — almost in slow motion — being sure everyone got a good look at the red number seven on the long pad of my right foot, before landing again on two feet and raising my front paws over my ears in triumph.

The curtain rose behind me as the applause died away revealing the

Great Mortoni, magician extraordinaire, and my master. I spun and danced my way back to his side, motioning to him and then raising my arms to the audience to get them clapping and cheering again.

Audiences loved us. Well, they adored me. They laughed at cheered at my antics, my smooth dance moves, and my winning smile. Mortoni's magic tricks only got polite applause unless I stoked the fire of their enthusiasm. He was competent, don't get me wrong. He just had no flash, no pizazz. But that's what he had me for. And we killed, night after night after night.

Life hadn't always been that good, though. Before he became the Great Mortoni, my master was just Morton the magician, playing dives in Reno. We weren't even in the heart of Reno. We played the fringes — the sleaziest bars and clubs on the very edges of Vegas's seedy little sister.

I wasn't even Big Red at the time. Sampson was my natural-born name. Morton found me in a discount pet shop where customers got great deals as long as they didn't ask questions. I was this cute, white bunny, barely old enough to hop, with a black circle around my left eye and a smudge of black fur on my right, rear paw. Morton bought me because I fit in the palm of his pudgy hand.

As I grew, he used me less and less in the act. Even then, I had enough sense to know that when I got big enough, I would go from being part of the act to being part of Morton's dinner. The only thing that had saved me so far was that as my feet grew, the black smudge on my back foot turned into a semi-passable figure seven.

So, even though Morton couldn't palm me anymore, he could still pull me from a hat and get some applause from the drunk gamblers in the audience by showing off my newly red-dyed birthmark. That's how I became Big Red. It's what gamblers call the large, red seven in the middle of a craps table. But even with that gimmick, Morton's career was headed nowhere, and I was just a few missed meals away from oblivion.

But then fate stepped in and changed everything. One night after a seriously bad performance where Morton's magic box broke, his impossibly long silk scarf tore in half and all his doves literally flew the coop, he holed up in his dressing room, which was nothing more than a storage closet off the basement furnace room and cried himself to sleep.

At least we had food because the drunken gamblers had all brought cabbages to the performance that night — a sign of just how bad Morton's act had gotten — and tossed them at us during the big reveal of my seven-emblazoned foot.

I grew cold after finishing my cabbage leaves, so I scrambled through a gap in the wall to the furnace room. I found some old clothes behind the large metal box and burrowed in for a nice warm sleep. In the middle of the night, something in the bottom of that pile that felt like a furry stick poked my belly and woke me up.

When I grabbed the stick between my back paws to push it away, I felt a change come over me. My front legs grew while my back legs lengthened and straightened, pushing out from the tiny bundle of rags to bump into the walls. My paws widened and splayed out, growing fingers and toes behind my claws. Finally, my nose flattened into my face like a button, my mouth grew from a little pointy opening into a broad smile, and my eyes sparkled open, as if I could really see the world for the first time.

I looked down at the stick and was bewildered — and at the same time horrified — to find it was a rabbit's foot. I quickly checked all my feet, which stuck up out of the pile of rags at weird angles. But I still had all four of mine, plus an extra, which now looked small compared to my own newly giant-sized paws. I didn't realize it at the time, but I had found an actual lucky rabbit's foot.

At that moment, Mortoni burst through the door. He'd been worried that I'd escaped or been taken for someone else's supper. I looked up at him, my arms and legs flailing around in the rags, not even sure how to get off my back.

"Mortoni!" I called. "Help me."

The magician just stood there, his jaw slack, his own eyes wide open, with equal measures of shock and fear displayed behind them. We stayed there, in tableau, for what seemed like an hour until Mortoni finally gathered enough of his wits to exclaim: "You can talk?"

The next few weeks were a blur. I'd always been nimble. I mean I am a rabbit, right? Once I found my feet and got used to the length of my legs, it wasn't long before I was running and dancing and leaping into the air.

As my abilities grew, Mortoni began to recreate his act, putting me out front as his assistant, distraction, and hype rabbit. It didn't take long for us to be headlining in the heart of Reno and then make the move to Vegas. Mortoni's magic improved a bit, but we both knew that it was me that brought the crowds to the show. So, I worked on my moves just as much, if not more, than Mortoni worked on his tricks.

Everything was perfect until that Sunday afternoon.

There was this girl, you see. She caught my eye in the audience. Cute little thing with kind of a big nose and red hair with bangs that hung over her eyes. I don't know what it was about her that stood out. I never paid any attention to the crowds. I always kept my attention on Mortoni and my routines.

But for some reason, I couldn't keep my eyes off this tow-headed moppet. I started playing to her, just her. Every flip I made, every high note I hit, I did for her. It was glorious. I hadn't felt that alive since I literally came to life in that pile of clothes when I found my lucky rabbit's foot.

I'd always loved the attention and adoration I'd felt from the crowd, but the feel of this girl's eyes barely visible beneath her carrot-colored hair, made me feel giddy inside. I loved her and wanted to be with her forever.

What I didn't realize at the time was that Mortoni was struggling behind me. As I jumped and flipped and danced for the carrot-headed girl, Mortoni was desperately trying to grab the key hidden in his straight jacket as the water poured into the tank where he was chained behind a curtain.

I should have checked on him. I was supposed to check on him after two minutes. It had been five and I was still dancing, still staring at the little girl in the audience. Finally, a stagehand rushed out and ripped the curtain down to find Mortoni, his face bloated and blue, floating listless, held in the center of the tank by the chains.

The crowd screamed as I landed a quadruple flip. At first I thought the screams were for me, but then I saw the horrified looks on their faces, all but the carrot-topped girl. She was still staring right at me, right through me, down into my soul.

After the chaos died down and the rescue workers left, I sat on my haunches backstage, alone in the middle of all of Mortoni's magic gear. I couldn't move. I couldn't feel. I was in shock. I should have been mourning Mortoni, but all I could think about was what would happen to me now that he was gone.

That's when I looked up and saw the orange-haired girl again. She had somehow convinced her father to come backstage and, in all the confusion, no one had stopped them.

"Can we keep him?" the girl asked.

"We'll have to ask the hotel, Lilly," her father answered. "I suppose they own him now."

"Nobody owns me," I replied, my smile returning. "I'm my own bunny."

Lilly smiled back at me as her father stared, dumbfounded.

"He really can talk," he muttered eventually. "Well, I'll be a monkey's uncle."

"Rabbit's uncle," I replied as I jumped into Lilly's arms, the twinkle returning to my eyes above my broad smile. "Let's go."

I didn't even look back at Mortoni's gear, not even the hat he used to pull me from. That probably makes me a bad person, but in the moment I was just happy to be with Lilly. Lilly Loller of Louisville. She had come to Vegas with her parents, Larry and Louise Loller, and her brother Lonny. They packed me in a cat crate, and we flew back to Kentucky where the Lollers ran a general store.

After the bright lights of Vegas, my life with the Lollers was absolutely bucolic. Their store was in a tiny neighborhood on the edge of town. We saw the same people day in and day out. They came in to meander slowly around the store, pinch the fruit gingerly to see if it was ripe, and chat gaily with each other and the Lollers before happily waving goodbye.

I was a big hit. Not like Vegas, bright-lights big. I just sang little ditties for the regulars, danced around the aisles with the ladies and their kids, and laid in the window by the carrots taking the sun during the slow times. I loved it.

While I was there, business picked up for the Lollers. I'm sure the word got out about the singing and dancing rabbit, but that wasn't what was bringing them in. Not always. One weekend a choir bus broke down on its way to a concert. They practically bought out the store. A week later, a terrible storm shut down the neighborhood and everyone came in to stock up.

There was always something driving business to the front door of the Lollers. They could even afford to get Lilly a new haircut, which allowed me to see her beautiful green eyes for the first time. After the haircut, Lilly's grades started to improve. She'd always been a whiz at English, but now her numbers were coming along. I helped out by singing songs about the multiplication table.

Lilly's dad, Larry, though, started to wonder out loud if there was something else going on that accounted for their good luck. He looked right at me as he wondered. Like I was a good luck charm or something. I mean, I still had my lucky rabbit's foot, but that was my luck, right? And I was the luckiest rabbit on the planet. I had Lilly and the little store and more carrots than I could ever eat. What more could I want?

But Larry wanted more, so when a champion billiard player came to town for a big tournament, Larry decided to play him, and he took me along for good luck. Lilly tagged along as well. I was her rabbit, after all. I don't know why Larry was so excited about playing this particular champion. He muttered something about revenge and that luck would be on his side this time, but I didn't care. I was with Lilly and that's all that mattered.

Larry was pretty good. I guess he had played billiards in college or something, but he certainly wasn't rusty at all. He tore through all his opponents as Lilly and I cavorted together nearby. Eventually, it came down to the final match between Larry Loller and the billiard champion everyone called Naughty Niner.

There was something about Niner that caught my eye. He was flashy, I'll give him that. Niner was a hip cat in a pink suit and a wild, multi-colored tie. I thought it strange that he never took off his fedora. Like Lilly before her haircut, I couldn't see Niner's eyes beneath his hat. He also chewed on a lit cigar the whole time he played and blew smoke rings, smoke lines, and even smoke curves from his mouth. Eventually the entire ceiling of the pool hall was covered in smoke.

I was enthralled. Even in Vegas, I had never seen anything like Niner. He was unique, one of a kind. Like me. For the first time during the tournament, I watched the match. Larry won the first game of nine-ball, but I could tell he was struggling by the end. During the second game, Niner broke and ran the table. I got so excited, I began clapping and dancing as the nine fell into the pocket.

"Stop that!" Larry yelled. "You're my good luck charm."

Chastened, I sulked into a corner as the third and final game began. I barely paid attention, but every time I glanced up and caught sight of Niner, resplendent in his smoke-ringed fedora, the champion sunk another ball and Larry moaned.

Finally, the crowd uttered a collective gasp. I ran over to see what had happened. There were two balls left on the table and Niner, true to his name had done something naughty. Unable to line up a winner, Niner had left Larry an impossible shot. The cue ball was stranded in a corner behind the yellow-striped nine with the black eight-ball clear on the other end of the table, poised perfectly at the edge of the corner cup.

If Larry couldn't hit the eight or grazed the nine, it was ball in hand for Niner. Larry had no choice but to try a trick shot. He needed to jump the cue over the nine down the table to hit the eight into the pocket. If he did, he won. If not Niner would easily clear the table.

I tried to watch the table, but Niner began blowing smoke rings and curves again. They came out and merged into perfect, floating nines. I'd never seen anything like it. It was amazing. I was entranced by his skill. As I watched the nines floating off into the distance from Naughty Niner, I heard a loud snap, followed by a horrible crack and a resounding gasp from the crowd.

I looked around to see if Larry had completed the impossible shot, but both the nine and the eight sat just where they had been. But the cue ball was missing. So, what had it hit? What had been that horrible crack? That's when I saw Larry drop his cue stick and rush around the table.

He skid to the floor past the other end of the table where Lilly lay, her head in a pool of blood, the cue ball still spinning beside her, spraying blood in a widening circle. Larry grasped Lilly in his arms and wailed. I realized at that moment that I had forgotten Lilly had even been there in the pool hall. My heart broke at what I had lost, and I turned and walked into the back room, where I curled up inside a suitcase filled with silk ties and reeking of cigar smoke and cried myself to sleep.

I awoke in a dark and confined space that constantly swayed back and forth and occasionally jumped up and then rattled back into place. It was one of those sudden bumps that must have awoken me. I didn't scream. I was used to sleeping in small boxes. I was still a rabbit despite my appearance and natural-born talent.

After a while I figured out that I was still in Naughty Niner's suitcase bouncing along on a train to somewhere. I don't know if I purposely chose to be with Niner after the death of Lilly or if was just happenstance that I ended up in his case. Either way, there was no going back. Even if Larry would take me in again after his lucky charm failed him so completely, I had no idea where I was or how to get back to the Lollers.

I decided to hitch my lucky star to Naughty Niner, but this time I swore I would never let my eye stray again. I'm no idiot, you see. Mortoni's death might have been a freak accident, and I just got lucky to end up with Lilly afterward. But after Lilly got beaned with that cue ball while I stared at Niner, it felt like death was following me and happened to those I loved when I forgot to keep them in my life.

I didn't know Niner, but I was certain he wasn't like Mortoni who was super nice if terribly naïve, and he wasn't like Lilly, who loved everything with open abandon. No. Niner seemed like the gruff kind of guy who wouldn't cross the street to save another soul. He was almost certainly a crooked pool hustler, but that didn't mean he deserved to die just because I came into his life. So, now that I was with him, I didn't dare leave or even look away.

Niner and I traveled the rails from town to town, back and forth across the Midwest where he did indeed hustle people out of their money in the pool halls. Well, hustled is a strong word. Most everyone knew Niner and, as I said, you could just look at him and see he was a hustler. Most people who came to play him were fully aware they were overmatched. They just wanted their shot at taking Niner down a notch.

After a while, I wasn't even sure Niner needed my lucky charm. He won so easily in the end every time that he hardly breathed hard, which was something considering how much he smoked. Unlike Mortoni or Lilly's family, I didn't notice Niner's life improve with me around. Of course, I didn't know much about him before I laid eyes on him in the Louisville pool hall, but it wasn't like we were swimming in money or fame.

I kept quiet most of the time I was with Niner, wondering if it had been my flashy ways that had made the luck sparkle so brightly that it burned my human companions. For his part, Niner never complained and never pressed me to bring him luck, like Larry had. Perhaps he didn't need it. If so, maybe I could leave him without leaving another body behind me.

This thought preoccupied my days while I kept my eyes on Niner at all times, like a doting mother on an adult son who still lives at home. The thought of what might happen should I ever shine my attention on anyone else kept me up nights and haunted my dreams when I did finally get to sleep.

I barely ate. I started drinking to get through the days and blunt the nightmares that came for me in the dark. Still, Niner said nothing. He stared hard at me through the haze of smoke most days as I tried to keep my tired, swollen eyes open and trained on him, but he never questioned why I was with him or what had driven me to this sorry state.

And then it happened. Again. But this time it was different. We went to the Station in Reading, Pennsylvania to grab the train to Scranton. Niner went off to buy his ticket while I rested on his suitcase. I hadn't had a drink in a while and my Seven paw was twitching from withdrawal. I spied a liquor kiosk across the terminal. After taking a long, hard look at Niner in line at the ticket booth, I hopped and danced over to the liquor stand.

It took a while to convince the seller that I was old enough to drink. I'm not, actually. Not in human years, anyway. Eventually, a wad of Niner's cash made my point for me and I turned to head back to the suitcase. Only it was gone.

I guess Niner assumed I had crawled inside to take a nap. I often did that on the train as it cut down on gawkers and questions about a second ticket from the conductor. But I wasn't' in the case. I had been distracted by a bottle of booze. I ran to the tracks to look for Niner. I had to get my eyes on him before something bad happened.

When I got there, though, the train was already pulling out. I ran after it, yelling and screaming. I almost caught up with it, too. As I got to the end of the platform, I took three long steps and leapt across the gap, my back legs splayed as I reached for the caboose rail with my front paws.

I hung there in the air between the platform and the train as time seemed to come to a stop between safety and oblivion.

And then I was falling. Eternity came crashing up to meet me as I tumbled onto the gravel between the tracks. I looked up to see Niner's train chugging off into the distance. I turned and ran away, not wanting to see what came next.

I heard the grinding of the brakes, and the rending of the metal behind me as I rushed across crisscrossing tracks filled with trains waiting to be moved. It turns out Reading was a major junction where a massive conjunction of trains arrived, switched tracks, and left again in a rush. The timing had gone wrong on one such switch, causing a massive pileup.

I learned later from the Junction Chief that 149 people lost their lives that day, including Naughty Niner. I didn't stay with the Junction Chief. I couldn't do that to him. I hopped on a freight train heading west the next day and didn't stop until I got back to where it all began. Right here in Reno, at this casino behind that very furnace there.

And now I know what I need to do.

\#   \#   \#

His story done, Big Red looked down at the tiny rabbit's foot clutched tight in his much larger, furry paw. Jerod noticed a bit of sparkle had returned to the old, drunken rabbit's eyes. They no longer looked sunken and out of focus. Perhaps the rabbit had found some peace from telling his tale, given him the determination to do what must be done — what he should have done long ago.

Big Red hopped off the wooden crate he'd been sitting on, tossed his lucky rabbit's foot in the air once and then again and walked toward the furnace door, behind which a roaring fire raged, fed by the coal Jerod had shoveled in there before taking out the trash.

At that moment, Jerod also came to a decision. He realized it had been fate that had brought Big Red to his alley today, fate that guided Jerod to find the drunken creature and then stayed his hand when he considered leaving

Red there to die or tossing him into a pot for supper.

Jerod was here to help Red finish his story. That classic tale of good luck and bad, of fortune and misfortune, of life of death, could only end one way: The heroic sacrifice for the good of other men. Well, for the good of one man … for the good of this one man here tonight who had to sit through that insipid chronicle.

As Big Red twisted the iron handle that locked the furnace door shut, Jerod stood up from his chair and stepped behind the rabbit. When Big Red raised his paw to toss the lucky rabbit's foot into the furnace, Jerod grabbed him by his furry wrist and twisted until the lucky foot fell from his grasp to clatter to the stone floor.

Jerod then grabbed Red by the neck, lifted his liquor-emaciated body off the floor, and casually tossed the talking and dancing rabbit through the iron door into the raging furnace. Jerod slammed the door shut and twisted the handle to lock Big Red inside.

Jerod didn't know what he expected to happen next. Surely screams of pain or crying. What he wasn't prepared for was the clear strains of a song punctuated by the crackling of the fire as it burned fur and flesh.

"You can call me Lucky because Lucky's my name;

Singin' and dancing,' that's my game.

I never did a whole day's work in my life;

But everything seems to turn out right…"

Eventually, the singing trailed off and all Jerod could hear was the fire and the blower of the furnace.

It was then that Jerod bent down to pick up the lucky rabbit's foot. He polished it between his thumb and forefinger, not sure how the magic would work. He didn't feel any different, but he knew that easy street was not far away now. The luck had always made the rabbit's life better. It only backfired on the people around him that he cared about.

"It's perfect for me," Jerod muttered. A small smile crept across his face. He'd been alone his whole life. He cared about nobody, and nobody cared about him. "What do I care if people die around me. As far as I'm concerned, the rest of the world can just go to hell. It's halfway there already."

Jerod flipped the rabbit's foot into the air, just as Big Red had before he tossed the dumb rabbit into the furnace. He considered getting back to work, but then Jerod realized that work no longer mattered, so he decided to sit down, take a nap, and wait for his luck to change.

As Jerod slept a small fragment of white-hot coal that had popped out of the furnace when Big Red landed inside smoldered in the corner near a pile of rags next to the coal bin.

#   #   #

The day maintenance technician found Jerod the next morning dead in his chair, asphyxiated from a smoldering coal fire that had filled the room with lethal levels of carbon monoxide and formaldehyde. After opening the door to the alley to clear the air and calling 911, the tech noticed a small, white object on the floor next to Jerod's chair. He leaned down to see what it was and found a dirty, smoke-covered rabbit's foot.

"I guess it wasn't that lucky for Jerod," the day tech said.

He thought about tossing the foot into the furnace, but holding it made him feel good. He felt light on his feet and a little giddy in the head, almost like he could break into a song and dance at a moment's notice. As the day tech heard the sirens coming closer, he pocketed the rabbit's foot and made his way to the side door. ♜

BREAK YOUR MOMMY'S BONES

By Katya de Becerra

In the morning we brush our teeth, and you should too!
Brush, brush, brush those baby teeth!

THE TV DRONED ON IN the living room. Lil' Twigglies were giggling and singing about teeth and dirty knees, and jumping for fun and splashing in the puddles, while Nika went room to room, picking up Ophelia's toys. *I swear to God,* Nika thought, *these toys are everywhere.*

The toys indeed were everywhere, in every corner of the house, under the staircase, and seemingly in every room. At only four, Ophelia had an incredible knack for breaching boundaries. She could get into any space, no matter how well-guarded or off limits. Baby-proofing did little to hold her back, and 'off limits' meant nothing to her.

Nika's eyelids were drooping, she suppressed a yawn. She could count on the fingers of one hand how many hours of sleep she got over the past few nights. Ophelia was a light sleeper, though 'light' was an understatement... Nika would never use words like 'bad' or 'terrible' in relation to her daughter, even when talking about Ophelia's sleep pattern. Because Ophelia was precious, darling, *perfect.* She just resisted going to bed, or staying in bed, or falling asleep, or staying asleep. Nika would never verbalize it, not to her husband, and definitely not to those other moms she chatted with at the park or at the swimming lessons or baby ballet, but there were times she wondered whether Ophelia had some sixth sense when it came to her mother's sleep. Because it felt as if the second the house grew quiet at night and Nika's eyes closed, Ophelia would start crying and calling for Mamma. It was always Mamma, never Papa. David slept through it all, night after night, rarely jolted by his daughter's cries for attention.

In the morning we wash our hands, and you should too!
Wash, wash, wash those baby hands!

Nika's Saturday mornings used to be quiet. With a leisurely coffee and a book, they'd stretch into eternity. Now, with Ophelia in the house, it was an unending parade of singing mice and talking dogs and dancing flowers. TV noise ran a constant background to everything all of the time.

But it was the Lil' Twigglies show that dominated all else. Nika couldn't remember the time when Ophelia wasn't obsessed with these round-bellied, bewinged creatures, played by four costumed actors who moved like clumsy bears and sang in high-pitched voices. The repetitive songs left Nika's head buzzing, but Ophelia loved them. Whoever scripted the thing must've been able to see straight into the mind of a child. Ophelia became practically glued to the screen whenever Lil' Twigglies came on.

Before Ophelia was born, Nika never paid any mind to how bizarre, even psychedelic, kids' shows were. Why would she? Before, Nika would binge on grimdark fantasy and obsess over B-rated zombie flicks, the more disturbing the better. She was a horror connoisseur, loved all things dark and strange, even fancied going back to university at some point to study scriptwriting. But life had other plans.

Nika loved Ophelia. So much. Loved her innocent eyes, her sweet voice, her ever-evolving logic. She loved her from the moment she first held her and even before, when Ophelia was just a growing presence in Nika's belly, brushing against her organs, tiny limbs stretching against her mother's skin, already testing boundaries.

Nika was also discovering new depths of patience and endurance every day.

It was barely ten in the morning now and she already scrubbed the breakfast dishes, disinfected the countertops, tidied up… And all that pre-coffee. She munched on a cookie, which had no taste. David was at work, he often worked weekends. His was important work, which often involved taking out clients to golf, treating them to luxury brunches. David's work paid for it all, the house, everything in it, Ophelia's toys and her swimming lessons and baby ballet classes.

Before Ophelia was born, it was decided Nika would stay home and look after her. And that was what Nika did. She took Ophelia to classes and 'baby dates' out in the park, where other moms gathered every day, sporting pricy leisurewear and posh sneakers. There were some nannies too and a handful of dads and non-binary parents in the mix, but it was a group of moms that dominated the group. They never missed their chance to remind everyone else how their babies were ahead of the curve, how they only ate organic food and sipped purified water from glass bottles.

Nika dreamed of going back to work, eventually, but it was better for everyone if she didn't, not yet, not now. David didn't want his child, his precious firstborn baby girl to be brought up by strangers.

Carrots are orange and delicious!
We love to eat them and you should too!
So use those baby teeth and chomp, chomp, chomp!

When Nika checked on Ophelia, Lil' Twigglies were still singing, holding hands and jumping. Their partially masked faces remained unmoving, while their mouths contorted in close-lipped smiles in between the songs. Ophelia was alternating between listening intently and crooning along.

Do Lil' Twigglies have teeth? Nika wondered as she folded laundry. *Do they get hot with all that fur? What do they do on their days off? Sing songs and hold hands and splash in puddles? Or do they shed their kid-friendly personas and speak in gruff voices and smoke cigars and swear? What are their wings for? They never use them…*

It was time for Ophelia's snack.

Lil' Twigglies continued to sing about the goodness of vegetables, of divine power of spinach. As Nika worked in the kitchen, peeling and slicing an apple and cutting up a banana, the song filled her perception.

Apples are shiny and juicy!
They are so good for you!
You should eat them and then…
You should trip your mommy too!

Nika's hand shook and the knife went sideways, nearly slicing through her finger. Her skin clammy and cold, she left the kitchen island and came to stand behind the couch, where Ophelia was watching Lil' Twigglies. The furry creatures were singing about apples, how good they were and how juicy. Nothing else. Nothing odd.

"Mommy, I'm hungry!" Ophelia said, turning her head enough to give her mother a side-eye.

Nika snapped out of it and went back into the kitchen. If she didn't give Ophelia her snack on time, the apple would turn brown and Ophelia would reject it. She was such a picky eater.

When Nika returned to the living room with a plate of sliced fruit, the couch was empty.

Where did her daughter go?

As Nika registered a flash of pink in her periphery, she exhaled in relief. Ophelia must've gone to the bathroom by herself like a big girl.

Nika took another step and then she was stumbling, falling. The plate flew out of her hands, slices of apple and banana coursing through the air.

Her knees banged against the wooden floor, her right wrist bending at a dangerous angle trying to stop the fall. Sliced fruit was all over the floor, and the plate shattered into pieces, glass everywhere. *Shit.*

"Don't come here—I need to clean this up! Go find your shoes…" Nika said, as Ophelia marched on toward the couch, unaware or uncaring about the broken glass, and undisturbed by her mother's accident.

"I want Lil' Twigglies!" Ophelia protested, not slowing down.

"Go find your shoes," Nika repeated, standing up and making eye contact with the toddler. Dull pain radiated through her knees. She needed to take ibuprofen and find her old hand sling. Her wrist was going to bother her all day, but it wasn't broken. She hoped.

That's when she spotted a striped snake on the floor, not far from the couch. The snake was one of Ophelia's countless plush toys. It must've been what tripped Nika.

But Nika put all the toys away earlier, didn't she? God, this was such a Sisyphus labor, this unending task of tidying up, picking up, sorting things into their correct places. Some parents gave up, their houses quickly descending into chaos. Nika couldn't be like that, couldn't stand the mess, her brain ached at the thought. But her daily fight against entropy was starting to get to her, along with her lack of sleep and poor nutrition.

She picked up the snake gingerly, half-expecting it to hiss, to bite her. But the toy was inert, a lifeless object.

Apples are shiny and carrots are juicy!
They are so good for you!

In the background, Lil' Twigglies went on singing.

Ophelia fetched her shoes and was waiting for her mother to help her put them on.

Suddenly, all Nika could think of was Lil' Twigglies' command she thought she heard.

You should trip your mommy...

Her exhausted mind made that up. Surely.

She knew that. And yet.

\#   \#   \#

Every day was the same, every morning was Saturday morning.

When Nika was a child, there were certain TV shows she could only watch on the weekend. She eagerly waited for those precious mornings, cherished them. They were special. Now, it seemed Lil' Twigglies were *everywhere*, all of the time, filling every silence with their puerile singing.

Days and nights passed, all blending together. Ophelia slept poorly, ate pickily, spread toys throughout the house, and watched her beloved humanoid creatures dance and sing on the screen. There were cuddles and laughter too. Nika took Ophelia to the park, to swimming lessons, to baby ballet, and they went shopping, ate ice cream and said hello to pampered dogs out for a walk with their dotting owners.

But something shifted too.

Nika kept finding herself tense whenever Lil' Twigglies were on. She studied her daughter, growing anxious as Ophelia froze in raptured attention, lips moving.

Time for Lil' Twigglies! Time for Lil' Twigglies!
Hello, hello, hello!
Join us in the yard!
Let's get your knees all dirty, dirty, dirty!
Let's dig things up…

Nika strained to understand the lyrics, which were perforated by giggles, singers' voices overlapping. Whenever she focused like that, it felt as if Lil' Twigglies' music deteriorated into nonsensical sounds. *Lalalalala! Hehehehehe! Wawawa!*

Was this supposed to be good for a child's development? What was Ophelia learning from this absurdity? But whenever Nika tried to change the channel, Ophelia protested, and then she cried, cried, cried.

#　　#　　#

Later, when David was home and spending much needed time with his daughter, Nika went outside to check on her long-suffering garden. She came from a gardening family, both her parents obsessed with growing their own produce, taking delight when harvest time came. Nika was trying to follow in their footsteps but her green thumb was lacking. Still, she dutifully planted a few things in the Spring. It was much to her surprise when many of the seedlings took off, despite her irregular ministrations. Last time she checked, green stems were emerging from the soil, leaves unfurling, and there were even a couple of yellow flowers on the verge of opening.

Today, the moment she stepped outside, she knew immediately something was wrong. Instead of green, her garden patch had the uneven brown color of the upturned soil. Nika's fledgling plants were gone, destroyed, torn out before they even had a chance.

Join us in the yard!
Let's get your knees all dirty, dirty, dirty!
Let's dig things up…

The words echoed through Nika's head, making her dizzy, sick.

Could this be… Ophelia?

It was pure madness to think that sweet Ophelia, Nika's darling baby, would do something so senseless.

But then there was also the snake planted in Nika's path the other day.

Nika rushed inside, finding David with Ophelia on the couch. They were watching Lil' Twigglies.

"I thought you were going to read together?" She struggled to keep her voice even. As she looked between them, two pairs of dazed eyes looked back. Their mouths were moving.

Join us in the yard!…
Let's dig things up!

No. That wasn't right.

David's mouth wasn't moving in sync with the ridiculous song. In fact, he had his mobile phone on his lap, likely checking work emails while Ophelia was being zombified by the TV.

"What's the harm," David asked. "She loves them."

"That's so not the point," Nika said, but then her attention drifted to Ophelia's knees.

Let's get your knees all dirty, dirty, dirty!

Ophelia's knees were dirty.

Not filthy, exactly, but smudged with brown and green.

"Did you go outside, Ophelia?" Nika demanded, anxiety swirling in her belly.

"No, Mommy," the little girl said.

"What's up with you, Nikki? Do you want to go upstairs and lie down?" David asked.

"I don't need to lie down," Nika replied. Though she was tired. So. Tired.

#   #   #

As Nika started paying more and more attention to the words in Lil' Twigglies' songs, there were times she had to force herself to look away from the screen. While those creatures, silicon masks partially covering the actors' faces, were creeping her out, they were fascinating her too.

What were Lil' Twigglies supposed to be? They had wings but didn't fly. They chatted and sang in little kids' voices but they had big heads and giant eyes and fur all over. One of them had an antenna on its head while another a tail that moved out of sync with the music. At some point, Nika thought one of them winked at her, while another smiled maliciously.

It all had to be in her head. Right?

#   #   #

Days went on, and Nika developed a new routine. After making breakfast for Ophelia, instead of cleaning and tidying up, she'd research the show and its writers. But there wasn't a lot of information available. The names of actors playing Lil' Twigglies weren't known to the public, to preserve the show's authenticity, its creator said. The creator himself, Martin Cotton-Doll, was rather mysterious too. There were no photos of him online, his bio was missing. Lil' Twigglies appeared to be his first writing credit. Same went for the rest of the team behind the show.

Nika turned to some parenting forums for information, searching for keywords and mentions, hoping to find something, *anything*. Maybe some other tired parent heard bizarre messages in Lil' Twigglies songs? But again, internet provided no enlightenment.

Nika read articles about hallucinations too, about noises and voices brought on by exhaustion or illness. But her family history held no precedents. As for her interrupted sleep and all the usual things that came with looking after a toddler… She's been in this state of exhausted alertness ever since Ophelia was born, but she hasn't been hearing kid show characters give her child sinister commands. Until now.

# # #

Another Saturday morning arrived in the haze of summer drizzle.

Despite the weather, David had to go out for another career-advancing golf session. The house was a mess, with Nika neglecting her clean up duties, losing time to observe her daughter consume one episode of Lil' Twigglies after another.

> *In the morning we brush our teeth!*
> *Brush, brush, brush those baby teeth!*
> *Wash, wash, wash those baby hands!*
> *Carrots are orange and delicious!*
> *Chomp, chomp, chomp!*

Nika's limbs felt numb, while her mind grew noisy, as if her head housed an angry hive and all the wasps wanted out.

Lil' Twigglies kept on singing, dancing, swirling. One of them was flopping its wings. On the couch, Ophelia was clapping her hands to the songs about spinach and digging up the yard and getting one's knees dirty.

The room swayed in Nika's view, air rippling like she was underwater, drowning. The TV's screen rippled too, stretching the dancing creatures into monstrous shapes.

Swept in the motion, Nika nearly fell to the floor but managed to hold on to the back of the couch. Ophelia sat motionless.

Lil' Twigglies paused in their tracks. Four pairs of unblinking eyes zeroed in on Nika.

"What…?" She swallowed the rest of the words.

The things on the screen were moving again, but their eyes were now trained on Ophelia. The girl's mouth was moving.

Her panic tasting bitter, Nika registered the words of the song her daughter was singing along with the creatures who lived inside the TV.

Break your mommy's bones!
Let her have it all!
Smash, smash, smash!
Kill. Kill. Kill.

Nika waited for the room to swing again, for her to lose balance. She needed help. She needed to talk to someone. She needed…

Ophelia's head turned slightly, followed by the rest of her until she sat facing her mother.

The room wasn't spinning anymore. Rubbing her wrist that was still sore from her fall last week, Nika stared into her daughter's adorable eyes. For a second, before settling into their normal grey, Ophelia's eyes turned as dark as those of Lil' Twigglies.

"Mommy, I'm hungry," Ophelia said.

It was time for Ophelia's snack. Nika nodded and went to the kitchen. She pulled out the cutting board and a clean knife and started slicing fruit into a bowl. From her spot behind the kitchen island she could see the back of the couch, and the top of Ophelia's head. She could hear the unending singing of Lil' Twigglies.

She got distracted, and when she looked again she couldn't see Ophelia anymore. A cold wave of terror surged her, as if she was standing on the edge of a cliff and looking down, down, down into the whirling water below.

"Mommy?" Ophelia asked.

Nika flinched, nearly letting go of the knife.

Her daughter was by her side, looking up at her. How long was she standing there, waiting?

"What is it, my darling?"

Ophelia opened her mouth to speak. For a moment, instead of her daughter's sweet voice, what Nika heard was the infernal singing of the TV creatures.

Break your mommy's bones...
Kill. Kill. Kill.

Shaking, Nika smiled at her daughter, waiting for the moment to pass, for this nightmare to end.

Her daughter smiled back. Everything was back to normal.

Nika continued preparing Ophelia's snack as the TV droned on.

CONTRIBUTORS

KATYA DE BECERRA writes atmospheric horror featuring determined characters, complicated families and enigmatic places. Critics called her debut *What The Woods Keep* "a thoughtful and compelling horror fantasy" and "a narrative that will keep readers enthralled", while her second novel *Oasis* earned a Starred review from Booklist. Katya regularly publishes short fiction in anthologies and literary magazines. She is also co-editor of the anthology *This Fresh Hell*, which reimagines and subverts horror tropes. As a child, Katya wanted to be an Egyptologist, but instead she earned a PhD in Cultural Anthropology. Katya is a short version of her real name, which is very long and gets mispronounced a lot. Her third novel, *When Ghosts Call Us Home*, is forthcoming in 2023. You can find Katya on Twitter and Instagram @katyadebecerra, follow her for updates on Facebook at facebook.com/katyadebecerra or visit her online at katyadebecerra.com.

JEREMIAH DYLAN COOK is a horror writer whose work has been published by The NoSleep Podcast, Castle Bridge Media, Tales to Terrify, Ghost Orchid Press, Cabbit Crossing Publishing, Timber Ghost Press, The Lovecraft eZine, Hippocampus Press, Necronomicon Press, and Eye Contact. He won Purple Wall Stories February 2021 Writing Competition, and the Ligonier Valley Writers 2018 Flash Fiction Contest. While pursuing his bachelor's degree at St. John's University, Jeremiah received the Mario Mezzacappa Memorial Award for Outstanding Achievement in Poetry and Prose. He completed his Master of Fine Arts in Writing Popular Fiction at Seton Hill University. Jeremiah is an affiliate member of the Horror Writers Association and the Managing Editor of New Pulp Tales.com. You can learn more about him at JeremiahDylanCook.com, where he offers free stories and posts reviews. He's easiest to contact on Twitter, @JeremiahCook1, where he discusses Resident Evil, Weird Fiction, and his favorite movies.

DENNIS K. CROSBY is the multi award-winning/bestselling author of the Kassidy Simmons urban fantasy novels—*Death's Legacy* (2020), *Death's*

Debt (2021), and *Death's Despair* (2023). *Souled* is his ninth published short story. Originally from Oak Park, IL, Dennis completed his undergraduate work at the University of Illinois-Chicago. With a bachelor's degree in Criminal Justice, he spent six years working as a Private Investigator. He later pursued a master's degree in Forensic Psychology which led him to shift his profession to community mental health services. Since 2008, he has worked primarily with men and women experiencing challenges with mental health, addiction, and chronic homelessness.

In 2018, Dennis completed an MFA program at National University. The bourbon loving Chicago Cubs fan and deep-dish pizza connoisseur continues to work on his Kassidy Simmons series and works on weird and creepy short stories in his spare time. A self-proclaimed geek and lover of pop culture, Dennis currently lives and writes in San Diego, CA.

To keep up with his journey, check out denniskcrosby.com.

P. J. (TRICIA) HOOVER wanted to be a Jedi, but when that didn't work out, she became an electrical engineer instead. After a fifteen year bout designing computer chips for a living, P. J. started creating worlds of her own. She's the award-winning author of over 40 books, including *Tut: The Story of My Immortal Life,* featuring a fourteen-year-old King Tut who's stuck in middle school, *Deadly Decisions: Into The Woods,* an interactive horror adventure with 80s slasher overtones, and the editor of *Castle of Horror Volume 6: Femme Fatales.* Under the Connor Hoover pseudonym, she is also the author of the popular *Pick Your Own Quest* series, which are *Choose Your Own Adventure* style interactive adventures perfect for everyone. When not writing, P. J. loves spending time practicing kung fu, fixing things around the house, and solving Rubik's cubes. For more information about P. J. (Tricia) Hoover, please visit her website pjhoover.com.

STEVEN PHILIP JONES writes novels, graphic novels, audio scripts, non-fiction books and anything anybody needs him to write. He enjoys working in all genres and his stories have been published by the likes of Aconyte Books, Actionopolis, Caliber Comics, Campfire Comics, IDW, McFarland Publishing, Malibu Graphics, and MX Publishing. Among his best-known credits are the novels *Henrietta Hex: Shadows From the Past* and *King of Harlem*, the comics series *H. P. Lovecraft Worlds* and *Nightlinger*, graphic novel adaptations of the films *Re-Animator* and *Invaders from Mars*, and the review text *The Clive Cussler Adventures: A Critical Review*. Steven graduated from the University of Iowa where he majored in Journalism and Religion and was accepted into Iowa's prestigious Writers' Workshop MFA Program. A proud husband and father, Steven currently resides in northern Utah.

TONY JONES has dined with royalty, supped Slings in Singapore and been taught by several Nobel Prize winners (though he could have paid more attention!) He is a writer and blogger based in the early 21st Century. A retired management consultant, he was Audio Drama Editor for Starburst Magazine, and now occasionally writes pieces for Cultbox. He wrote a few Doctor Who stories for Big Finish (and several fan publications) and is now dabbling with self-publishing, horror stories and rediscovering his love for D&D.

ALETHEA KONTIS is a storm chaser and New York Times bestselling author of over 20 books and 50 short stories. She has received the Jane Yolen Mid-List Author Grant, the Scribe Award, and is a two-time winner of the Gelett Burgess Children's Book Award. She was twice nominated for both the Dragon Award and the Andre Norton Nebula. Alethea also narrates stories for a myriad of award-winning online magazines and reviews books for NPR. Born in Vermont, Alethea currently resides on the Space Coast of Florida where she watches K-dramas with her teddy bear, Charlie.

SCOTT PEARSON is a freelance writer and editor working across multiple genres in both traditional and indie publishing. His published works include short stories and novellas in humor, mystery, horror, urban fantasy, and science fiction in various anthologies, including *Castle of Horror* 4, 5, 7, and 9. Scott's *Star Trek* fiction appears in anthologies and the e-book exclusive *The More Things Change*. For several years he has copyedited the *Star Trek* novels and edited and written for the *Star Trek Adventures* roleplaying game. Scott and his daughter, Ella, cohost the *Generations Geek* podcast. Scott and his wife, Sandra, live in the wilds of Minnesota. Visit him online at scott-pearson.com and generationsgeek.com. Follow him on Twitter @smichaelpearson or Hive, Mastodon, Post, Spoutible, and Tribel @scottpearson. (But who has time to post on everything? Even copy-pastes? Not Scott.)

JOY PREBLE is the author of a medium-long list of young adult novels and short stories, as well as a children's picture book forthcoming in 2025. She is fond of clever conversation and clever cocktails, teaches writing at Writespace Houston and is also the Children's Programming Director at Brazos Bookstore. Visit Joy at joypreble.com or follow her on Twitter or IG @joypreble.

HEATH W. SHELBY has spent his entire life looking forward to Saturday mornings. As a child, Saturday mornings represented a bowl of Raisin Bran, Saturday morning cartoons, Channel 5 Championship Wrestling and time at his grandparents' farm. As an adult, Saturday mornings are a time when Heath tries to sleep until the crack of noon, dreaming about those good ole childhood Saturday mornings. When he is wide awake, Heath lives in Searcy, Arkansas, where he is the father of two incredible kids (his son Collin and his daughter Caitlynn) and his Maltizhu, Leia. Heath spends his waking hours writing, working as a College Admissions Rep, listening to 80s music in his Mustang and hoping his 49ers will win one more Super Bowl within his lifetime. As a writer, Heath's work has so far appeared in Castle of Horror Anthology Volumes 5 and 8.

BRYAN YOUNG (he/they) works across many different media. His work as a writer and producer has been called "filmmaking gold" by The New York Times. He's also published comic books with Slave Labor Graphics and Image Comics. He's been a regular contributor for the *Huffington Post, StarWars.com, Star Wars Insider magazine, SYFY, /Film,* and was the founder and editor in chief of the geek news and review site *Big Shiny Robot!* In 2014, he wrote the critically acclaimed history book, *A Children's*

Illustrated History of Presidential Assassination. He co-authored *Robotech: The Macross Saga RPG* has written two books in the BattleTech Universe: *Honor's Gauntlet* and *A Question of Survival*. His latest book, *The Big Bang Theory Book of Lists* is a #1 Bestseller on Amazon. He teaches writing for Writer's Digest, Script Magazine, and at the University of Utah. Follow him on Twitter @swankmotron or visit swankmotron.com.

CASTLE BRIDGE MEDIA RECOMMENDS...

If you liked this book, you might also enjoy reading the following titles from Castle Bridge Media available on Amazon or by order at your favorite book store:

Animal Charmer
By Rain Nox

Austinites
By In Churl Yo

Bloodsucker City
By Jim Towns

THE CASTLE OF HORROR ANTHOLOGY SERIES
Volume 1
Volume 2: *Holiday Horrors*
Volume 3: *Scary Summer Stories*
Volume 4: *Women Running From Houses*
Volume 5: *Thinly Veiled: The 70s*
Volume 6: *Femme Fatales**
Volume 7: *Love Gone Wrong*
Volume 8: *Thinly Veiled: The 80s*
Volume 9: *Young Adult*
Volume 10: *Thinly Veiled: Saturday Mournings*
Edited By Jason Henderson and In Churl Yo
*Edited By P.J. Hoover

Castle of Horror Podcast Book of Great Horror: Our Favorites, Top Tens and Bizarre Pleasures
Edited By Jason Henderson

Dream State
By Martin Ott

FRENCH DECEPTION
A Forgery in Paris
By Janice Nagourney

FuturePast Sci-Fi Anthology
Edited by In Churl Yo

GLAZIER'S GAP
Ghosts of the Forbidden
By Leanna Renee Hieber

The Hermes Protocol
By Chris M. Arnone

Isonation
By In Churl Yo

Junk Film: Why Bad Movies Matter
By Katharine Coldiron

MID-LIFE CRISIS THRILLERS
18 Miles From Town
By Jason Henderson
Lost Angel
By Sam Knight

Nightwalkers: Gothic Horror Movies
By Bruce Lanier Wright

THE PATH
The Blue-Spangled Blue
By David Bowles
The Deepest Green
By David Bowles

SURF MYSTIC
Night of the Book Man
By Peyton Douglas
Dark of the Curl
By Peyton Douglas

Yesterday's Tomorrows: The Golden Age of Science Fiction Movies
By Bruce Lanier Wright

Please remember to leave us your reviews on Amazon and Goodreads!

THANK YOU FOR SUPPORTING INDEPENDENT PUBLISHERS AND AUTHORS!
castlebridgemedia.com